"Intelligent and moving . . . Tamara'[s] . . . expansive view marks this as a lumi[nous novel.]"

"A feisty narrator . . . Tamara is an engaging character."
—*The New York Times Book Review*

"Willis's writing is clear and fresh, capturing the emotional edge of childhood and the search for home in one's heart."
—*Library Journal*

"Heartfelt . . . Whenever it would appear that no more successful variations on the American coming-of-age novel remain, an engaging new book arrives. Willis's is the most recent." —*The Miami Herald*

"Unerring emotional accuracy and taut, seamless prose."
—*Austin American-Statesman*

"Memorable . . . [Tamara is] smart and perceptive. She tells her story in strong, short words that pack power." —*Booklist*

"[Willis] has created an astute protagonist who . . . remains consistently compelling . . . [the novel] is quirky and believable, and it illuminates that time of life when, as Tamara observes, one is 'a traitor' to one's own desires." —*Los Angeles Times*

"Set in 1954, this tangy debut is [a] fully imagined coming-of-age story . . . Even though Willis's light, funny take turns deeper and more nuanced when Liz contracts tuberculosis and is quarantined in a sanitorium—effectively ending Tamara's adolescence—the novel never loses its edge." —*Entertainment Weekly*

"With likable wryness and honesty, *Some Things That Stay* portrays an amusingly itinerant, unorthodox family—one whose members are deeply rattled and ultimately steadied by their needs for one another." —Martha Cooley, author of *The Archivist*

"[A] rich novel . . . Tamara is wholly lovable even as she misbehaves . . . she is strong in spite of herself, endlessly interesting and funny. Willis's ability to startle and delight, page after page, makes this old story brand-new." —*Pittsburgh Post-Gazette*

Some Things That Stay

Sarah Willis

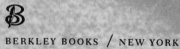

BERKLEY BOOKS / NEW YORK

A Berkley Book
Published by The Berkley Publishing Group
A division of Penguin Putnam Inc.
375 Hudson Street
New York, New York 10014

Copyright © 2000 by Sarah Willis
Interior design by Jonathan D. Lippincott
Title page photograph by Anna Bushell

PRINTING HISTORY
Farrar, Straus and Giroux hardcover edition / February 2000
Berkley trade paperback edition / May 2001

The Penguin Putnam Inc. World Wide Web site address is
www.penguinputnam.com

Library of Congress Cataloging-in-Publication Data

Willis, Sarah
      Some things that stay / Sarah Willis.—Berkley trade pbk. ed.
         p.   cm.
      ISBN 0-425-17960-5
         1. Teenage girls—Fiction.   2. New York (State)—Fiction.
      3. Moving, Household—Fiction.   4. Children of artists—Fiction.
      5. Tuberculosis—Patients—Fiction.   6. Atheists—Fiction.
      I. Title.

PS3573.J4565557 S66 2001
813'.54—dc21   2001025101

For My Parents

Some things that stay there be
Grief, hills, eternity . . .

—Emily Dickinson, "The Secret"

Some Things That Stay

Sarah Willis

One

We move each year in spring, like birds migrating, except we don't go back to a familiar place. We never go back. We pack up who we are and the few things that cling to us, and drive away. We are good at packing. Good at leaving behind.

We traveled three hundred miles today, and five hundred miles yesterday, pulling behind us a small humpbacked metal trailer that wobbles and slows us down. My father would be happy without that trailer, but he needs it to haul his canvases and art supplies, allowing us the rest of the space inside for our things as an afterthought. "Oh, I suppose we need clothes," he will mutter, as we load in our cardboard boxes filled with my mother's encyclopedias, my brother's comics, my sister's stuffed animals, my record player and 45's. "But what's the rest of this stuff? Do we need it?"

An hour off the highway, a half hour past the last poor excuse for a town, my father turns toward the three of us in the back seat. "We're almost there," he says as my mother drives down a two-lane blacktop road exactly like every other two-lane road that has brought us, last year and the years before, to almost there. These roads inevitably lead to dirt lanes which we travel up, or down, or around some river, or through some bog, to where we will live for the next year, places where the occasional house stands out like a bright rainbow on a dark day. Today we turn right, onto a narrow but paved road: Moore. The woods are dense, arching over the road like arms reaching for each other in fright.

My teeth are clenched and my jaw hurts. As always, I have convinced myself that *this* time we will be living in a suburb of some sort, or maybe the tail end of a town, where there are sidewalks, and porches, where people watch neighbors come and go, asking them in for tea and cookies. I once lived in a place with a sidewalk, but I was three and don't remember.

We drive over a hill and down the other side. "This must be it," my father says. "It's a mile since we turned. Yes. There it is. This is it, kids."

I can hardly breathe, because what I notice first is that I don't know which house he means, because there are *two* houses, directly facing each other from across the road. One is a pretty farmhouse with brown shingles, white trim, a front porch, and a big red barn. There are acres of mowed grass and a cow pasture that spreads out behind the barn and up the hill. I can see lace curtains wave from the open windows. Across the road is a tar-papered house, with no porch, and a half-dozen cars scattered about a mangy yard, the grilles glistening in the late sun like the teeth of rabid dogs. If my father turns right, into *that* drive, I will not get out of the car. I would rather die.

We turn left, onto the stony driveway of the farmhouse. I want to shout with joy. I am so relieved it's the pretty farmhouse, and so excited we have actual neighbors, but as I get out of the car I look again at the house across the road and shudder, imagining who must live there: an old hermit with warts and a beard down to his knees. Just my luck.

It is the spring of 1954. I will be fifteen in two weeks. For the next year we will live in the farthest outskirts of Mayville, in western New York, so my father can paint. His scenic oil paintings make everything seem lovely, idyllic, beautiful. But actually living in these places is quite different. From up close, the country is a deadly boring place, where people rust like old cars.

Even as we drive up, I imagine us leaving.

These rented houses come fully furnished, a must for my father. The owners have always moved far away and we never see them, but this house belongs to a Mr. and Mrs. Burns who have gone to live at her sister's house right in town, while she stays with a dying aunt in Albuquerque.

They have left their dog here. It barks at us when we get out of the car, staying hidden under a hydrangea bush by the front porch. As my father unlocks the trailer, he yells at us to leave the dog alone, that it needs to get used to us first. I've never had a dog before.

Entering a new house for the first time is like getting on a ride at the amusement park. The anticipation is always better. I imagine secret tunnels through closets, hidden rooms, forgotten diaries, maybe even a canopy bed with gauzy white lace just for me. I should know better by now.

Carrying my pillow, I follow my mother along the flat slate stones that lead from the end of the drive to a side porch, which opens up into a bright and airy kitchen. There is a round pine table with two wooden chairs, floral cushions tied to the seats. The green linoleum floor is covered with a road map of fine lines and gray scuff marks. I figure this is where the Burns ate, not in the dining room, which looks formal and dark. In the back of the kitchen is a big mudroom, with steps leading down into the basement. The refrigerator is in the mudroom, empty and well scrubbed, the door propped open like a hungry mouth. In a year, I will clean it out and leave it just like this. It is my job.

In the living room there is an overstuffed couch, a matching chair, and end tables covered with starched old-lady doilies. No family pictures, just landscapes, which my father will hate because they are dull and uninspired. It doesn't matter what is on the walls though, because within the next hour my mother will take them all down and put up my father's old paintings. The first to go up will be the painting of my mother, completely naked, sitting on a chair with her legs crossed, one arm folded over her head, the other barely covering her crotch. She'll hang it in some prominent spot in the living room, where you can't miss it no matter how hard you try.

My mother modeled nude for art classes and that is how my parents met. When kids ask me if that's my mother on the wall with the big boobs, I lie and say no, it's just someone who looks like her. If she hears me, she'll correct me, and tell the story about how she met my father, with more details than anyone wants to know.

Robert, Megan, and I run upstairs. There are four very small bedrooms, one in the front of the house with a double bed, which we leave for my parents. I call the bedroom that faces the road and the tar-papered house. The room has yellow wallpaper and a picture of a baseball player sitting on a bench, holding a bat. I don't know who he is, but I'll leave it there. I have nothing to put in its place, unless I want to put up some of my father's paintings, which I don't. The bed is neatly made with a plain white quilt. No canopy. I throw my pillow on the bed to claim it. Megan and Robert fight over one of the other bedrooms. They know better than to mess with me.

Going back downstairs I see my mother moving an end table over by the front window. Then she moves a chair up against a wall, and asks me to help her move the couch. In the dining room we slide the heavy table up against the wall so there are only three sides to sit at, and then we cover a small dark mahogany cabinet with a sheet and carry it into the basement. We are making room for my father's stretched canvases, his two easels, his toolbox, cut lumber, rolls of canvas, boxes of paints, brushes, and charcoals, and his crates of linseed oil and turpentine. By nightfall, my mother will have removed the curtains in the living room, so more light will come in. This shifting of furniture always makes me nervous. I worry we are not where we are supposed to be, that some mistake has been made. These people may be out to lunch and come home. I will feel this way for weeks.

We unpack the trailer quickly, competently, just as we packed it, as if those minutes we save will make our stay seem longer, as if by emptying the trailer and stashing it on the far side of the barn, we can pretend we have lived here all along.

The dog, whose name is Kip, comes out from his hiding spot, and with his tail between his legs he inches up to us and sniffs our feet. He is an old beagle with sad eyes and short brittle hair that seems to break off rather than shed, and his ears hang almost to the ground, caked with dried mud. My father says the Burns didn't take Kip with them because they now live next to a busy street, and they are afraid he might get hurt. He is supposed to stay outside.

There is also an enormous black bull, two dozen beef cattle, and a milk cow. The beef cattle stay in the back pasture and Mr. Burns told my father we should just ignore them. The milk cow has another pasture, off to the right of the barn, and the bull has his own pen, about two acres, between the barn and the beef cattle.

Before we moved here, my father assured the Burns he knew about cows, then my mother went to the library. She will be in charge of milking the dairy cow.

Just after my mother leaves to go get some groceries, some people pull up the driveway and get out. My stomach turns. But they wave and address my father by name. The Burns have come to see us get settled. Luckily we are outside when they come, so we don't have to open the door and ask them in.

Mr. Burns is a heavy man who is almost bald; he has more hair coming out his ears than covering his head. Even though he's bald, I don't think he is as old as my father, who's almost sixty and has a full head of thick white hair. Mr. Burns wears overalls and a plaid flannel shirt, and his round basketball belly presses taut against the front of his overalls. Mrs. Burns is very short and just as round as Mr. Burns, but her head is covered with tight brown curls. Her eyes are the green of wet grass. She wears jeans and a plaid shirt, and the clunkiest brown shoes I have ever seen. She glances over at the house, and her face kind of freezes as if she is lost in thought. Mr. Burns touches her on the arm and she turns away. They smile at us, but just quick smiles, with their lips closed.

Mr. Burns shakes our hands, and Mrs. Burns nods and says hello. Mrs. Burns' voice is gravelly, like it was used too much and wants to quit working.

"We won't come in," Mr. Burns says. "We don't want to intrude. Just introduce ourselves and make sure you got in all right. Any trouble finding the place?"

My father says the directions were perfect, and thanks for the letters they sent with maps and notes about the house. The dog has scrambled out from under the hydrangea at the sound of the Burns' car and is beside himself with excitement. He rolls on his back and Mr. Burns squats down to scratch his belly. His tail thumps on the ground, scattering pebbles in its wake.

"Well, you must be worn out," Mr. Burns says, straightening back up. "But there are a few things I think you might want to know." He tells us kids that we are allowed to wander in the milk cow's pasture, which is fifteen acres and has a pond we can swim in, as long as we have some adult supervision. He also tells us to stay away from the bull, which doesn't really need saying. The bull looks as if he has a constant headache and if you glance at him funny he might decide to kill you. He has horns about a foot long that curl into deadly points.

"There're some tools out in the barn," Mr. Burns says to my father. He pulls at his earlobe and nods his head toward the barn. "Let me show you where they are." It's my mother he should be showing. The only thing my father can do is paint.

"Well," Mrs. Burns says, "I was hoping to talk to your mother about the cow." She looks at me, since I'm the oldest, but I don't know what to say. After a minute of uncomfortable silence, she says, "Well, I guess I should show you then."

I nod, and return her tight smile, but I still don't know what I'm supposed to do.

"Well, follow me," she says.

Megan and Robert stick close to me as I follow Mrs. Burns to a gate where the barbed-wire fence meets the back right corner of the barn. Mrs. Burns unclips a hook, and the gate swings open. The cow, white with black splotches, is in the field, right past the muddy area behind the barn. It raises its head and stares at us. "Just don't move too fast," she says. "And watch where you step." The cow freezes in mid chew as we approach. She holds so still you can tell she's alive only by the fact she's standing. As we get a few feet away she stumbles backwards, but Mrs. Burns calls out, "Hey, sweetie, come here, sweetie," and the cow freezes again. Mrs. Burns puts her hand on the cow's wide nose, and it moos. Robert jumps a foot.

"Come on now," Mrs. Burns says. "Let her get used to you. Give her a pat. You've been around cows before, right?" Remembering what my father has told us, we all nod. Megan, the youngest, is the first one to touch the cow, then me. My brother, Robert, hangs back, as if he is waiting his turn, which, if it's up to him, will be never. He's wearing his stupid Davy

Crockett hat, as if he is some brave hunter, but he's really just a coward. A fat little chubby coward. His ears stick out under his hat like handles.

The cow feels like the dog, sort of bristly yet soft. She's warm to the touch, and her skin moves against her body as if it's not connected to the muscles in the same way ours is. She smells like nothing I ever smelled before, which is what I presume is the smell of cow, which is hard to separate from the smell of manure, which is everywhere.

"You say your mother knows how to milk a cow?" Mrs. Burns says, sounding concerned, maybe even doubtful we have a mother at all.

We nod. If reading dozens of books can teach you how to milk a cow, then my mother knows how.

"Well then, all right. Let's go back now." Mrs. Burns is so bent over she has no problem looking where she's walking. And now I know why she wears those shoes. Mine are covered with mud, and probably manure. I'd throw them away, but they are my only pair of sneakers. Mrs. Burns shows us how to close the gate. "Always make sure you close it behind you," she says. "I wouldn't want the cow to get out and wander on the road."

Their car is the second car I've seen on this road since we came here. The cow would probably be safe taking a nap right dab in the middle of the road, but I tell her we'll be careful.

"What's her name?" Megan asks in her sweet little voice she does so well.

"Well, I guess she doesn't have a name. She's a cow."

Megan and I look at each other.

Mr. Burns and my father are waiting by the Burns' car. "If you don't mind," Mr. Burns says, "I'd like to come by on Sundays after church, to check on the cattle, set out some fresh hay. I won't be a bother to you at all."

"Not a bother at all," my father says.

"We go to the Methodist church in Westfield, about a forty-minute ride from here," Mrs. Burns offers. "There's also a nice Baptist church right in Mayville and a Presbyterian church way over in Jamestown. We can give you directions."

"Don't worry," my father says. "We'll be fine."

There is silence for a minute while Mr. Burns looks at all of us, tugging again on his ear. "Gosh," he says. "I didn't think to ask if you all are Jewish. With a name like Anderson, I didn't think about you being Jewish." He looks over at Mrs. Burns, as if maybe this is a problem.

"Oh, we're not Jewish," my father says. The Burns look relieved. They even laugh.

"All right then, we'll see you Sunday, about one." They get in their car. Kip moves quickly and hops right over Mrs. Burns and into the front seat. Mr. Burns has to drag him out. Nose almost scraping the ground, tail between his legs, Kip goes back to the hydrangea bush. "See you Sunday," Mr. Burns says, maybe to the dog, maybe to us. They drive off.

If my mother were here she would have told them right out that we're atheists. But my father is like me in just this one way: we don't mention things if we don't have to.

No one's ever asked us if we're Jewish before. I wonder which is worse.

We move in spring because my father wants to see the land bare, before it fills in with the flesh of green that summer brings. He would move us in the dead of winter, but my mother refuses him this, saying it would be too disorienting for us to change schools halfway through a year. Except he gets so edgy during that time when things begin to bud that my mother packs earlier and earlier each year, and my father just happens to find us houses that are in need of tenants in May, not June. So we are pulled out of school and shuffled into a new one for the last few weeks. My mother excuses these moves while school is still going by saying this way we can get to know a few kids first, and we'll have someone to play with during summer vacation. The fact that we never get invited to other kids' houses, or invite anyone to ours, doesn't change her mind. Things that are rational should work. She has a hypothesis. She will just repeat the experiment until she is proven right.

It is a wonder we even survive these moves. My mother, who does the driving, refuses to wear glasses, even though she needs them for distance. When I was six, she went to an eye doctor who told her she had to get glasses, and she dutifully went out and bought a pair. But she didn't like what she saw.

"Oh," she said. "Everything has such sharp edges. I didn't know that." Then one day as we were driving on the highway she got upset. "I hate these signs they put up, all these advertisements for such junk! The words jump out at you. It's distracting." She took off her glasses. "Much better," she said. That was the last I ever saw of her glasses.

My father hardly ever drives, even though his eyes are fine. He doesn't drive because of what he does see. Lines and colors and shapes moving past him too quickly to get a hold of. He used to drive at least half of the time during our long trips, but he drove slowly, weaving and stopping randomly, until my mother simply said *I'll drive,* and she did.

My father never told my mother to put her glasses back on. My mother never told him to keep his eyes on the road.

In the morning, my mother milks the cow as we all watch. She has trouble at first holding on to the teats, and getting the milk to go in the bucket. The cow makes funny low sounds as if she is trying to sing with a stomachache. Finally my mother gets the hang of it and milks her dry. Holding up the bucket, she asks us who wants to try some milk. We decline. Watching it come out of the cow changes everything. I may never drink milk again.

She names the bull Harry after her father, who died of tuberculosis, and the cow Edith after her mother, who drove into a tree four months later. The beef cattle remain nameless, which is for the best since they are just walking hamburgers and pot roast.

While my mother is gone, registering us at the new school which we will start attending on Monday, Megan, Robert, and I find a boy's bike in the barn. It's carmine red, with rusted handlebars and flat tires, but it's still a find; we have never had a bike, our own or anyone else's. When our mother comes back, Robert begs her to take us into town to have the tires filled. She agrees, after phoning the Burns to ask if it is all right that we ride the bike. It's too big for Megan, but Robert and I could give her rides, and she is just as excited as we are.

On the way to the Texaco station on the far side of town, my mother informs us that the bike belonged to the Burns' son, Timothy.

"He died," she says. "Last year. He was only sixteen. He died of leukemia. That's cancer of the blood. It's very sad."

"Did he die *in the house?*" asks Robert, who reads the same horror magazines over and over again—*Chilling Tales, Worlds of Fear,* and *The Vault of Horror*—scared each time, maybe *more* scared each time. He tapes the pages back together when they fall apart and stubbornly packs them up in his cardboard box, refusing to leave them behind, even though my father thinks he should. It is the only time Robert ever defies my father. I think having horror magazines makes him feel protected. They are *his* villains, *his* monsters. He hasn't brought any on this short trip, too distracted by the bike.

My mother pauses as if she might not answer his question, but, of course, she finally does. She is a big believer in information. "Yes, he died in the house," she says.

My brother gasps. "No!"

"Where?" I ask.

She pauses again. "In bed," she says.

"Which bed is that?" I ask.

"Yours," she says. "But Mrs. Burns said she bought new sheets and blankets, just for you."

"Oh, great," I say. "I'm so glad. That makes all the difference." I wish she would have lied. There are many times I wished she would have lied, but this time I really wish she could have. Sometimes lies are preferable to the truth.

We spend a half hour at the gas station as my mother asks the attendant how the bike should be oiled, what the tire pressure should be, what bolts should be tightened. The attendant, a twenty-year-old acne-faced nerd with gray teeth and oil-stained fingernails, does more than answer my mother's questions. He fixes the bike for us—*for her*. She is good at this, getting people to like her, because she asks so many questions, then listens intently to the answers. Besides, she is breathtakingly beautiful, with golden-blond hair, green eyes, and big breasts. You wouldn't know we were related except for those breasts. Even with big breasts, I'm no looker. My hair is the color of wet sand, my eyes are ordinary brown, and my lips are lopsided, the top lip larger than the bottom. He wouldn't have fixed the bike for me.

Before we go back to the rented farm with the now slickly oiled bike, she takes us to the library, her favorite place on earth. She tells Robert to find a book on bike maintenance and Megan and I are to find books about the area we now live in, as if anything interesting might have been written about Mayville, New York. I would complain, but it is good to see her acting like her old self. She hasn't forced us to go to the library for months. She hasn't discussed, page by page, the latest *National Geographic* for even longer than that. But today she seems lively and overly anxious to teach us. Just like old times.

At dinner my mother says the Burns rented this house because they couldn't bear to be in it any longer after their son died. She says they should sell it, but can't, because their memories hold them to the house like an anchor. She says those memories can pull them under so they can't breathe any longer. She says they have jumped ship, but not swum far enough to escape the undertow. My mother loves metaphors almost as much as she loves the bare facts of life.

I am sleeping in a room where someone died. A kid, like me. Right here. Right in the space I'm in. Every time I hear a strange sound my eyes fly open and I am sure, for a brief moment, I see something, so I close my eyes again.

The attic of the house, which can be reached through a trap-door in the ceiling, is filled with boxes of the dead boy's stuff, and we are not allowed to go up there. I hear noises coming from up in the attic. I can hear the boxes whisper.

Out behind the house, just past the garden, where the ground begins to rise into the hill, is a half-completed bomb shelter made of gray cinder blocks and cement. There is a doorway, but no door, and steps leading down to the cement floor six feet below. The walls are finished and they extend two feet above the ground. There is no roof. I suppose the Burns stopped building it when their son died.

I try to imagine my parents without us kids. I can.

Two

At first I just watch them from my bedroom window.

One is a skinny boy, about my age or maybe a year younger, with light-orange hair and a pale round face. It's kind of exciting, the idea of a boy right across the road. It's certainly better than no boy, or a dead boy. It's hard to tell from this distance if he's cute at all. At least he's not fat, like my brother.

It's rained a lot in these past three days, but whenever the rain stops, he comes out of his tar-paper house and takes off into the woods carrying something: a board, a tin pot, a mug, a box of crackers.

Sometimes his sister follows him. She is the same height as her brother, and skinny, but with a narrow face and tangled hair the color of sawdust. I wonder if they're twins. He yells at her to get lost, but she still follows him. She doesn't stay away long. When she comes back, her arms are folded across her chest, her face even longer than before.

Today they are in their enormous and overgrown vegetable garden, with their older sister, a large-boned girl who must be past school age, maybe almost twenty. She has hair that falls in dark-red curls to her waist, tied back loosely in a thick ponytail. She has her brother's round face and she is fleshy, but not fat. She moves in a slow, peaceful way. Although I am too far away, I'm sure she hums as she works; the way she pulls the weeds from the ground, tosses them aside, then bends down again, has a rhythm that comes only from music. I believe I can hear the music as I watch.

The thin, tangled-haired girl puts down her basket and runs over to the tire swing. The tire is tied by a rope to the thick limb of a twisted ancient maple at the back of their house, an unfinished house that looks like it will never be finished. The girl is too big for the swing and her butt hardly fits through the hollow opening of the tire. She turns herself around until the rope gets twisted real good, then lets go and it spins her like a top. I'd be too embarrassed to play on a swing at her age. I grow dizzy watching.

They have a mother who comes and goes, wearing a tan uniform when she leaves in the morning, then comes home around four, goes inside for a half hour, then comes back out wearing a dull gold uniform, both shapeless dresses with big square pockets. She drives a dark-blue car and the door shrieks when she closes it. The back of the car has a huge dent on the driver's side, and the bumper wobbles like a broken jaw. If her car were an animal, I'd shoot it.

The father has only come outside a few times, to carry garbage to the compost by the garden, and to work on one of the junk cars when it's not raining. His face is very narrow, and he's as tall as my father, a little over six feet. He keeps his right leg straight all the time and kind of has to throw it around his body in a half circle to take a step. My brother calls him Frankenstein.

I will write their names in my diary when I meet them, so I will remember them. It is the only way I remember the names of people I have met, and sometimes even the names don't bring back a face. Some people are so forgettable.

.   .   .

"Hey! Come here!" the skinny girl yells at me from across the blacktop road. It's our fourth day here, and finally it's stopped raining.

She stands on a lawn that is mostly dandelions. The furry yellow flowers weren't there yesterday. In the woods behind her house, the trees have tight green buds as if someone squeezed the trunks and green burst out at the tip of every branch. Spring has come with the rain. It's May and finally warm, not a false warmth but a promise.

From up close, she looks like she's been hibernating. Her skin is white as a ghost's and her hair is a mess. Her face is very plain and she has a long, thin, triangular chin. What I notice most is her elbows and knees, which are knobby and make her arms and legs look even thinner than they are.

Instead of walking down our pebbly driveway in my bare feet, I jump across the ditch in front of our house, my jump not good enough to clear the pebbly edge of the road. Stones scatter in all directions as I skid and slip backwards into the ditch filled with a good four inches of cold water, which immediately soaks straight through my jeans and into my underpants. Embarrassment heats my face like a sunburn, but I will it away. In a year, I'll be gone. It is this girl who will have to stay in this nowhere place with the embarrassment of her tar-paper house.

I pretend I don't even notice my pants are wet as I get up and cross the road.

"Hey," she says. "You moved into the Burns' house, huh?"

"Yeah," I say, thinking she sure is bright.

"You know what happened in that house, don't you?"

"Yeah," I say. "Their kid died. I'm in his room." I say this like it doesn't bother me at all.

"Ewww! I couldn't sleep in there. Not a chance. My name's Brenda." She sticks out her hand.

"I'm Tamara." I shake her hand.

"What?" she asks. Everyone asks that.

"Tamara."

"They call you Tammy?"

"No. Just Tamara. Like *tomorrow* with an *a*."

"Oh."

We stare at each other. She has a smudge of dirt running all the way down her right cheek.

"My brother's Rusty," she says. "And my sister's Helen."

I think Helen is a perfect name for her older sister, like Helen of Troy. And I bet they call her brother Rusty because of his red hair. Then they should call this girl Mop Head. I feel myself grinning and bite my lip. "My sister is Megan," I say. "My brother is Robert. Megan's seven and Robert's eleven. I'm almost fifteen."

"I'm fourteen too!" Brenda says. "I turned fourteen on April 10th. Rusty's fifteen, and Helen's nineteen. What's your dad do?"

"He's a painter," I say. "He paints pictures that get hung in galleries in New York City. He paints landscapes."

Which is why we move each year. We find houses to rent, then leave them behind like a snake sheds its skin. My father outgrows the landscape. He needs new lines, new hues, new inspiration.

"Are you going to go to school here?" Brenda asks.

"Sure." We came on Thursday. Tomorrow is Monday. There are only about three weeks of school left. I've only finished the same grade in the same school once.

"What grade are you in?" she asks.

"Tenth." I'm ahead a grade, just like my brother and sister.

"So, you'll ride on the bus with us?"

"Yep."

"I'm in eighth grade," Brenda says. "I hate my homeroom teacher. Mrs. Burt. I call her Mrs. Butt. You'll get Mrs. Green or Mrs. Hawthorn. They both seem nice. We gotta be out here at seven-thirty. The bus won't wait. It's Mr. Matthews. He hates kids. You want to come in and meet my family?"

I shudder. I'm not going in that house. "No, thanks. I got to help my mom. Nice to meet you."

"Okay." Brenda rubs at her face with the back of her hand. The smudge grows bigger. She shrugs. "See you at seven-thirty. Better be a little early."

"Okay," I say, knowing my mom will drive us to school on our first day. I don't want to tell Brenda. She might ask for a ride. I don't want to show up at school on the first day with Brenda. I've got a good feeling she's not too popular. If she is, I'm in more trouble than I thought.

We always live in these backward places where the schools are easy; even a grade ahead I get straight A's. My mother was a science teacher, until she gave it up for my father, and my father was a math teacher, until he gave it up for art. They are both so full of information they are likely to burst. They ease the weight of so much knowledge by passing it on to us, like other parents might pass a football or a platter of brownies.

They are so alike inside and so different on the outside. My father is six feet four with an abundance of white hair, and piercing light-blue eyes. He's almost sixty, much older than my mother, but he still looks imposing because of those eyes and his height and the way he holds himself up so straight. Some people think him a snob, but he doesn't realize it. He's not a snob, he just doesn't know how to carry on a normal conversation. I understand my father, I just don't like him.

My mother doesn't know how to carry on a normal conversation either, but that doesn't stop her. She's only as tall as me, five feet six, and her blond hair and pale skin make her look soft and vulnerable, but she lets you know that's a mistake pretty quickly. People think she's charmingly eccentric. My mother loves my father, more than us, more than herself, and he loves her, even more than art, so I forgive him his trespasses. He loves us too, but we come after art.

The only family member I think is interesting is my grandmother, my mother's mother, who died when she drove into a tree. When my mother speaks of her, which is not often, she describes it as an accident. "My mother died in a car accident," she will say, in a tone that stops all other questions. But I think my grandmother killed herself from grief, after her husband died. I imagine her behind the wheel, headed directly toward that tree, firm, unflinching. It's an image that sticks with me. I want to be strong like that. Determined. I feel my jaw tighten as I pretend I am her.

I used to wish I could paint, like my father. With pastels I drew trees and hills and suns. I could draw them all separate, and you'd know exactly what they were, but I couldn't put them together. I could never figure out depth. It's like music, which I love. When I try to sing, I can get each note, but the notes never slide together, become a melody. I'm good at math. I like taking apart the functions. I like the way things add up to a right or wrong answer. I like the fact I'm good at it.

But sometimes I take out my pastels. Sometimes I wish I could sing.

Only occasionally will my father pack up his easel, canvas, and paints, and drive to some other valley or hilltop. Mostly he wakes up, walks around the perimeter of whatever house we are living in, stops at some particular spot looking out toward the trees, and nods as if in greeting. Then he goes inside and gets his easel and sets up for the day, painting that same view for the next few weeks; a morning version and a late-afternoon version. He begins with a sketch in pencil on paper, which will take countless revisions, then moves to canvas and oil. He has a cigar box filled with gum erasers he tosses across the yard in frustration, and it is our job to collect them at the end of the day. He pays us a penny apiece, and still we don't always find all of them. We leave erasers behind us like bread crumbs. As a child, I used to imagine tossing them one by one out the car window as we moved, so I could find my way back.

A few months ago, I decided to be rational and try to talk my father out of our constant moves. I set up my questions like a math problem, believing I could lead him to an answer that would prove we didn't have to keep moving. As he set up his easel only ten feet from the back door of our house in Diamond, Georgia, I calmly approached him and asked him why he always painted so close to the house.

"Look out there," he said. It was early morning and our back lawn was three acres of mowed grass, dotted with a few old magnolias casting shadows like black ink on the dewy grass. Beyond the lawn was the edge of a national park, thick with tall weeds and muddy swamps. "Look at the robins, how they stand guard over the earth, watching for a worm to escape. Today is the first time I've seen robins this way. I've seen them before as birds in flight, or perched on the tops of trees to sun themselves in the late afternoon. I've seen them as color—*used* them for color—placing them where I need them, but I've never seen them this way, like prison guards. I want to capture them this way, see what it will do to the rest of the painting. It is the small things that bring a painting to life. There is a challenge right here, where I stand, that I can't resist."

I thought about that, how it fit into my equation, and I asked my next question carefully. "Then why do you drag us across the country each year? When you get done with the views from this house, why can't we just move a mile or two away, to a place you haven't painted yet? Why drag us so far away just to stand in the back yard?"

"To jar my soul," he said. "Or because I am afraid. Now, I have to sketch the robins before the light changes, but good try, Tamara." He turned away, to look at the lawn, to raise his pencil to the canvas, and even though I didn't step back, I was gone. Erased.

That was, and will be, my last attempt at rational argument. When my mother told us we were moving to Mayville, New York, I threw a fit for days, my best fit ever. I refused to eat dinner but sat at the table and glared at my parents. I threatened to slit my wrists, but when I took the blade out of my father's razor, I got scared and sliced up my pillow instead. My mother bought a new pillow without a word of comment. I hid the car keys until my father said he'd break all my records. I even tore a hunk of hair out of my head that is only beginning to grow back. The day we moved I refused to pack the trailer, so my mother did my part. When it was time to leave I said I wouldn't get in the car, but she just stood there holding the door open. She was so pale and tired-looking I got in the car, but I'll never do that again. I'll never move again.

In the school cafeteria I carry my tray over to a table with six girls whom I met in my class today, all of them with the latest short haircuts and tight-belted candy-colored dresses. Some are taller, or fatter, but interchangeable in their perky bright-eyed way. Across the room are the girls with the long braids or frizzy hair, wearing last year's fashions and scuffed dull shoes. Brenda waves to me from over there. I can't wave back since I'm holding my tray. I have already looked her way more than I am supposed to. I turn away and ask if I can sit with the popular girls.

They say sure, eager to decide if I am a yo-yo or if I am cool. If they decide I'm cool, they will accept me temporarily. I will still have to prove myself in the long run, but I won't have the time. When the summer begins, I will never see them. The cool kids are the ones who live in town, where they can easily get together. Those of us who live on the outskirts, where distance is too great for the constant collisions that form friendships, are forgotten. By fall, when I come back to school, I will have lost the advantage of being the new kid, and will be in the void of the slightly familiar.

By next winter, I will be sitting on the other side of the cafeteria. By spring, I will be gone.

The girls at this table study me as I sit down. They have no past history of me to ease them into who I am. Who I am is not a thing, like a ticket, I can take out of my pocket and hand over for admittance. But there is an advantage to this, if only for the last three weeks of school. I can be someone new this time.

Last year a boy asked me if I was a communist, a red spy. "You don't go to church," he said, loud enough for everyone to hear.

"I am an atheist, not a communist, stupid," I said.

Denials were no good. From that moment on I was an atheist, a communist, and a red spy, a deadly combination, especially with Joe McCarthy pointing his finger at everyone and sending them to jail. Adults would walk by us in town with their lips pressed together in tight smiles, as if they were afraid to breathe too deeply near us. Even my mother's charms could not win them over.

My mother said I did the right thing, telling the boy we were atheists. She only reprimanded me for calling him stupid. "He might have been willing to listen to you explain the difference between communists and democratic atheists if you hadn't offended him," she said. "It's his loss," she sighed.

But I learn from my mistakes. "Where are you from?" a girl in a blinding yellow dress asks me, who might be a Debby, or a Trudy, or a Maggie. One of those.

"Austria," I say. "We lived there for the last few years." What the hell. I have only three weeks to keep this lie together. By fall they won't care.

"Wow," says a Susi or a Holly, or maybe this is Maggie. "Tell us about it."

I picked Austria because I did a report on it a couple weeks ago at my last school. I tell them about the Alps, the thin air, the goats. They nod and look at each other with wide eyes and I know I will be sitting on this side of the cafeteria, for now.

Robert, Megan, and I ride the bus home. Brenda sees me and hollers that she's saved me a seat. There is nothing I can do. Her brother, Rusty, who is near the front of the bus, smiles at me, then looks out the window. A cute, shy smile. He has freckles everywhere. My brother, Robert, sits across the aisle from Rusty and looks at him like a puppy looking at a bone that belongs to a bigger dog. Megan follows me and tries to sit in my lap, but I push her off and tell her to go find a seat of her own. The only seat left is next to a boy with slick, oily hair who is wearing a black leather coat. Megan glares at me with narrow eyes and sits with her legs turned toward the aisle.

Brenda tells me about everyone on the bus, whispering hoarsely in my ear. The boy with the glasses and a thick ear has a mom who is blind. A girl with a cast on her leg fell off the cement ledge of the school building while trying to show off. The girl wearing the pink sweater with a hole in the sleeve had lice this year and last year. A fourth-grade boy sucking his thumb had a father who was killed by a mine. One girl eats dirt. Another has BO. There is something the matter with everyone on this bus.

I can't help thinking about the Burns' boy. If someone new came to school last year, Brenda would have been saying, *See that boy there? He's real sick. He might die.* He's the one I want to hear about. I wonder what he looked like.

I have this feeling he's still in the house. That he's angry at me for using his room. That I should apologize to him for something. I tell myself I don't believe in ghosts, but when I get off the bus I look up at the window of my room. The curtain moves.

When I go in the house my mother is sitting at the kitchen table writing on a yellow legal pad. There are crumpled pieces of paper all over the table, the floor, and even in the sink. She looks up. Her green eyes are round and glassy. Robert, Megan, and I all stop, piled up between the door and the table. "Well?" she asks. "Were there any? Tell me there were."

"No," I say. "Not a single Negro in the whole school." I know exactly what she is talking about because on the car ride from Georgia she heard on the radio that the Supreme Court ordered an end to school segregation. When she asked us if there had been talk about it at school, we had said sure, there were rumors some Negro kids were planning on coming to our school and lots of white families were going to protest by keeping their kids home if the Negroes came. This made my mother crazy.

"They'll think we pulled you out because we support them! If I only knew. How could I have missed it? What can we do? They need to know the truth! I'll have to write and explain. What must they think of us!"

It is this "us" that makes *me* crazy. Everything is always "us." When I pulled my hair out, she said, "Look what you have done to us." It was *my* hair. And I had nothing to do with moving us from a school that would have to be desegregated to this school that is definitely going to stay all white. Even the really poor people around here, the ones who live in those trailers, are white. I bet my parents couldn't have picked a whiter place if they tried.

"Are you sure?" she asks, as if we might have missed just one colored kid.

"I'm sure," I say.

"It would have made it so much better if I could have written that we chose a school that was integrated. Now I don't know what to say. Every time I start this letter I get so upset. Maybe I should wait a few days until I'm not so emotional about it." There is a tear running down her face. This is so odd we can do nothing but stare and nod.

Megan helps my mother pick up the yellow balls of paper. Robert opens the refrigerator. I go upstairs to my room and put on my 45 of "Hey, There" and play it over and over because there is something about Rosemary Clooney's deep voice that always calms me down, takes me away from the things that are bothering me. But it doesn't work this time. I remember the last letter my mother wrote, just two months ago. She read that the government might add "under God" to the Pledge of Allegiance and wrote a letter to President Eisenhower, *and* to our teachers, informing them that "the phrase *under God* is offensive." She didn't have any trouble writing *that* letter. My teacher pinned the note on the bulletin board. The few friends I had never spoke to me again, except to taunt me. Robert and Megan lost their friends too, but they had each other to play with. I wanted to kill my mother. Just remembering it makes me so mad I bite my arm until I can't take it anymore.

At dinner, my mother is still weepy and upset. Every time she speaks, her words come out watery like she's talking right through a throatful of tears. My father suggests she go to bed early and she agrees. Then he tells us to clean up.

"She's tired from the move," he says when he comes into the kitchen to see how we are doing. He looks at Robert washing the dishes and Megan drying. "This move was especially difficult for her," he says directly to me.

I get the point. I begin to wipe the counter, and he leaves.

·   ·   ·

Tuesday the Girl Scouts and Boy Scouts have their meetings
after school in the gym. Brenda is a Girl Scout. Every girl in the
school is a Girl Scout. Or a Brownie. Every boy is a Cub Scout or
a Boy Scout. Everyone wears a uniform to school. Everyone has a
badge. This school has four hundred and ten kids enrolled, from
kindergarten to twelfth grade, and they are all walking around
in freshly pressed greens and browns like perfectly wrapped
packages. I pass my brother in the hall and I catch myself looking at him with hope. I want to feel like I belong somewhere,
even if it's just part of my stupid family, but he is looking at
the passing boys with such obvious longing it makes me sick,
and instead of a smile and a wave like I was planning, I stick
my foot out and trip him. He falls. His books go flying. A Boy
Scout helps him up. Another picks up his books. More badges, I
suppose.

Helen is helping my mother in the garden. They are both kneeling
on the ground, turning over the earth with trowels. Helen wears
a sleeveless gingham dress and a yellow sun hat tied under her
chin with a white ribbon. She's barefoot. It's not really warm, but
she doesn't seem to mind. Next to Helen, my mother looks awkward and bony. My mother has always been well padded, as she
used to say. But she isn't anymore. I try to remember when I first
noticed she had lost weight, but I can't.

Helen lifts up a fistful of dirt and squeezes it. The dirt falls
from her hand like dark-brown rain. "It's good earth because of
the night crawlers," Helen says.

The garden is about fifty feet by twenty feet. Nubs of old
dry growth stick up all over like partially uncovered bones. My
mother and Helen have been out here for hours and only turned
over the dirt in a small corner. "Tomatoes do very well in this
sun," Helen says. "We should plant five or six varieties. Mrs.
Burns had the beans over there. But really, we should get the

lettuce and spinach in soon. I don't think it will frost heavy again this late in May, it's been so warm. Maybe a light frost. Would you like to help, Tamara?"

I can't think of anything I want to do less than kneeling in dirt, but there is something about Helen that makes me want to please her. I love the way her hair spills over her shoulders and curls around her face in tiny little ringlets. My hair is so straight and thin. And Helen seems so happy, so pleased. I want to know why. I say, fine, I'll help.

"And Robert and Megan could help too," Helen says. She smiles at my mother. "Would you like me to come into town with you, to get some seeds?"

"Why, thank you, Helen," my mother says. "I think I'd like that."

Helen stands and steps back to look at the garden, like my father steps back to look at his paintings. I can tell she is seeing this garden full, thick with vegetables, bees pollinating flowers, tomatoes ripening. I look at the garden, trying to see it with Helen's eyes. It just looks like a big mess to me.

My mother was a rebel. At the age of sixteen, following the death of her mother, she moved to New York City to live with her aunt and uncle. She never talks about her parents or her life before they died, but more than once she has told the story of how on her very first day in New York City her aunt and uncle took her to Saint Patrick's Cathedral, and suddenly, looking around at the stone arches and carved saints and tremendous stained-glass windows, she began to think about all the wars fought in the name of religion, of the millions killed and tortured. Nailed to crosses and burned. When she thought of all the horrible things in the world—starvation, rape, crime, disease, and accidents—she lost all belief in God, all her belief in religion, which was that of a good Presbyterian. It was like having something taken out of her hand, something she had been holding tightly for so long, yet once it was gone, there was no memory of its weight, of its shape, of its purpose or use. And, she says, she felt stronger, as if instead of losing something, she had gained something new. She says becoming an atheist had nothing to do with the death of her parents.

Then she went to college, and became a science teacher. She got a job at a high school in the city, and joined a small group of underground communists, but she was bothered by their anger and propaganda, and quit. To find something interesting to do with her spare time, she began modeling for art classes at the Art Students League, in the nude. The rest is history. She taught school for only three years, unless you count the time she kept us home for a year and tried to teach us herself.

She often talks about teaching, how much she loved it, but lately she doesn't even talk that much. I wonder why she gave up teaching, but I think it was because she got pregnant so young. I was conceived before they got married. That's another story she tells, how I was conceived in bright and beautiful love. She doesn't actually say that I am also the destroyer of great rebellious dreams.

No one mentions that my mother has slowed down, that she wraps her arms about her chest instead of dragging books home from the library or writing letters to *Time* magazine, that she has hollow pockets under her eyes. That she coughs and can't stop. That she sometimes walks off and doesn't come back for hours. Megan has started following her, as if she's afraid my mother might not come back. Sometimes when Robert and I fight, instead of lecturing us she just sighs. The sigh is worse than a lecture. We don't say anything about her being sick, because she doesn't. We are all like Kip, who hides under the hydrangea bush.

Three

My mother pats the cow's hip. "Go on now, Edith, go on." The cow lumbers to the barn door, where it stops, halfway in and halfway out. She blinks, the sun in her face. It looks like she's thinking, trying to make a difficult decision. Finally, her heavy square head nods up and down a few times, as if she is agreeing on something she has decided. Still, it takes her some time to get back into motion, then climb up the hill. Cows move slowly, except when they are going to get fed a special treat, something other than hay and grass. We give Edith a special grain in the early evening, and she knows by the angle of the sun just when that's going to be. She comes running down that hill like all get-out, more stumbling forward than running. A galloping cow is the silliest sight I've ever seen. The first time we saw her do that we laughed until tears leaked out of our eyes. My mother fell on the ground, right down, as if her legs gave out, holding her stomach as if it might explode. That is when she began to love Edith. She has always loved awkward things.

· · ·

On the way into town, Helen sits in the front seat next to my mother. Robert, Megan, and I are in the back seat. We each have a dollar we can spend in town. That means ten comics for my brother. He is so excited he's bouncing on his seat and I elbow him once hard in the ribs. "Leave off, duffus," I tell him. "Or else." He sticks out his tongue at me. He's so immature.

"So, Helen," my mother says. "Will you really be able to help me with this garden? You must be busy. Do you have a job, or plans to go to college?"

"No," Helen says. "I'm waiting for God to tell me what to do. I'm helping out at home right now, so that must be what He wants. It's hard for our mother, having two jobs. My dad's a mechanic, but the gas station he worked at burned down last summer. He hasn't found another job yet, and he has trouble moving around because of his injury from the war."

Robert and I look at each other. We both want to know more about this injury, but my mother hasn't heard a word past the God stuff.

"Waiting for God to tell you what to do?" my mother says. The way she says this, her voice both low and very firm, I know my mother wants to grab Helen and shake some sense into her. A lecture on the folly of religious belief is forming inside her like storm clouds. The car slows.

"Yes." This is all Helen says.

My mother sighs. "I can't believe it," she says. "So foolish." She shakes her head.

It is obvious Helen is completely baffled by this. Still, she doesn't get mad. She thinks she must have misunderstood. "Pardon me?"

But we are in town now, and my brother spots the five-and-dime. "Over there!" he shouts. "That store! They got to have comics. Park there! There's a spot! Park there!" He's bouncing again. The smelly tail of his coonskin hat swings against my face. I grab it off his head and hold it out the window.

"No!" he screams at the top of his voice.

My mother screeches to a halt in the middle of the street. I bounce forward and smack my chin on the back of Helen's seat. Megan falls to the floor.

"What?" my mother shouts. "What?"

Robert and I both try to explain, our stories quite different.

"Never mind," she says. "Just be quiet." She pulls into the open spot in front of the five-and-dime. Robert grabs his hat out of my hand and hops out of the car before she can even turn it off.

"Robert!" my mother shouts, then looks at me, with the same exact look my sister had when she had to sit next to the guy in the leather jacket. She's looking at me as if this is all my fault. I think she's just upset she didn't get to debate Helen.

"They'll have seeds here," Helen says, getting out of the car and shutting the door gently. She does everything gently.

My father sells his pictures in galleries in New York City, but he doesn't make quite enough to support a family of five, so he also paints pictures to order, to match the interiors of people's homes. He calls them couch pictures. People send samples of their couch upholstery, little folds of wallpaper, swatches of curtains, patches of carpet. One lady sent a dessert plate of her best china, and wanted him to copy it. It's best not to be around my father when these missives arrive.

He runs ads in newspapers all over the country, using a fake name. But now most of his customers come to him by word of mouth. Many of these people not only want him to match the color to something that they already own, they are also specific about what kind of picture they want. *A Monet, but not a Monet,* one woman wrote. *Blend the spots together a bit more.* Another wanted a picture of seven trees in a meadow. The trees represented her family and were to be age specific. She sent a long list of the personalities of her children, hoping he could capture those qualities in the trees themselves. She also listed the types of trees she felt were appropriate. A regal maple for her husband, a pin oak for herself (with the acorns showing, her seed, which produced the children). Her children were to be all different kinds of trees. Obviously, the acorns went through some form of metamorphosis, or they were adopted tree-children. My father sent a note back saying he didn't think he would be able to accomplish all she asked, and maybe she should try someone else. It was the only time I know of that he refused.

He paints these pictures inside, from noon to three, five days a week. He frowns and mutters under his breath. If you get near him, he will snap at you. The rest of the time he is okay. Not chummy or very warm, but if you sneeze, he says gesundheit.

My father paints one picture a year that isn't a couch picture or one that he sends to New York City. He paints a simple head-on view of the house we're staying in at that time, and leaves it as a thank-you for the people who are coming back from France or wherever else they have gone for the year. When we see him start on that picture, we know we have less than a few weeks.

My father finds these rented houses through a man he pays to look through newspapers and magazines. The man sends my father clippings, with notes scratched in the margins. I have the urge, when I see those manila envelopes come in the mail, to grab them and throw them away. But I don't.

Because I throw fits when I find we are moving again, they never tell us until the last possible moment. From the time my father starts his farewell painting until we actually move is always the very worst.

.   .   .

When the Burns come on Sunday after church, my father is inside painting a couch picture, my mother is planting petunias in a spot of freshly dug earth by the barn, Robert is trying to scratch his name on one of the flat slate stones, Megan is climbing a small apple tree in the field, and I am bored silly, wearing cutoffs and lying in the sun to get tan. As soon as I see their car I want to shout. *Get out of the tree! Turn the stone over! Hide the petunias! Get out of their house!* I am the only one not messing with their things, but then I realize I'm lying on their towel. I want to apologize for us, for taking their place, for not having a house of our own.

There is an awkward moment while my mother introduces herself. She turns to the house, expecting my father to come out and say hello, but he doesn't. I have jumped up off the towel and am standing up, thinking it rude to lie down while they are here. I imagine us all standing up for the rest of the afternoon. How can we sit down if they won't? Mr. Burns excuses himself to go tend to the cattle. Mrs. Burns asks my mother how everything is going.

"Wonderful," my mother says. "It's a lovely house. We couldn't be happier."

I turn red, not because of the sun, but because this house was such an unhappy place for the Burns that they left it, and can't even walk back inside. Mrs. Burns looks at me and I blush more, thinking she can read my mind and knows I am thinking about her dead son. She says hello, but then her eyes get kind of glassy and she holds perfectly still, staring at me, but not at me. It's like she is seeing something else—or someone else. I think maybe she sees me as someone who might have been here visiting her son, a girlfriend maybe. For a moment, I feel that way too, that I am not part of my family, but part of something that might have been.

Mrs. Burns blinks, and turns back to my mother. "Are you planting annuals?" she asks, with an edge to her voice. "I never would have thought of planting flowers over there, but it makes perfect sense. You'll be able to see them from the kitchen window. Would you like some help?"

"Please," my mother says. "I'd love some." Together they walk over to the barn.

Mrs. Burns looks back at me one last time. Her eyes do that hazy thing, and I think she frowns. It's hard to tell, because she turns away so quickly. I think I am a reminder that most children grow up healthy. I think she's not sure if that's a good thing to know.

Taking a left at the end of our driveway and walking about a half mile along Moore, we come to an intersection with another road, Potter. It leads up and up and up a steep hill, part of the ridge behind our house. The top of this hill is called Valley View Hill by the locals. From here you can see dozens of miles into the distance, hills following hills like folds of heavy cloth. Houses dot the hillsides; they are small boxes of secrets. I want to pluck off the roofs, see what's inside. From up on top of the hill I feel very big, and everything else seems very small and silent.

Every evening, a half hour before sunset, my mother and father lead us up this hill, making us walk on the stony berm of the road, in case a car comes over the top, which it never does, but my mother is cautious. Sitting on flattened hay we watch the sky over the rolling hills turn pink, then magenta, then deep violet. Straight above our heads the sky stays blue, the blue of that particular day: light blue, cerulean blue, French ultramarine, even blues my father can't name. Just after the sun sets there are bolts and streaks of brilliant color reflected on clouds like oils fresh from a tube. Looking at the sunset, I swear I smell oil paint mixed in with the hay and the smell of warm blacktop.

There are times, though, when the sky just goes dark, without the grand showcase of colors, as if it is in a lousy mood and doesn't feel like pleasing anyone. I like those skies too, the drama of night falling without the rose-colored pretensions.

After the sunsets, Megan, Robert, and I run down the hill, on the berm, always on the berm, because my mother shouts that out as we run. *Stay on the berm,* she yells as we move down and away, as if we can't think for ourselves. But it is true: if she weren't here, I'd run down the middle of the road, arms outstretched, eyes closed. I'd run as fast as possible to someplace I would never leave.

As Robert, Megan, and I run, our feet pick up speed, going beyond our means, and we tumble into the tall grass and away from the road. It is one of the few times we do anything together.

My father says a beautiful sunset is the day taking a bow. From the bottom of the hill, we hear him clapping.

Brenda is not afraid of my father, like most other kids are. She comes up right behind him and asks him questions about painting. "Why do you put the white on last? Why do you go out of your lines? Why did you move that tree? Can you do that? How come you been standing there for so long and not painting? Did you know you have red paint on your ear?" He will answer her for a few minutes and then say, "I guess I better stop telling you my secrets now, Brenda, or you are going to be my competition soon." She doesn't know what he means, but she always laughs and goes away. Yesterday she told me she thinks my father is cool, which no one has ever said, ever. Then she said, "But your mom scares me." When I asked her why, she just shrugged. I told her I wouldn't be her friend if she didn't say why and when I turned to walk away she grabbed my arm. "She acts spooky sometimes, you know. All talky or really quiet, like she went to sleep with her eyes open. She's okay though. Really." I jerked my arm out of her hand and walked away. She shouted that it wasn't fair, 'cause she told me what I asked, but I kept going. She should talk. Her father limps like Frankenstein and hardly speaks, and her mother doesn't ever smile. I was never going to speak to her again, but today she begged me to play marbles with her in the middle of the road and gave me a bag of her marbles to keep. She won most of them back, but it was fun playing in the road. My mother was out by the pond, or somewhere, otherwise she would have thrown a fit.

When Robert and I were young, Megan *too* young, our parents sat us down and taught us the meaning of the word *atheist*.

My father dragged over his easel and clipped on a large pad of cheap white paper. He drew, with a gray pastel, six blobby circles. My mother narrated. "Amoebas," she said. "In the oceans. Billions of single-celled creatures just floating about. Then, over *millions* of years, they began to change, to grow, to adapt." My father drew tentacles hanging from an amoeba.

"They became many-celled. They evolved into fish, amphibians, reptiles, birds, mammals, and dinosaurs." My father drew quickly. Now the blobby shapes grew legs and tails and long necks. One looked like a rat, one like an alligator.

"Then there was some kind of disaster and most of the creatures died," she said gaily, and with a flourish of motion, my father tore off the top piece of paper, wadded it up, and tossed it across the room.

"Some animals survived. No dinosaurs, but reptiles and mammals. And the mammals came to be the dominant life-form, through the survival of the fittest."

My father drew furiously. Monkeys. Apes. Ape men. People with all their private parts showing.

"No Adam," my mother said. "No Eve. No creating people out of dirt. No God. It was evolution. Say that. Ev o lu tion. Four syllables. Please say it."

"Ev o lu tion," Robert and I repeated. Megan, maybe two, sucked her thumb harder.

"There's a big dispute," my father said, pausing for a moment by his easel. "We just want you to know what side of the fence we're on."

"We don't believe in God," my mother said, as if we hadn't caught on to that yet. I'd heard of God in school. He was like a principal.

My mother sat down on the low flat table in front of the couch, facing us. "We're atheists. There are not a lot of people who are atheists, not right now, although someday everyone will be one. Right now there are just a few. But that's okay. We can be atheists, even if it's not popular."

"Are any of the kids in my school atheists?" I asked. I must have been about nine.

My mother bunched up her face and thought about it. "Probably not," she decided. "But maybe. They may be in hiding. They may be scared to admit it."

"Scared of who?" Robert asked. "God?"

"Well, son," my father said. "They wouldn't be scared of God if they didn't believe in Him."

I wasn't so sure about that.

"Oh," Robert said. "Then where did the amoebas come from?"

I winced. He hadn't learned that a question like that would take up the next hour of his life.

"Good question," my mother said, and stood up. She waved my father away from the easel and took the pastel out of his hand. Then she tore off the sheet with the naked people and thick-eyebrowed apes and handed it to my father, shook her shoulders, stretched out her arms, and drew a big black ball in the middle of the white paper.

"There's a new theory, the big bang theory. There was all this matter in the middle of the universe surrounded by . . . Oh. Do you know what the universe is, Robert?"

"No."

"How about the solar system? Do you know what that is?"

He shook his head no.

"Well, let's start with some basics then." She tore off the paper with the center of the universe and dropped it on the floor. "Let's start with the sun and the planets, and their moons." She drew the sun in the center and started on some planets, but before she got done with all of them she stopped, stepped back, and looked at her picture. "I'd like to do this in color." She looked around the room and found my father's box of pastels. With cerulean blue she colored in the third planet from the sun—Earth, I knew—then put back the blue and took out an emerald green. As she started coloring in continents, my father spoke up.

"You know, Liz, if you're planning on getting to the big bang, you might want to skimp on the details."

She thought about this. "Okay." She finished drawing the rest of the planets with the green pastel. "It doesn't look right, but . . . Now, Robert, do you know what an orbit is?"

"Yes," I said, before he could reply. She didn't seem to notice that I answered, she was so busy drawing in moons. "Okay. So everything is moving, nothing holds still . . ."

We are, I thought.

We stayed on that couch for what seemed like all night long as my mother explained the solar system, the galaxy, the universe, and, finally, the big bang. The floor was littered with large sheets of paper that she stepped on without the slightest notice. The crinkle of paper still reminds me of the big bang theory.

Nothing ever pleased my mother more than last year's August issue of *Life*. A dinosaur on the front cover. Fifteen pages on Evolution. She bought each of us a copy. We discussed it at dinner for a month. It's on our coffee table right now. You'd think she wrote the article herself.

•   •   •

Sex is also a subject approached with the easel and white paper. The pictures were drawn prior to the talk. They were very detailed, although I think my father must have gotten carried away with the pubic hair. Certainly there can't be that much. The balls on the man hung down like a dog's. Not like my brother's at all. Not like my father's either, from what I've seen. I think he drew them hanging down so far so we could see them better from behind all that pubic hair.

After the explanation of how babies are made I was numb. I think it was the year after the big bang, so I was about ten. To have sex explained by my mother, as my brother sat next to me on the couch and my father pointed with a painting knife to the erect penis he'd drawn, was a little too much, even for someone used to this kind of stuff.

They both explained, at the end of this session, the importance of love. They said sex without love was only lust. I didn't ask what lust was, I was much too embarrassed and I didn't want any more pictures drawn or explanations given. I never looked the word up, but I think I've got it figured out now.

They imagine themselves great teachers. They swell with pride at their openness, their boldness, their ability to get out the facts. But they started with us much too early, and now, when a frank talk about sex might actually interest me, they have collapsed into themselves, like those distant galaxies, the hot air and gas all burned up.

The tar truck comes. We can hear it from way down the road, so we gather on our lawn for the show, crossing our legs under us, getting comfortable on the warm grass. Rusty and Brenda come out and sit on their lawn. Brenda is wearing the same plaid shirt she wore yesterday, and probably the same jean shorts. It's hard to tell, since all her shorts are cutoffs with fraying threads hanging down like spit out of a dog's mouth. Rusty's curly red hair picks up the morning light and glows like a fuzzy sun. His hair needs to be cut, but I like the way some curls fall across his forehead. Brenda shouts hi to us. Rusty just nods. We stay on our own side of the road. The truck moves slowly, spewing out black tar like spreading night over dusk. The truck driver waves to us, a thick fleshy hand, and grins pleasantly, like a man in a parade.

My mother comes out and stands behind us, hands on hips. "They are paving the road," she says, as if she is telling us something we don't know. But we are not little anymore, and her knowledge has its limits. She must realize how stupid it sounds; she doesn't say anything else.

Following the tar truck comes a truck that drops tiny pebbles into the hot tar, pebbles that tumble and bounce, then find their place, stuck forever like the dinosaurs. This driver also waves to us. Robert makes the motion of pulling down an invisible rope, and the driver answers with a blast of his horn. Robert claps and hollers as we watch the back of the pebble truck move down the road. Our road now glimmers in the afternoon sun, the curves of pebbles reflecting the light in dozens of directions, becoming something grand.

Finally the big, wide roller comes, pressing the pebbles down into the tar, taking away their shape and their dimensions, until they all lie flat and lightless, until the road is once again just a road. I close my eyes. The smell of hot tar makes me think of cities, with tall buildings, busy people, buses, taxis, car horns, sidewalks. I open my eyes. Brenda is scratching her armpit.

Until the road cools, no one will cross to the other side. But even when we do, we are divided just the same. We are smarter, they are poorer. I will never understand how they can stand to live like they do.

Forever we have lived among people who don't shape up to our standards.

Behind me, my mother sighs, unsatisfied by something she hasn't said. I know that sigh. She turns away and goes to the barn, and I know she will milk the cow, her hands needing the motion her words have lost. Tomorrow she will go to the library to find something she can teach us about paving roads.

I feel sorry for her, and for me, watching the road get paved as if it were a great play.

While I'm writing an essay, "My Personal Hero"—I have chosen Amelia Earhart because teachers love her—the school siren goes off, jarring the silence of our supposedly deep thought and causing at least three girls to scream, one directly behind me. I know what this siren means; all my schools have had this same siren with the same deafening blare.

"A tornado!" someone whispers harshly.

"No, a bomb, stupid!" someone says.

"The Communists," someone else agrees.

"The Communists are dropping the H-bomb on us!"

I almost expect everyone to turn toward me and point, but then I remember my mother hasn't been to school to protest anything yet, and just for a minute I'm thankful she hasn't been feeling well. The teacher yells, "Hush up!" and motions for us to get into line. The girl behind me has the hiccups now. "This could be the real one," she whispers. I roll my eyes, thinking that even the Communists wouldn't be stupid enough to waste a bomb on Mayville, New York.

We file into the hall and down the steps to the first floor, where all the classes are jammed up together waiting to file down the steps to the basement. I am pressed up against a glass cabinet with the sports trophies. Dozens of trophies and plaques proclaim Mayville to be second or third place in baseball, football, and wrestling. Considering there are hardly enough boys in the tenth, eleventh, and twelfth grades to even make a football team, I guess they did pretty good. Plus with everyone missing practice for Boy Scout meetings, it's amazing they placed at all.

With a minimum of shoving and stepping on feet, we all arrive in the basement, lined up against the damp, clammy walls of the boiler room and hallways. We crouch down and cover our heads with crossed arms. Way down at the end of the hall I see my sister with her class. A few of the smaller children are crying, but not Megan. I don't see my brother, who probably is crying. I'm not scared at all. It's a drill, like all the rest have been. It had better be. It would be so embarrassing to die in this stupid town in a boiler room with a bunch of third-place football players and hiccuping girls in poodle skirts. This is not where I want to die. I don't know where I want to die, but I'm not there yet.

The siren stops. It stops so suddenly it's as if we have gone deaf, and everyone holds their breath; I can feel lungs expand on both sides of me, right through the bodies pressed against mine. We wait as long as we can, listening for the whine of a falling bomb, then exhale, words tumbling out of our mouths, like "Oh," and "Ah," and "Told you so," and for a minute I don't even realize I have said something, until the girl next to me says, "Yeah, I thought so too." She laughs softly, like little bubbles rising to the surface of water. All around me, kids are laughing and nudging each other. They are thinking about the rest of the day being right there for them, like a frosted cake on a platter. I get this funny feeling, like a rush of having too much, like I actually want to hug the hiccuping girl next to me, and it hits me, this weird thought: I don't like anyone, because I'm only going to move away, but since I'm not going to let that happen ever again, I can like people if I want to.

The teachers tell us to stand up and file back to our classes. I turn to smile at the girl beside me, but she is talking to someone else. I look for my sister, but she is gone. As I head up the steps, I see my brother. His eyes are all red and he turns away so I can't see his face. Such a sissy. When we get to our classroom, the teacher tells us to sit down and finish our essay. We have ten minutes left. I finish it in five. These kids are pretty stupid.

. . .

I listen to my parents talk when they don't know it. Late at
night, when they think we are all asleep, I creep to the top step
and sit down carefully so the boards don't squeak. Sometimes I
can catch only a few words, other times their voices float right
up to me.

By the time I sit on the top step tonight, they are already in
the middle of some conversation. The acoustics in this house
are good, maybe because of all the bare wood floors. I can hear
everything perfectly.

"All I'm saying is this isn't what I expected," my mother says.
She sounds weary, as if the words are an effort. She coughs, then
goes on. "The house is fine, more than fine. I really like it. I've
really liked them all. What I mean is, this isn't what I expected
when we left the city. Not that I miss it. It was full of stuffed shirts
and stuffed minds—even those who pretended to disagree. But
what I'm wondering is, haven't we become . . . aren't we now just
like *them*? We were going to live in beautiful places, immerse ourselves in the land. We were going to live for the moment. In the
moment. In the land. But that hasn't happened. The cow, she's just
a pet really, and the beef cattle, we have nothing to do with them.
We're just like baby-sitters. That's all we do. Baby-sit homes. It's
like baby-sitting somebody else's children, Stuart. Finally you
want your own. I want to have some effect on something. I don't
want to just move the furniture around, I want to buy some. I
want to plant a perennial garden. I want to run for town council."

There is a long pause. My father likes to think before he
speaks. Then he says things that sound final, and he thinks they
are.

"No," he says. "It's not like we planned. But it was your idea
I give up teaching. If it weren't for you I would never have
believed I could earn a living from painting, that I could make
money doing something I love. You said it never mattered if we

owned a house, or a fancy car. You said I was a great painter. And I believed you, in everything, and here we are. I can't go back. I couldn't teach math anymore. Too much has changed. And I wouldn't want to. I love what I do. What you showed me I could do." My mother starts to interrupt, but he talks over her. "I don't paint what's popular. It's a miracle I sell what I do. But landscapes are what I love. And not everyone likes this new modern crap. Splatter art. It can't last. I paint what I see. I need to see the land, spread out, open, free from cities and smog. You can't deny me that, can you?"

She sighs. "That's not what I meant. I mean, I just need to take a long, deep breath, and maybe here is the place to do that."

There is another long pause. His pauses drive me nuts. "It is beautiful here, Liz, but if I have to move on, find someplace new that will help me grow as a painter, you'll come, won't you? You're not saying you won't come?"

"I'm just saying I'd like to talk about it."

"Fine. We will. But not now. Let's just enjoy it right now. We'll talk about it. I promise."

A long pause, then he speaks again. "Come, here. Come on over here."

From the lack of further conversation, I assume she does.

The only other time I ever heard them disagree about anything other than politics was about a year ago. My father was trying to convince my mother to let him paint Megan. Nude. Megan had just turned seven. She has blond-white hair the color of the winter sun, and light-blue eyes. She has legs like a gazelle and a little heart-shaped butt. She is fragile-looking and plays this feature to the hilt. She is quite the actress.

"She's too shy," my father said, as part of his argument. "Posing nude will help free her inhibitions. She hides from life.

She thinks she is incapable of so much. Through my eyes she will see what a solid body she has, that she's beautiful and . . ."

"Crap," my mother said. "Sometimes you can convince yourself of such crap, Stuart. You want to paint Megan because she's at that perfect age. Flawless. Well, forget it."

"But don't you see . . ."

"I see enough. Not another word."

He was silent. After five minutes or so he asked her what she thought about something McCarthy had said. He knew that would change her mood. At least she'd be mad at someone else. Being atheists, with McCarthy pointing his finger at everyone, made us all angry, me more scared than angry.

I didn't like thinking about him being out there, making plans to have us put away. He was like the boogeyman. I tiptoed back to bed.

I lay in bed, long after my parents had gone to sleep, wondering at what age my body left its flawless stage. I touched my breasts, trying to remember them flat. Our family never cared much about nudity. It was not a big deal if one of us walked from the shower to a bedroom without covering up. We sometimes peed with the door open, or walked around looking for a shirt. I knew what a penis looked like, both my brother's and my father's. I knew bodies changed, grew hairy, breasts sagged. Yet I could not figure out what was wrong with me, why he didn't ask to paint me. I would have posed willingly.

From that night on I covered myself up, never again walking nude around the house. I was embarrassed by my body. I imagined I had a scar that never healed right. You could see the sutures.

Four

Tuesday, the eighth of June, my birthday, is Spirit Day at school. You are supposed to wear your class T-shirt, the one you got last year, and green or white pants or skirts. If you weren't here last year, you could have ordered a class shirt right before Easter break. Too late for us. Too bad. I bet the dead boy's class T-shirt is upstairs, in our attic. I think about him a lot today. As my mother carries in the cake and everyone sings me "Happy Birthday," I imagine him sitting on this chair to blow out his candles on his birthday, not knowing he would be dead before his next cake. I wonder what he wished for.

As I blow out the candles I feel a puff of air on the back of my neck and turn around quickly, sure I will catch sight of him. But if he's here, he's stuck up in the attic with his stuff, packed up and waiting like a wish.

"Shit and Goddamn!" Brenda swears constantly; like a heartbeat it keeps her going forward. When she isn't swearing she looks stuck for words. Swear words are vowels to her, an intrinsic part of spoken English.

School is over. It ended yesterday with a party on the school's front lawn, the band playing, egg and tuna sandwiches for everyone.

Brenda will flunk if she doesn't attend summer school. I have offered to help her with her studies. It's something to do. I tell her to go and get her math book.

I don't want to go into her house. It looks dim and dusty in there when I look through the screen door, and her father is in there. I tell her we'll study at the picnic table, even though the whole thing is just one mass of splinters being held together by a prayer.

"Every math equation has a formula to solve it, or a series of formulas. The trick is to memorize the formulas." I write the formulas for finding the area of a triangle, a circle, and a square. Then I go through solving some of the problems in her math book, real basic stuff. She isn't even looking.

"It's not so hard, Brenda. Just give it a try." I write out a simple problem.

"Fuck it," she says.

No one swears in my family. I take a deep breath, absorbing the sound of *fuck* into my throat, rolling it around in my mouth. I position my mouth for the F sound, then stop, too afraid to actually say the word. I touch Brenda's arm and she jerks as if I hit her.

"Brenda, math is like a code. A game. You just need to know the rules."

"And fuck you too," she says. She knocks the math book onto the ground and walks into her house.

Fuck you, I whisper. I like the sound. Brenda has a lot to teach me, I think.

As I turn around on the picnic-table bench and stand, facing the woods, there is a flash of red hair and the pale white movement of an arm. Rusty. He's hidden now behind an oak, but a shoulder shows like a soft fleshy bump on the bark. He must be wearing one of those T-shirts with the sleeves cut off. As if I can see right through the tree, I imagine his eyes, blue with white eyelashes, blinking in nervousness. I imagine the way his body must be tense behind that tree, like a deer, ready to bolt. It's exciting to be watched like this; I can feel my lips grin. I can feel my body. It's a funny feeling, as if I never really knew it was there, or as if I'm naked right out here in the open. I walk away, slowly, not looking back until I cross the road. Then I can't help it. I catch Rusty's eyes just before they disappear behind the oak.

The next day, Helen sits at our kitchen table, breaking the ends off of string beans. Her long reddish-brown hair is tied back in a thick braid and she is wearing a simple homemade dress of blue cotton. She's at least five ten, but seems bigger because her hair is so thick and she has shoulders like platforms. Her hands are callused and her nails short. She is the opposite of calendar girls, and most likely boys think her homely, but I can't take my eyes off Helen. She has something special. I guess, even though she's large, I'd call it grace.

Helen is helping my mother, not because my mother needs help but because Helen needs something to do at all times, unless, I suppose, she is praying.

The Murphys are Baptists, and even though Brenda uses swear words when her parents aren't around, I know she believes in God. Helen has taken belief a step further. She is determined to save us. My mother must have told Helen we're atheists, because for the last week, as they poked holes in the ground with the tip of a pencil, dropped in the seeds, then smoothed the earth back over as if they were tucking them into bed, you could hear my mother's voice like a man hammering the same nail, and the murmur of Helen's voice, like water rolling over stones. A few years ago I'd be betting on my mother, but now I'm betting on Helen. It strengthens Helen's belief to have it battered by my mother. She leaves our house standing straighter, more pious for her effort, sure she has won a minor battle toward our salvation. The funny thing is that when she leaves, my mother is sure *she* has won the day. Belief, even nonbelief, is a mighty thing to break down.

"I'd like to take Tamara, Robert, and Megan to church with us this Sunday," Helen says. She snaps a bean and puts it into the copper bowl in the center of the table.

"I don't think so," my mother says. She drops a bean in the bowl.

Helen snaps another bean, but this time, she pops it in her mouth. "I know you don't believe in God, Mrs. Anderson, but your children should be exposed to all the options, so they have a choice. I won't preach to them, just take them to church." She keeps her eyes on my mother's face. They have both stopped snapping beans.

I have been drawing, using charcoals, trying to capture Helen's hands. What I've drawn looks like a deformed crab. I don't know why I bother. I look at my mother. Her eyes look bruised. Tired as she is, she can't resist a good argument.

"You *will* preach to them, Helen. You always do. It's part of your religion. It's compulsive. They've bred it into you. You probably don't even know you're doing it." She says this all kindly, but firmly. She likes Helen.

"I merely point out God's offerings to them, like these beans." Helen scoops up a handful and holds them out, an obvious answer to all my mother's doubts. "Just because you bought these in a store doesn't mean they didn't come from God. Surely, when your garden prospers, when you can pull the rewards from the earth, you must wonder at the miracle of food coming from soil."

My mother takes a slow breath and lets it out just as slowly. She has a gift for this; she has made an art form of the long breath and the sigh that follows. "Helen, everything is a miracle, I don't deny that. It's a miracle that amphibians crawled out of the oceans to live on land. It's a miracle apes evolved into Homo sapiens. It's a miracle that birds fly. But it doesn't mean there's a God who controls it all. There is scientific evidence for evolution. Everything *you* believe comes from a book of fiction, written by fanatical people decades after the supposed events. There is no proof."

"I disagree," Helen says. "The proof is right here, plain as day." She places the beans back in the bowl, and smiles at me, a warm, sweet smile. I smile back.

Helen looks at my mother. "You have such bright children, Mrs. Anderson. It's because you have allowed them so much knowledge. You and Mr. Anderson were teachers. You must believe in learning everything life has to offer."

My mother nods. She looks a bit nervous, as if she has missed a beat. Helen continues. "All I'm saying is I'd like them to learn something about my religion. Religion is a powerful force in the world today. They are going to be at a disadvantage if they know nothing about it. Certainly, it can't hurt them to learn something new. They can make up their own minds what they think of it, can't they? You're not afraid of that, are you?"

My mother looks at me. I try to look bored, indifferent.

"Fine," my mother says. "They can go with you if they want. No preaching. They are just to observe. I doubt they will want to go. You may not pressure them. Just ask."

"Thank you," Helen says. She looks at me. My mother looks at me. "Would you like to come to church with me?" Helen asks.

"Yeah. Do I have to wear a nice dress?"

"Yes, you really should."

"Okay," I say. I'm excited. God has been this big mystery. To my mother and father, God is a fraud, an impostor, a superstition for the masses. The word *God* is like a bad taste. But for a while now, I have wanted to see what God is all about for myself. I could be missing out on something. According to Helen, my soul is involved. I don't know if my mother believes in a soul. She's never brought it up. But I like the word. I like the implication of it. I like the way Helen talks about my soul, as if it's something she loves. I want to go to church to find out if my soul is real, if God is real. But if He is, it will break my mother's heart.

My mother begins to snap the beans again. Her face is calm, but she breaks the beans roughly. She has fought against God, time and time again. She has alienated us from our classmates all our lives, and now she has given in, all because Helen found the right argument. Helen is very smart. Or maybe God is helping her.

"I'll go ask Robert and Megan if they want to come too," Helen says as she stands up.

"I'm sure they won't," my mother says to the beans. "They aren't quite as enamored of you as Tamara is." This isn't said with the same kindness the conversation started out with. My mother doesn't like losing.

Robert and Megan say yes.

My mother stands by the fence separating our yard from the cow pasture. She's looking away from the house, away from me. I walk over and lean on a post.

The bull glares at us.

"It's okay I go to church with Helen?"

"Look," she says. "The cattle on the hill, they look like spotted clouds from here. Cows in the shape of clouds. How silly. That makes the grass a green sky. I guess it's all how you look at things." She laughs. It's a sharp laugh, a little escape of something pent up inside her. I know how that feels.

She reaches over and strokes my hair. "Go to church. Take a look and see. You can make up your own mind what you think of it all."

That's not really what she means. She wants me not to believe, to just trust her about all this. She wants me to see the world as she does. But maybe believing in God is like wearing glasses. Maybe some need God.

I wonder what God will look like.

That night, I dream of God. He looks like Albert Einstein.

My father's parents don't talk to us, don't write, anything. I have never even met them. They are very religious. They blame my mother for turning my father away from God. And away from being a math teacher. They say she's the devil. My father told them they couldn't speak to her that way, and so they said they wouldn't, and turned their backs on both of them. My mother's getting pregnant before they were married didn't help.

I think my father has a little bit of religion in him, because every now and then he looks up, as if there is an answer to something above him. He doesn't do it when my mother's looking, and if she saw him, he'd just say there was a crack in the ceiling or isn't the sky blue. I think he'd like to believe, but my mother is too important to him to risk it.

I wonder if he's just a bit pleased we are learning about God. Maybe he thinks if we get religion, he can talk to his parents again. I don't know why he does everything my mother says. Maybe that's what lust does.

We all squeeze into the Murphys' station wagon. Mr. and Mrs. Murphy and Helen sit up front. Robert, Megan, Brenda, Rusty, and I sit in the back seat, pressed tight together, our legs and feet all in a row. We look like a giant centipede.

We are all scrubbed clean. Brenda's hair is tied back, so you can't tell so much that it's all tangled. Rusty has on a suit coat and slacks and looks very uncomfortable in them. I decide I like him better in cutoffs. He has small ears, but not too small. His skin is beginning to get pink all over, and he has more freckles than I thought possible. He glances at me, blinks, then looks out the window.

Helen has on a pretty flowered dress, much more stylish than I have ever seen her wear before. Mrs. Murphy, Brenda, and Helen are wearing white gloves. I feel slightly undressed without gloves and fold my hands under my arms so you can't see them. Mr. Murphy wears a dark-blue suit, pressed and clean, although his nails are stained and the lines on his hands look etched in coal. It was hard for him to get in the car because his knee doesn't bend right. I tried not watching, but Robert downright stared. Mrs. Murphy, who is driving, wears a light-green dress with a little green hat. She looks like a mother, which surprises me, because I always think of her as a waitress. I think of Helen as the mother.

Mr. Murphy takes his wife's hand as we walk from the car to the church. Except for his limp, they look like all the other parents walking toward the church, not like people who live in a tar-paper house. Everyone is dressed fancy, with gloves and hats and purses and shiny shoes. They stop and say hello to each other. They glance our way and I am sure they are talking about us. They all know each other. I bet they love having something new to talk about. The heathens have come to church, without their parents. The phones will be busy this afternoon.

Helen's church is a small brick Baptist church on the main street of town, next to the hardware store. It's not much of a church to look at, not like the ones I've seen in *Life* magazine. You could easily miss it if you weren't looking for it.

We go up three steps and we're inside a little front room. There are open doors that lead into the real church. Helen presses a hand to my shoulder and leads me forward. I follow her parents to an open pew, and we all file in. There are a few dozen people in the church already, but no one in this row. I can tell right away people sit in the same spots every week, and this is the Murphys' pew. There is just enough room for Robert and

Megan and me to squeeze in with them. Helen sits on the aisle, next to me. Brenda is on my other side. I am boxed in.

The church smells of wax and dust and heat. Sun streams through the stained-glass windows, which are not large or elaborate, but still beautiful. They are on fire, the colors brilliant because of the angle of the sun; oranges and reds, yellows and golds. They are just a composite of small rectangles, with a symbol on the top under the arch; a gold star, a gold cross, a white lily, a gold candelabra. I think my father would like this place, the high ceiling, the open spaces. There is something about sitting here that is like finding a clearing in the woods. It feels safe and special, waiting for me to find it.

My heart beats hard as the lady at the organ starts to play. This is really it. There is no backing out. I'm terrified God will figure out I'm an atheist in his church. It's like I'm a rich person stealing food, or a Negro pretending to be white. I will be found out, then what? I remind God I'm not an all-the-way atheist. I'm just the product of my environment.

The church is mostly bare of decorations. I don't know if it's the style of Baptists or if it's just a poor church. The pews are made of a dark, highly polished wood, worn as smooth as satin, and there is a lectern on a platform in front, with two folding wooden chairs off to the left. And there is the organ of pale wood that looks like an ordinary piano, but the music vibrates and I can feel it on my skin. On the wall behind the podium is a plain wooden cross. I thought Jesus was supposed to be hung up there, on the cross, head down, wearing a crown of thorns. I know I saw that in a picture. I'm afraid that the little I know must be wrong, that I'm not prepared for this at all. I jump when Brenda whispers something to me. I don't answer Brenda. I don't know the rules. Maybe she can break them, since she's saved, but I'd better be careful. I don't quite know how powerful God is, but I bet if He gets mad at you, the worst place to be is in a church.

Suddenly I want to be outside again, where not believing is safe.

The lady quits playing the organ and two men walk out from a door in the back of the church, each wearing a maroon smock over regular clothes. One man has one of those white things around his neck. He sits in one of the wooden chairs. The other man moves behind the podium and says something I miss. Everyone stands, so I follow suit, glancing at my brother and sister. They stand. Their eyes are big and round. I can hardly blink. The lady plays the organ again and everyone sings. Robert looks at me and raises his eyes in question. I'm afraid to even shrug. Helen hands me a book from a pocket in the back of the pew in front of me. She points to a page with notes and verses. By the time I find my place, the song is over.

The man behind the lectern says, "We will now sing 'His Name Is Wonderful,' page 64." I quickly turn the pages and find the right one in time to join in, but I just mouth the words. I don't have the courage to sing a song I don't know at all. The voices fill the church, and it's as if each voice has a place, like they fit together perfectly. It makes me sad and happy at the same time.

Now the man behind the podium says a short prayer, and we sit down when he's done. Then we sing again, while sitting. A song about obeying Jesus. I thought maybe there was some rule we had to stand when we sang, but I guess not. I wonder which songs you *do* have to stand for, and why, and how long it takes to remember which is which. Maybe there's a formula, like in math. Maybe for all songs about God you stand and songs about Jesus you sit. I wonder if there's a book in the library about all this. While I'm thinking this, another thought creeps into my head. I think I hear my sister's voice. I look over. She *is* singing. I don't believe it.

After the song, the man behind the lectern asks if there is anyone special we should include in our prayers today. A tall, hunch-shouldered man in the second row stands up and tells a story about his son and daughter-in-law, who have moved to Montana. He says he hopes we can pray for them to find a good congregation in their new town, a good Baptist community. This seems like a very small thing to be bothering God about. Shouldn't we ask Him to make sure no one drops the H-bomb on us? Or for world peace? Then again, He's their God. I'm certainly not going to ask Him for anything yet.

Now a lady with a pale pink hat says her mother is in the hospital and she is very sick. She wants us to pray for her recovery. The man behind the lectern writes this stuff down, then asks if there is anyone else. To my complete horror, Helen rises to her feet.

"We have new neighbors, the Andersons, and they have no beliefs of their own. They do not know Jesus or accept Him into their hearts. I would like to add to our prayers that they find Jesus and be saved."

"Yes, we can do that," the man says. He writes it down. "Is there anyone else?"

No one speaks.

"All right, let us pray to Our Lord Jesus Christ, first for Mr. Henry's son and his wife . . . "

Everyone bows their head. My face is burning; it's so hot I think I might pass out. I want to kill Helen, and yet, at the same time, I hope it works. I tell God this is it, this is what I came for. I want to be saved. Helen has told me if I am not saved I will burn in hell for all eternity. The man behind the lectern prays out loud. When I hear him say, "We pray, too, that the Andersons, who are new in town, will discover the love of Our Lord Jesus Christ and find salvation," I prepare myself for God to appear in the rafters, the bright and blinding face of a wise old man with a beard, who will call out my name. Tell me He loves me. Tell me I'm saved. But all I hear is the man in the maroon robe. When the prayer is over, I'm just the same as I was, except my arms and legs hurt from being so tense.

We stand and sing "God Bless America." I just mouth the words, even though I know them. I definitely hear my sister *and* brother singing. If they were just saved and I wasn't, I will kill them. I was the first one to say yes to Helen. They are just tagging along. We sing another song, about praising Father, Son, and Holy Ghost. I thought they didn't believe in ghosts, just heaven and hell. But this ghost is holy, I guess, so they do make exceptions.

The man behind the lectern introduces the man who is sitting. He's the minister, and he stands up. The first man sits. The minister is short and fat with a red face and puffy lips. His cheeks are so high they push up his eyes into permanent squints. He talks in a huffing way, as if he has just run up a hill.

The minister tells us a story about himself, when he was young and found Jesus. It's a long story about growing up in a happy family, where everyone loved each other and helped each other, then one day he realized a family down the street wasn't so lucky. The father lost his job and their child died. The minister's mother helped the family by baking them things. The minister's father helped them paint their house. One day the mother from the other house comes over with some wildflowers and starts crying. The minister's mother takes the crying lady to her church, they just walk over there, and the minister, who is then fourteen, tags along. In the church they pray. The mother tells her son to pray as hard as he ever has, and he does, and Jesus comes to him. Jesus tells him he has to devote his life to God. And the boy does. Which is obvious, since he's up there preaching to us. He tells us that the family did fine after a few years. The father got a job. The mother learned to live beyond her grief and love Jesus again. So now I know you can pray hard. Does that mean there is such a thing as a weak prayer?

We sing another song, "Something for Thee," still sitting. I didn't know there would be all this singing, but I like it. Then they say a short prayer that everyone knows the words to, then all of a sudden people are standing and moving out of the aisles and the lady is playing the organ. I missed some clue.

As soon as we get outside of the church, I miss it. I want to go back. I keep thinking if I just sat in there one more minute, God would have found me. He was busy with all those prayers and songs. If I had just stayed . . .

On the ride home I sit next to Rusty. We are so tightly pressed together I can feel his chest expand with each breath. I am warm as toast in the back seat, a warmth that moves inwards. It's a very nice feeling. Rusty smiles shyly at me and I can't help grinning. We've never even talked to each other, but, like my mother says about the thunder, I know exactly what he's saying.

When we get home, my father is just about to start on his couch picture. He places the easel down in the middle of the living room and switches on the little oblong light that's attached to the top of the board. The painting is of a dove on a mountain-ash branch. The orange berries will match some lady's curtains. "Well?" he says. "How did it go?" He sounds like he's really interested. He pauses with his head tilted. Waiting.

"Okay," I say. Robert and Megan say the same thing.

"Where's Mommy?" Megan asks.

"I think she's taking a nap," he says.

Megan goes off looking for her.

I don't want to see my mother right now. I don't want to see her be happy that I didn't find God today. I go outside and sit on the porch, looking for Brenda or Rusty. No one comes out. The whole family stays inside.

·   ·   ·

The next day, no one is home at the house across the road. I sit on our lawn by the edge of the road, near the ditch. I play a game I used to play when I was young, piling sticks at cross angles to make a tiny campfire. I pretend I am lost in the woods, all alone, and must survive by eating berries and killing rabbits. I take a stick and rub it between my palms, feeling the heat of friction, imagining the sparks fly.

My mother yells out my name in a sharp, scared voice, so unusual I jump to my feet and turn around, expecting the house to be on fire. Ten feet away from me, to my left, is the bull. He stares at me with crimson eyes. He snorts and scratches at the ground. I run. Toward the house. Toward my mother on the steps. I move so fast my feet leave the ground and I fly, above the grass. The porch is thirty feet away and my feet never hit the ground until I land on the top step. My mother grabs me, pulling me inside. The bull has actually chased me and stops at the bottom of the steps. We face each other through the screen door. In my ears I can still hear my mother scream. I must have screamed too, but all I really remember is flying.

My mother calls Mr. Burns, who comes and puts the bull back in his pen and fixes the fence where the bull escaped. Mr. Burns apologizes fifty times.

Later, when we are all calm, I ask my mother if she saw me fly. She says I am imagining things.

But my father was outside, painting a picture of a stand of pine trees. He says I flew. He says he turned when my mother screamed and he saw me fly. He shakes his head as he says this, as if he doesn't believe what he saw.

"It's very strange," he says. "Very strange indeed."

My mother doesn't disagree with him, but she shakes her head in the same way and walks off. Robert and Megan, who missed the whole thing, ask me a million questions. They want to believe. My brother says he's heard of stuff like this happening.

Ladies lifting cars off their children. Men bending spoons. He follows me around all day.

That night my mother comes to my room. "Your father has a good imagination, you know that, don't you, Tamara. You both do. An imagination is a great thing to have."

"I flew," I say.

"Well, good night," she says. "Just don't try jumping off a roof."

As I fall asleep I wonder if this is the miracle I was asking God to perform so I would know He was real. It might be, but I'm not sure. Maybe I flew because my body was going through a metamorphosis, like fish crawling out of the oceans and breathing air. Survival of the fittest. Maybe I'm a new species.

I'm worried now because if this was God's sign to me He might get mad because I'm not totally convinced yet. I better go back to church. I'll ask Him for another sign, something I can't misinterpret.

Three years ago my mother decided to teach us at home. She wanted to invest in her children's education. We were the perfect age, she said. Finally, she could go back to teaching, and her students would be the most important students in the world—who else should she teach if not us? Anyone else, I would say now.

She approached the whole thing with enthusiasm and abundant energy. School lasted from morning to night, from opening our eyes to laying our tired, heavy heads back down on the pillow. It is that year that I remember falling in love with the comfort of a bed, the anticipation of silence, the dark gray that became an empty black inside my head as I drifted out of consciousness.

But near the end of that year her enthusiasm lessened. She became sluggish, tired, drained. She cut back our school hours, or left us for long periods of time in the library to do our own research, rather than picking out books for us and turning the pages as she sat next to us. This home schooling, which was meant to be a forever thing, lasted from one move to another. Two years ago, when we moved to Deer Isle, Maine, we were simply enrolled in a new school. No debate, no questions. No arguments.

During that year, I learned fifteen new words every day. I knew the botanical names of every plant and flower, the species, subspecies, and genus of every bird, insect, and animal, and every word in our dictionary to the letter *R*. I knew a million words, which have since escaped me. I feel lighter for their absence. If those words were still in me I would have been gored by that bull, too heavy to fly. I would be dead of an overdose of vocabulary.

A few days after the bull charged me, I walk by my father as he paints. I stop and stare. In his picture there is a child flying, not me, but a kid about nine or ten. She looks a little like my sister. She is not obtrusive in the picture, nor is she flying very high, only about ten feet off the ground. She's flying in front of the pines. It's not a picture about a flying girl, but you can't ignore her. She catches your eye and because of her the pines take on a whole new feeling. They become mysterious. I begin to wonder what might be in that pine forest.

It's the first time in quite a while that I have really looked at one of my father's paintings. It's a wonderful painting, very stark, very moody. I just wish that girl looked a little more like me. If she had breasts it would ruin the whole thing, but she could have my face. That wouldn't hurt the picture at all.

He finishes the painting in two days, a record for him, and begins to sketch a new one of the cow pasture. By the edge of the field, there is a girl flying, naked, arms spread out to catch the wind. My mother comes outside and walks over to look at the sketch. She shakes her head and sighs.

This flying girl looks even more like my sister now, but I must admit that even though this painting is hardly done yet, it is more alive than all his other paintings. He paints right through the time he usually paints the couch pictures. In the evening he wants to play Scrabble. Megan and my mother team up together and are beating us all when my mother starts coughing. She coughs so hard she knocks the table, and the letters on the board scatter and lose their place.

My father says it's time for bed.

Five

Today my mother comes back from the market with something more than food. She has a white box, a gift box, but it's not anyone's birthday. "Don't touch," she says, with a sly grin, then puts away the food: chicken in the fridge, cereals in the cupboard, canned food on the back hall shelves. It's a bright blue day outside, but Robert, Megan, and I hang around in the kitchen; we even help to put things away. We scoot around the kitchen chairs, open cupboards and close them. I notice my mother glancing at the kitchen table every minute, at the box.

"Careful," she says, to no one in particular.

Finally, without comment, she opens the box and pulls back the crisp white tissue paper. Inside is a very light cadmium-green vase, a glass vase; the glass unbearably thin. She lifts it slowly out of the box like a baby, with both hands. She walks it over to the sink and fills it with water, then places it on the kitchen table. "Don't touch," she says as she goes to a drawer, takes out the scissors, then goes outside. We look at each other, unsure whether to follow her out or look at the vase.

We don't buy fragile things. It's an unspoken law. We do not allow ourselves breakable things in our life. Nothing that is not easy to move. Only tin pans, clothes, a few board games and puzzles, canvas and paints, frames and framed pictures, boots and shoes.

My mother carries in fresh-cut flowers, naming them as she snips the stems under running water in the sink. "Foxglove. Its other name is digitalis. It's used for medicines, but it's deadly if ingested. Poppy. It's where opium is derived from. Yarrow, used as a dye. Columbine. My favorite." As she talks and snips, she turns to place each flower, one at a time, into the vase. When she's done, she steps back and just looks at the flowers arching out of the green glass. A drifting sigh comes up and out of her lungs, through her open mouth, like a butterfly on a warm day.

"It's pretty," Megan says.

"Thank you," my mother says. "It is, isn't it?" She picks up the glass vase and walks around the house, all three of us following. She puts it down on different surfaces, steps back, then moves it again. It stays, finally, on the glossy table between the couch and the overstuffed chair. But in the morning it is on the kitchen table again, and at dinner it's on the dining room table.

That night, at dinner, my father brings up the subject of the vase. "Yes, it is lovely. I can see why you were tempted. It'll be hard to move. It might not make it."

Another rule: we do not mention moving until it's too late. I wish he hadn't said what he did. It's like breaking the enchantment of the vase. It's almost like breaking the vase itself.

But over the next week the effect of my father's words mellows to a point where the vase grows stronger. Thicker somehow. We don't tiptoe when we walk by, wherever it is placed. We don't even always look at it. It is part of us now.

We become more careful about this house, and more careless. We are careful not to spill juice on the carpeting, or scuff the floors, or bump the walls, but our belongings begin to be absorbed by the house as if it were a sponge. We lose a shoe, a garden glove, a box of markers. We keep a Monopoly game, even though we have lost three of the properties; we assume they will turn up someday under the couch or a rug, even though we have looked already. Never before did we keep useless or broken things. Fixing things is something people do someday, and our somedays have always been limited to a year. We throw broken things out when they break. We move only what is whole.

But this time we begin to occupy this house as if it belonged to us.

It is seldom that I go to town. There is no reason. I imagine this town would be a comfort to someone old, who has seen too much change in the world; this town holds on to yesterday with a fierce grip. One block still has wooden sidewalks with wooden rails, as if we might need to hitch up a horse. The market has a minimum of staples, mostly those things, in combination, that can be the basis of all else. Flour and salt, eggs and potatoes, fresh fruit and canned fruit, fresh vegetables and canned vegetables, whole bodies of meat hanging in a back cooler to be dragged out and cut to specific sizes and shapes. Lots of tomato paste. Nothing foreign. No green olives. Rarely a pineapple or plum. It is a town that has been frozen, pre–World War II, except for the newest addition, seven years ago: the granite stone outside city hall with the names of forty-eight dead.

I don't like this town. There is a statue in the town square of two children huddled under an umbrella, the fountain sprinkling down a constant rain upon them. There is something so old about these two children in their perpetual wait for a sunny day. There is also a sadness to their lack of privacy. I try not to look at the statue; I imagine them at night, alone, in a dark, steady rain, their feet planted in cement. They are the stuff of nightmares.

Today, though, I have asked to be given a ride into town when my mother does the shopping.

I leave her at the market and walk across the street to Myra's Merchandise. Brenda says Myra is an Indian, an Indian princess with magical powers, and she has everything you would ever want, or need.

When I walk in the store she is standing behind the counter. She has long black hair and black eyes and she watches me closely as I look around at the stuff that's piled all over the place. There are typewriters and seashell-coated cigar boxes, a brass trumpet with a dent and a lamp with maroon trim on the shade. There are dishes and rugs and old clothes and wooden guns. Everything. I walk around but I don't see what I want. My mother will get mad if I don't hurry.

"Do you have a mirror?" I ask.

"What kind of mirror?" she asks, her voice soft and smooth.

"A hand-held mirror," I say. "With a handle," I add stupidly.

"Yes, I have two." She squats down behind the counter, slides open a glass door, and from nowhere brings out two mirrors, one wooden, one ornate silver. There is no question which one I want. I reach for the silver one and it is in my hand before I know it.

The mirror is a perfect circle, the glass clear, the image sharp; but it's an old mirror. On the back the thick, tarnished silver is shaped into vines with leaves spiraling inwards to the center, where there is one rose, fully opened. The mirror is smooth and heavy; a weight of something more than I can handle easily, but there is no giving it back. It is already mine, even though I don't know how much it costs.

"Five dollars," she says. "If you don't have it all now, you can owe me."

"No, I have it." I brought everything I have, which is exactly six dollars. I hand her five.

She takes the money and folds it into her pocket, then holds out her hand for the mirror. "I'll wrap it for you," she says, placing a white box on the counter.

"No, thanks," I say. I'm not wrapping anything up again. I'm not putting things in boxes. I hold the mirror to my chest and leave, turning back just in time to catch Myra's smile. I believe Brenda. She is an Indian princess. I just wonder what she's doing here, in this town. Maybe her ancestors are buried nearby. Maybe she can't leave. Maybe the dead won't let her.

Maybe I've been reading too many of my brother's comics.

There are mirrors in this rented house, as in all our rented houses. Round mirrors above bedroom bureaus, square mirrors above bathroom sinks, long rectangular mirrors above dining room cabinets, oblong mirrors behind candles stuck to the wall, but they all reflect a foreign place; the reflections from those mirrors are like pictures of a vacation, like postcards of me visiting a foreign country. The reflection is of a person in a place which she will soon leave. But I'm not moving again.

With my new mirror, the exact size of my face, there is only a hint of what lies behind me, someplace vague and shiny and out of focus: it is the place that I will someday call home. Holding the mirror close, I see my face, my high cheekbones, my heavy and too hairy eyebrows, my uneven lips and plain-as-mud hair. The mirror doesn't lie, but for once, I like the way I look.

I lay the mirror facedown on the dead boy's bureau.

Above me, a board creaks.

Dinner Saturday night is tense. Robert, Megan, and I have decided to go back to church with the Murphys tomorrow.

"I don't understand," my mother says. She is walking around the dining room table carrying a bowl of salad. "Why do you want to go back? Did you find God there?" She says this as if it were offensive, like finding a slug in your shoe.

"No," I say. "I didn't." I emphasize the I, looking at Robert and Megan. They have been behaving very piously all week, offering to do chores, never talking back. You would think she would want us to keep going to church by the way they are behaving.

"But then why?" She sits down. Our plates are full and we all begin to eat, except she doesn't. She just keeps looking from one of us to the other. She looks confused. Betrayed. She looks like she might burst into tears.

"I like the possibility," I say.

"I like the windows," Megan says. "And the singing."

"I like the singing too," I say, not to be outdone.

"And you?" my mother says to Robert.

He shrugs and ducks his head. He's such a baby. I could tell her it's just because Megan and I are going and he doesn't want to be left out, but she should be able to figure that out if she's so smart.

"It's their choice," my father says. "They're just balancing the scales."

My mother looks sharply at him, her lips thin. "We are talking about religion, not weights and measures. We're talking about a form of brainwashing. I find it frightening."

"If you're wrong, we will be condemned to hell for all eternity," I say. "You're risking our souls."

"Damn! It's started already. Damn Helen!"

We are all shocked. Damning Helen is like kicking a puppy. Worse even. My father lays down his fork and clears his throat.

"I don't like it any more than you, Liz, but we've brought them up to think for themselves." He gestures to us, as if we need pointing out. "Going back to church might be the best thing for them. The more they go, the more disenchanted they will become. It's like a crush right now. If we don't fight it, it will get old and lose its appeal."

My mother opens her mouth but no words come out. She stands. She hasn't touched her dinner.

"I'm not very hungry right now." She goes outside.

We eat in silence for a while. Finally my father speaks. "Well, did anything interesting happen today?"

"I got the new *Haunt of Fear*," my brother says, animated, eyes bright. "It's great. It's just so great. The Crypt Keeper tells this story about a man whose wife dies and she comes back and her skin is all falling off and . . ."

"You know I don't like those magazines, Robert. You may read them, but I don't want to hear the gory details."

Robert looks back down at his plate, and we eat.

It's different at church this time. I know where to sit. I can find the song in the hymnal quicker. I still don't sing, but I say the words in my head. Best of all, Helen doesn't stand up, so I begin to relax.

Several people do stand. They ask us to pray for a daughter who is having a difficult pregnancy, an uncle who has stopped bathing or taking care of himself, a grandson who can't control his temper. When we pray, I add my own message. I tell God that if He saved me from the bull, I'm grateful, but would He please keep trying to convince me. I suggest a message in the sky. I apologize for being such a pest, but it's hard, since my mom raised us to be good atheists.

After a few songs, none of which I sing out loud but kind of hum in my head, seeing if I have the timing right, the minister reads a Bible story from Luke about going after a lost sheep. I think he's saying that God will look after people who get lost, but then I wonder about the ones that were never found in the first place, like me. This is the part I don't get. God saves people who believe in Jesus, and everyone else will go to hell. What about kids in India who never heard about him in the first place? What if I never met Helen? Would he damn me because I was born to my mother? I'm guessing, from what I've heard, God's not all that friendly. Or fair. I can understand how my mom might get so mad at Him. I make myself stop thinking this stuff. I am here to believe. I wish God would make it easier for me.

Next, the minister tells another story about himself. He was in a storm on the lake and his sailboat tipped over. He was wearing his life preserver and floated in the cold water for over five hours before he was rescued. He says Jesus is like that life preserver. He's there for us, but we have to wear Him, we have to have Him in our heart for Him to help us. He pauses a long time before he speaks again. He lets his story sink in. Then we sing. Then we pray. Then we sing again. I really like the singing and I think I'll sing the next song and God will come to me, but then everyone gets up and leaves.

Once again I feel as if I was almost there. The warmth of the church, the comfort of the songs, the belief of all those people radiating all around me, was just beginning to get to me, and then it is over and I'm outside and everything looks the same. It's a dingy little town, still four blocks long, still smack dab in the middle of nowhere.

After we return home from church, I go into the barn to look for my mother. The smells hit me. Hay and manure, cow's milk, warm wood. Cool air. The barn is muted and hazy, except where the sun peeks through holes in the roof, casting beams of golden light like pillars in a temple. I tense, thinking God might speak now. It feels holy in here. I wait. Nothing happens. I wave my hand through a beam of light. Dust motes swirl. My mother isn't here.

She can usually be found in the barn, even when she isn't milking the cow. Sometimes I find her sitting on a hay bale, staring at nothing. Maybe she likes it in here because it relaxes her eyes. The barn holds in the distance of the outside world, sets limits to what can be seen. It's relaxing in here. Like church.

She loves to milk Edith. She sits bent forward on the stool, motionless except for the pull, pull, pull of her hands. She is the only one of us who drinks the cow's milk. The rest of us don't like the thin-looking stuff that comes out of our rented cow, or the way the fat floats to the surface when it thickens in the fridge. Even when my mother shakes the glass bottle before she drinks it, you can see little bits of fat, like tiny frogs' eggs, floating in the murky white.

The other place I can usually find my mother is at the pond. The pond, three times the surface of the barn, is grown over in spots with weeds, but it's deep enough at the far end to swim in. It also has fish. Bass and sunfish and a few catfish. My mother fishes in the pond, although she doesn't bring home the fish to eat. She gently takes the hooks out of their mouths and tosses them back in. She talks to them too, telling them not to worry while she takes the hook out, she won't hurt them. I bet that's hard to believe with a hook stuck through your cheek.

Even though she likes these peaceful places, my mother is not peaceful. She's constantly restless and there are lines around her eyes I never noticed before. At night, I hear her get up and go to the kitchen. Last night I heard her coughing down there, the repetition of her cough so constant it actually put me to sleep. My father never wakes when she goes downstairs. He is a heavy sleeper. We could play a tuba in his room and he wouldn't wake. I wonder if he knows she isn't sleeping well. No one mentions my mother's health.

I walk to the pond, following the path that leads off to the right of the barn and curves up over the hill. I pluck a piece of long grass and chew on the sweet end. Bugs attack my bare legs. I have been in places just like this dozens of times, but I like this better than the rest.

My mother is fishing, sitting on the grass by the deep end of the pond. I've never seen her sit and fish. Always before she has been standing, casting and reeling in the line, casting again. But now the rod is propped between her legs, her arms folded atop her knees. If a fish bites, she won't be able to grab the reel quick enough to hook it. I guess she doesn't care. I sit down beside her and she smiles at me.

"How was church?" she says.

"Okay."

"Find God?"

"No."

"Don't hold your breath." Slowly she picks up her rod, reels in her line. "Let's go back home," she says.

I wince. We are usually very careful. We usually say the *house*. Let's go back to the house.

"Are you mad at me?" I ask on the way back.

"What?" She stops and turns to me. She didn't hear me because I was walking behind her.

"Are you mad at me for going to church?"

"No. I'm not mad. I'm sorry you think that. I'm just disappointed. But not in you, Tamara. And I'm tired. Very tired."

"I'll make dinner," I say.

"All right. Thanks."

We go back to the house. Robert is outside the barn, just standing there looking at the bike. We never ride it. Every way out of here is up.

I'm eating potato chips and reading *Life* magazine at the kitchen table when Brenda knocks on the screen door. "Hey, Tamara!" she says, squinting through the screen, holding a book.

"Come on in," I say.

Something's happened to her hair. There are whole chunks cut out of it.

"What happened to your hair?" I say. It's easy to ask Brenda blunt questions because that's the kind she always asks, and because she wouldn't get it if I *weren't* blunt. You can't talk around things with Brenda; she gets frustrated and gives up.

She plops the book on the table and shakes her head back and forth, letting her hair fly. Most of it is untangled now, except for one lumpy spot on the top right of her head. Some of her hair is its old length, way past her shoulders, and some is four or five inches long. It looks truly terrible. "I cut out some knots," she says, actually grinning. "Beats trying to comb them out." She puts a hand up to her hair. Her fingers get stuck in that one bad spot and she bites her lip.

"I can't cut this, it's too close to my head, and it hurts too much to comb."

"I got an idea," I say. "Let's try putting some oil on it."

She makes a face like I'm nuts, but then that look vanishes and she shrugs. "Hell, okay. You always got good ideas. It can't hurt."

"Sit down," I say. I go get a towel and a safety pin and wrap the towel tight around her neck, then pin it. Then I get my mom's corn oil and my sister's good comb. "Okay, now hold still." I pour some oil on her head, right above the knot. Half of it runs down her hair and drips right onto the towel, so I feel pretty smart about thinking about the towel. I start rubbing the oil in with my fingers, trying not to make the knot worse, then I pull my fingers through the knot a little at a time, quitting when it tugs at her head.

"That feels good. Hey, you know, I like this. My mom used to, like, play with my hair when I was little. I used to love that."

Now I get the comb, and very slowly, from the bottom, start combing out the knot. I make it looser with my fingers. It's the size of a small robin's nest. It takes some time, but it works. Finally, one half of her head is all shiny and perfectly combed. But it's so uneven it still looks bad. And the oily side looks shiny and healthy; the other side looks like straw.

"I got the knot out, but it needs to be evened up now. I'm going to comb out the other side too. Just trust me."

"I could sit here forever. Go right ahead."

So I pour more oil on the other side and comb her hair over and over until it's real sleek, then I get my mother's scissors and cut off the long ends. I get a little carried away and I change her part from the middle to the left side, and cut the whole thing to make it as even as I can. Brenda doesn't say a thing, even though she's got to see the hair falling on the floor. I stop at about an inch under her ear. Now I cut her bangs real short. When I'm done I take the comb and curl her hair under a little, taking the end of the towel to press out the extra oil.

"Okay," I say. "Now don't move. Promise?"

"Uh-huh."

I run upstairs and get my mirror and run back down, but halfway back to the kitchen I think of something else and turn around and run back up to get a barrette from my sister's room. When I come back down, Brenda hasn't moved an inch. I put in the barrette, to hold the hair back on the right side, then hand her the mirror.

"Oh my God! Oh sweet Jesus! Oh God!"

My mouth goes dry.

"Oh God, I love it! I look just like Audrey Hepburn! Don't you think I look like Audrey Hepburn? My hair's a different color but I look just like her! Oh, Tamara, thank you. You're the best! Wait till my mom sees!" Brenda moves the mirror out to arm's length and turns her head from side to side. I do think she looks better, not at all like Audrey Hepburn, but I'm glad she's happy. It's partly because of the mirror. The mirror makes things look better than they really are. Maybe it's because it cuts out all the other things that we don't want to look at. Brenda doesn't see anything but her hair and her smiling face. She imagines the rest, like the life of Audrey Hepburn, the riches, the movie contracts, all right out there beyond the mirror, where hope is.

I unpin the towel, which is spotty with dark oily stains, and carry it over to the laundry chute. Brenda won't stop looking in the mirror.

"At least move so I can sweep," I say. She stands up and sidesteps over a few feet. I sweep up her hair and throw it away.

"I got to show Helen!" Brenda says, handing me the mirror and hugging me. Then she runs out the door, leaving her book behind. I look at it. Math. She's forgotten her homework. If I had helped her with her math we probably would have gotten into a fight, and now, instead, I'm like God. It makes me think: maybe being a hairdresser is more important than being a scientist. It's a weird thought.

I have another thought. I wonder if making Brenda so happy is like a little miracle from God. Nothing as big as flying, but still . . . Maybe instead of one big miracle I'm going to get a bunch of little ones. I better keep track of them.

Looking at Brenda's book I realize she's probably going to forget all about her math. She won't be able to think about anything but her hair for the rest of the day. I'm going to have to take her book over there. I get a creepy feeling every time I go near their house. I'm worried I might catch something from them if I go inside, or get fleas, or come out limping. But I should take Brenda her book.

I pick up her book and cross the road.

Rusty's standing by the side door, just leaning against the house like he's waiting for a train. "You cut Brenda's hair?" He pinks up all over his face when he starts talking.

"Yeah." We both know this, but I don't know what else we could talk about.

"She sure do look different. Better, I guess," he adds, to be nice.

"Thanks. She forgot her book." I hand it over.

We both just stand there.

"Guess I'll go give it to her," Rusty says. He moves the book up and down, as if I might not know what he means.

"Okay," I say. I can hear the sound of someone talking on the radio, big words drifting out through the screen door, words I bet none of the Murphys ever use.

"Adios," I say, and turn and walk away.

In the early evening I come into the barn, looking for my mother. She is asleep, sitting on the short stool, her hands fallen into her lap, her head resting against Edith's wide belly. I can hear my mother snore, a raspy sound, like a dry brush against thick canvas. Edith just stands there. So do I.

Every house we rent has something unique I will never forget. Woods and rivers, fields and valleys blend together. It is the smallest of things that stay with me.

When I was born in the early summer of '39 we lived on a ranch in Arizona. I know what it looked like only from the paintings: open and distant, flat and lonely. We lived there until I was almost two. Then we moved to Pencer, Minnesota, near Beltrami Island State Forest, where we lived for less than a year. When the war started, my father tried to enlist, but he was forty-five years old and married with kids, and they wouldn't take him. So in March of 1942 we moved to Monterey, California. My mother says that was the house with the sidewalks. I don't remember the sidewalks. I didn't know how rare they would be in my life. I must have taken them for granted.

My father gave up painting for a few months and tried to get a job helping out the war effort. He applied for a job working with radios. That's when they found out he had a punctured eardrum. He was told the best he could do was work in a factory, making airplane parts, which he did for less than six months. His schooling in mathematics and his talent for painting did not prepare him for hard labor, or monotony. He made mistakes. He quit, or was fired, which is my opinion, since no one talks about it at all, and we moved to a cabin in the Rocky Mountains, where my brother, Robert, was born three months later. I remember only the log railing coming down the front steps. I slid down it and dozens of long thick splinters pierced my hands and thighs, as if the railing were a porcupine in disguise. I have heard the story so often I don't know if it's my memory or not. Either way, my hands twitch at the thought.

When I was five we moved to Moab, Utah. We lived near the town, but not close enough for sidewalks. My father would drive out to Arches National Monument early in the morning and return in the evening. He would have been just like every other dad, just this once, except all the other dads were in the war.

We stayed in Moab until right after I turned six, then drove halfway across the country to Bloomington, Indiana. We were in the bottom of a deep valley, with a creek next to our house. When it rained, the creek flooded; it was like living in a shallow lake. This is where I started naming our houses. It was The Hammock House. The hammock stretched from an old oak tree to the front right corner of the house. The rope of the hammock was worn soft and the metal chain creaked as it swayed back and forth, until it—and I—came to rest. And then it was quiet, oh so quiet, and no one would bother me. I could pretend I was all alone on a desert island, shipwrecked, having pulled only the hammock and a few boxes from the sea. In all my daydreams, I am alone.

I started school in Bloomington, and am told I never spoke a word in front of anyone. A little over a year later, when I was seven, we moved to Nags Head, North Carolina.

Nags Head was The House of the Sandy Wind. I walked everywhere with my head bent down and eyes half closed. Half the time I had to walk backwards. Sand lived in my hair and my toes and my crotch. Sand came in the house and sat down for dinner. Sand slept in my bed.

My father was never really happy there because of that sand. It got into his paints and stuck to his pictures. I think he wanted us to move right away but my sister was born soon after we moved to Nags Head. My mother tried to convince the doctors to let Robert and me watch her give birth. The doctor said he thought that letting my father come in the delivery room was enough. Still, my mother told us more than we ever wanted to know about the whole thing.

We lived in Nags Head for a year and a half because my mother was exhausted after having Megan. Then we began our tradition of moving in spring. I spent my ninth birthday in the car on the way to Snowball, Arkansas, along the Buffalo River, in the middle of the Ozarks, a place more lonely than all the rest. It took over an hour to drive to town, up and down narrow dirt roads; there wasn't a level foot in all of the Ozarks. Houses were built into hills, and trees never grew perpendicular to the earth. The river changed like a living thing, sometimes creeping up to our house like a visitor who wouldn't come in.

This was The House of the Laundry Basket, because of the large wicker basket my sister could fit into, with thick bent handles reinforced with white tape. We used it to carry books to and from the library. Once a week we drove to town, filled the basket with dozens of books, and brought it back, placing it just inside the front door, too heavy to carry very far. I don't remember the living room, or the kitchen, but I remember the basket.

Next year, we lived in Valentine, Nebraska, in The House of the Bad Smell. Something had died in the floorboards. It was obvious why the owners had moved out. Then there was The House of the Seashells, in Crane, Oregon. The lady who owned it had a thing for seashells. There were seashell ashtrays, seashell spoon holders, seashell boxes, seashell wind chimes, seashell everything. When I was almost twelve we moved to Parshall, North Dakota, The House of the Squeaky Mourning Doves, named for the sound of mourning doves as they took off in flight from the abandoned flower garden next to the house. A year later we moved to Deer Isle, Maine, to The House of the Owl. There was a carved wooden owl on our door. Then last year we lived in Diamond, Georgia: The Yellow Roses House.

I used to believe that everyone lived like we did, moving from house to house like musical chairs.

When I was in third grade, living in The House of the Laundry Basket, I was invited to a girl's house after school. I forget her name. I asked her where she lived last year.

She squinted up her face. "Here," she said.

"Well, then, the year before," I asked.

She shrugged. "Here."

"How long have you lived here?"

"Since I was born."

I didn't believe her. The idea made me itchy. Her house suddenly felt like a trap.

At home I asked my mother if it was true, what the girl said, expecting to hear it was only a lie.

"Yes, it's true," she said.

"Is it just us who move? Everyone else stays in one place?"

"Pretty much," she said with a sigh, not a heavy sigh, but still a sigh. "Other people move sometimes, but not as much as we do. Possibly some do. I imagine so. But I've never met anyone who does."

"And these kids go to the same school, every year?"

"Yes. But this way you get to meet so many more children. It's quite an opportunity."

This coming from a woman who didn't have a friend in the world besides my father.

At every house we leave something behind. A sweater, a hat, an umbrella, a favorite book. My father once said he thought my mother did it on purpose. She doesn't, but it gave me the idea, and I have done just that ever since. Last year I left a bracelet with two seashell charms in a drawer by my bed. The year before I left a plain silver ring on a windowsill. I imagined I could see it flash in the sunlight as we drove off. The year before that I left a brush with some of my hair still in it, right in the bathroom cabinet. If the boxes in the attic hold the things that Timothy loved, and he's stuck in them, still part of the things he touched, then there are pieces of me all over this country. Maybe that's why I feel like there is something missing in me. Sometimes I poke myself with my mother's sewing needle, just to see the blood come out.

Six

I go across the road to see if Brenda's home, and when I get up the courage to actually knock on their door, Mr. Murphy appears on the other side of the screen. He tells me Brenda's not home. I say thanks and he's gone before I can even turn around.

"Psst . . ."

It comes from behind the big maple the swing's tied to. I wonder if it's Brenda. As I move around the tree, Rusty grabs me. I yell, only because he's scared me, not because I didn't want to be grabbed. "Shhh," he says. The tree is so thick it hides us from the house.

"What?" I say.

"You know," he says. "You been looking at me too."

"And so?" My heart's going a million miles a minute.

"I want a kiss." He blurts it out all in one quick breath, so he has to suck in air quick. He blushes by turning a solid hot pink. I grin.

"Why sure," I say. I close my eyes and in a second I feel his lips touch mine. We move our lips around, seeing how to make them fit. He puts his hands on my back and I put my hands on the back of his neck, which is very warm, and somehow feeling his warm neck with my palms is more exciting than the kiss. He moves against me and I fall back, my head bumping the tree.

"Ow!"

"Sorry," he says.

"You should be," I say, but then his face falls and I feel bad. "The kiss was good," I add. He grins. I like to see him smile. He has a great smile. The corners of his mouth are like the points of my father's quills, and when he smiles he shows all his teeth and the pink of his upper gums. It's a silly and helpless smile.

"Again?" he says. "Could we do that again?"

"Later," I say, and walk away.

I want this kiss to be a *one* thing, not a *many* thing. I remember one things better, like the one firework I saw burst in the sky fifteen minutes before the show was supposed to start. It was a mistake. Someone had set it off too early. I can't remember the shapes and colors of the following fireworks. Only that first one stays with me.

I plan on kissing Rusty a lot more, and those kisses will get bunched up, like a bouquet of flowers. But this kiss I will keep separated from the rest. I go to my room and lie on my bed, close my eyes, and remember the hard pressure of soft lips. The taste of someone else's mouth. The sound of breathing that isn't mine.

It is the third Sunday that we have been invited to church with the Murphys, and Robert, Megan, and I are just finishing breakfast when Brenda knocks on the door. She's sobbing, making gasping noises, and we all stand up and just watch her, terrified. Looking at her making that horrible noise through the screen door, I am reminded of the pictures in my brother's comics of the women freshly tortured by monsters, and I bet Robert and Megan are thinking the same thing because no one moves to open that door and let whatever has hurt Brenda into this house. "What?" I say, almost a shout. "What?"

"They're dead! They're dead!" and then she blubbers more. My brother gasps and takes a few steps backwards. I imagine her whole family slaughtered by ax murderers. I am ready to slam the front door closed and bolt it when she says, "Last night Jimmy Hills and Pete Myers and Cindy Lewis all got killed in a car accident! Cindy's my cousin. I had dinner at her house two weeks ago! I left my sweater there and maybe she was wearing it! They all died! Jimmy drove his dad's car right straight into the wall of the lumberyard. Rusty says the car is flat as a pancake!"

By now I've opened the screen door and Brenda is walking around the kitchen table in circles. She picks up a piece of my brother's jelly toast and stuffs it in her mouth, but keeps talking even with the food in her mouth and grape jelly on her face. My parents come in the kitchen and start asking questions, and Robert and I are asking questions, and Brenda's answering them all by saying, "They're dead! They're dead. Smashed like pancakes!" until my mother puts her hands on Brenda's shoulders and stops her from walking around.

"Shhh," she says. "Now calm down. It's okay. You're okay. Shhh," and then she pulls Brenda into a hug and just holds her while Brenda cries. Megan looks pretty scared and she goes over to my mother, who puts an arm around her too, so they're all kind of hugging each other. My dad puts his hand on Robert's shoulder. I don't know what to do, but my legs are shaking so bad I want to sit, but it seems wrong to sit when I just heard about three kids getting killed, so I don't. I try to picture the face of any of these kids, but I can't. Finally Brenda stops crying so loudly, although she's still crying some, and my mother leads her to a chair and sits her down.

"This is very sad news, Brenda. You don't have to tell us anything more right now, all right? Just sit quietly. Can I get you a glass of water?"

Brenda shakes her head no. "We have to go to church now."

"But is that a good idea? You are so upset. Maybe you should . . ."

"No, we got to go."

"Well, maybe it's not such a good idea for Tamara, Robert, and Megan to come today."

"No, they can come," Brenda gulps. "That's why I came. To get them."

My mother looks at us. Part of me doesn't want to go now, but I'm not going to admit it. "I'll go," I say.

Robert and Megan decide to stay home. They both look like they're a bit afraid of Brenda right now. She does look pretty scary. She stands up and holds out her hand, so I take it, and we walk across the road, get in the car, where everyone else is waiting, and drive to church.

On the way there Mr. Murphy tells us Jimmy Hills had been drinking, and the car had been going over a hundred miles an hour. Mrs. Murphy says this should be a lesson for us all. "I can't imagine the pain the Hills must be suffering right now." Then suddenly she turns to Rusty, her face so contorted she looks like her eyes might fly out of her head, and says, "Don't you ever do anything so stupid, do you hear me!"

Rusty bends his head down and says, "Yes, ma'am."

Mrs. Murphy turns back around, facing forward. She makes this sound like sucking in a lot of air, and then her shoulders start to shake. Mr. Murphy takes one hand from the wheel and puts it on her shoulder. He doesn't say anything. Neither does anyone else.

Church is different this time because instead of everyone having peaceful looks on their faces, they are all red-eyed and teary, and everyone hugs each other tightly and they don't let go for a long while. No one hugs me, but they look at me with such kindness, as if the loss of three children makes them like me more. I am not a stranger, or a new neighbor, but a child close to the same age as the ones who got killed, and I fit into their lives in a different way now. I feel somehow more valuable. I don't know if I should. I should feel sad and I should be crying, but all I feel is warm. Sitting in our pew I am scrunched up tight between Brenda and her mother, because there are more people in church today than ever before, but instead of feeling uncomfortable, I feel cozy and almost sleepy.

The service is held pretty much like it had been before, except when it comes time for people to mention who we should pray for, the minister talks about the three children who were killed, and everyone cries again, except me, and I think maybe I should fake it, but I can't, so I just look down in my lap for a long time. Then we sing and pray and sing and the minister tells his Bible story, which of course has got to do with Jesus dying so we can be saved, and then his personal story, which is about an afternoon he spent with Jimmy Hills when they were doing some kind of Clean Up the Town Day, and, of course, the minister cries and gets everybody going again, and even I'm beginning to feel weepy, even though it's a funny feeling because it's not for the dead kids but for the people in the church. Then the minister raises his hands and everyone sings. We pray and sing and it's over. It's very quiet. It's like after the siren went off at school and we were waiting to breathe again. Waiting to know we could.

No one gets into their cars. Little groups form and talk softly. I stand with the Murphys and two other families. The mothers plan on making chicken casserole and other things to take to the families that lost their children, while the fathers say something should be done about the sharp curve on Route 17. All the kids say the same thing: "I can't believe it." "Can you believe it?" I guess they have to say this over and over so they can believe it.

What I can't believe is what Brenda tells me in the car. That every year some kid gets killed on Route 17. It's like a curse. I can't believe they go through something like this every year. I don't feel so warm and cozy anymore. When I get home I go sit in the bomb shelter by myself. I tell Robert and Megan to get lost. I sit on the concrete floor and look up at the sky, wondering if you could really see a bomb dropping. At what point do you know it is a bomb?

During dinner, I think about all the families carrying casseroles around from door to door. I think about these same families coming to this house just last year, for Timothy, all the food he couldn't eat. When I go to bed, I tell Timothy I'm sorry he died. And I really am. It's like I know him, because I talk to him. It's funny, because I kind of miss him.

My father sells pictures from galleries in New York City, not the big prestigious ones, but galleries all the same. Twice a year he goes to New York to visit the galleries that show his work, and meet with people in the art world. We never go with him, although when he comes back he always says we would have loved it, that he'll take us next time.

Usually my mother gets quiet in the days before he leaves, but this time, as my father packs canvases into heavy, reinforced cardboard boxes and addresses them to be shipped out, my mother's not acting different, because she has been quiet for a long time now. She hardly seems to be here at all. My mother is fading like cloth in the sun.

She has always made sure we read, going to great lengths to help us pick out books. Now she drops us at the library and we're lucky if she comes back in less than a few hours. She just glances at the books we carry. She doesn't ask us questions about what we've read. She doesn't make Megan read out loud to her, something I always had to do. Megan reads though, it's about all she does. She's been reading more and more. She's taken on my mother's quiet as a means of communication. Simultaneous non-communication, like nonviolence, a statement in itself.

My mother also used to drop strange mathematical problems, written on torn pieces of paper, onto the kitchen table as I sat bored, as if she were carrying around an algebra question like one carries around a mop or a broom, a useful item to place in idle hands. She used to point out physics laws as we filled glasses with water or heated water for corn.

And, always, she tried to keep us occupied. But now she lets us do whatever we want. She doesn't care where I go or for how long. The days are long. The only entertainment is ourselves.

From my step I listen to my parents talk about my father going to New York City for a few days. I can't hear everything they say, because they are talking softly. They must be sitting very closely. ". . . just a cold," I hear my mother say. Then, "It's important." Then later, ". . . need the money." I hear my father say something about love, and then my mother say, ". . . not now." I go to my room. I don't really want to hear any more.

Today, when it is time for my mother to drive my father to the airport, she walks slowly out of the barn, rubbing her eyes. We stand around the car and wait for her. There is manure on her tennis shoes. My father points this out, and she looks down.

"Oh. Well, yes." She shrugs and gets into the driver's side of the car. When she turns on the car it makes a deep coughing sound, then I realize it is her.

My father gets in the other side. We are to stay here.

"Be good," she says. "I'll be back in three hours. Give your father a kiss."

He sticks his head out through the open window and we file past him, planting kisses on his cheek.

"You'll be the man of the house while I'm gone now, Robert. Take good care of your mother."

"Yes, sir," Robert says in a soft voice, and suddenly I am angry at my father. Robert can't take care of her. My father should, but he's leaving for four days.

"Take care of your sister," my mother says to me.

As they drive off I walk across the road, looking for Rusty.

While my father is in New York City, my mother spends more time at the pond pretending to fish. I have begun to cook dinners. I make Campbell's tomato soup and tuna casserole, Campbell's tomato soup and meat loaf, Campbell's chicken noodle soup and hamburgers. When my mother comes back from the pond she nods a thanks to me, but she doesn't eat.

At night she coughs for hours. I get on my knees and pray, saying the words out loud. I would shout if I thought that would work better, but I don't think He's listening either way.

My father calls and my mother tells him we are all fine. When he talks to me he asks how we are, and I say fine. My mother nods, pleased with my answer. She nods a lot now, rather than speaking. Sometimes a word comes out as a cough and we don't know what she's said. She will just wave us away, as if whatever it was wasn't important enough to repeat.

Sunday, the Fourth of July, the Murphys drive us into town, where we eat cotton candy, hot dogs, and candied apples, listening to the school band blare out the national anthem. Mr. Murphy hobbles around the crowded park by the lake. Every time I see him, some man is slapping him on the back or shaking his hand. He eats three elephant ears that I know about, probably more. Mrs. Murphy is quiet and whispers into other ladies' ears, cupping a hand to her mouth. I see the Burns, and recognize some kids from school, who wave and shout hello as if they are actually thrilled to see me. They don't come over to talk. When we sit on the blanket by the lake to watch the fireworks, Mr. Murphy stretches both legs out straight in front of him and

Brenda lies down with her head in his lap. He hollers as the fire-works explode, echoing light and sound off the dark water of the lake. Even Mrs. Murphy gasps and claps as the fireworks blossom in cracks and booms and shower down almost onto our heads. "Oh, look at that one!" she says. "Did you see that?" As if we could have missed it. My mother doesn't come.

Robert, Megan, and I go with my mother to the airport to pick up my father. The airport has a small waiting room with plastic chairs, and some offices in back. That's the whole airport. I have never flown before—in an airplane—and my heart pounds with the rumble of the airplanes taking off and landing. I don't believe in airplanes. I don't believe they are possible. I'm an air-plane atheist, but, *here they are,* right in front of my eyes, lifting up into the sky, staying up in the sky, traveling long distances through the clouds.

I want to go inside the waiting room, where my mother sits, and tell her that airplanes exist. I want her to understand how impossible things can happen. I want her to believe in God, because I think He is punishing her. I don't like Him one bit, but I am beginning to believe.

My father's plane lands, a small twelve-seater with Alle-gheny Air printed on its white rivet-covered body. A man in a uniform and earmuffs pushes a staircase up to the plane, and then the plane door swings open. The first person out is my father. He stands on the top step and looks around—not for us, but for the view, taking in the countryside from a new angle. I can see his fingers twitch for a pen or brush. A lady from behind taps him on the shoulder, and he moves down the steps, to us.

His face changes from a grin to a puzzled frown as he sees my mother. He has been gone only four days, but during that time my mother has lost the ability to pretend she is well.

"Are you all right?" he asks, placing the back of his hand to her forehead.

"I have an appointment with the doctor. Tomorrow," she says.

His white eyebrows raise up like albino caterpillars arching. His eyes widen. I hold my breath. I don't believe what I heard. I can never remember my mother seeing a doctor, except when she was pregnant.

"What time?" he asks. We are still standing by the airplane. People walk by us and stare at my mother.

"Eleven."

"I'll take you."

"Thank you." They are very polite. I want to scream.

In the car she asks him how it was in New York City.

"Great. Great. I should have taken you all. Renny loved the new stuff. He says it will really sell. He even wants me to sell a few sketches, before I get to the oils, but I don't know. Renny found me a gallery, but they're right in the middle of renovating. I'll have a show with just one other man, who does paintings of buildings. Almost my own show. In about a month."

There is silence for a minute. He must be expecting my mother to say something, but she's just nodding. He finally figures out that's all he's going to get. He clears his throat.

"I'll have to go back. I have to see the space. I won't let them hang my paintings without me. You know that. But it's all pretty exciting. Huh, kids?" He asks us, since he needs to hear somebody say something.

"Sure is, Dad," Robert says. No one else speaks. It's very quiet in the car.

My sister coughs, just a quick clear bark of a cough, but my mother jerks and swerves the car into the center lane. A car horn blares at us as she pulls back into the right lane. I have grabbed my brother's hand. I let go.

·   ·   ·

That night, fireflies come out in the thousands, as if they are born in the air as we watch. The whole Murphy family crosses the road to join my family on the side lawn between the house and the barn, a large open space that is now alive with lights. We have never all been together before. Fireflies cruise slowly around and above us. They talk with light and the absence of light. There are so many we can't move without one brushing through our hair or landing on our clothes.

My father walks over to Mr. Murphy. "Ever seen anything like it?"

"Yeah. Once. A night just like this. When I was twelve. Never forget it. Must be something special about a night like this."

"Must be," my father says. This is the most they have ever said to each other that I know about. Now they have nothing left to say and stand in silence.

Brenda and Rusty have brought jelly jars with them. In minutes the jars are crawling with the greenish-yellow glow of trapped fireflies. Megan lies down on the grass and looks up at the sky. "You can't tell them apart," she says. "They look like stars. Like shooting stars."

My mother lies down next to my sister and holds her hand. They lie there whispering to each other. I can hear oohs and aahs. I'd like to lie down with them and hold my mother's hand, but I'm too old to do that.

Mrs. Murphy stands perfectly still, her hands clasped in front of her. A firefly has landed on her forehead and stays there, blinking. Mrs. Murphy is smiling, a big, wonderful smile. I have never seen her smile before.

Robert runs inside the house and brings out a glass jar. He skips around scooping fireflies out of the air. He has forgotten a lid, so he holds his hand over the top so they won't escape. "They tickle!" he yells.

I walk over to Helen, who is standing alone, holding out a hand palm up, waiting for a firefly to land. When I get close to her, she puts her arm around my shoulder and pulls me right up next to her. "This is God's gift to us," she says. "A tiny piece of heaven, right here on earth. Do you know how lucky we are?"

"Will heaven be like this?" I ask.

"For me it will, Tamara. It will be just like this. And I hope you'll be there with me."

That makes me think of heaven as a place, a destination. Two thoughts cross my mind. I picture my family moving there, pulling our stuff behind us in the tag-along trailer, so my father can paint heaven. Then, I wonder, where will we go after heaven?

Robert runs over to me and holds the jar upside down above my head, trying to shake the fireflies out. They only crawl upwards, even though the way out is down. A few fall out on my shoulders, but most stay inside the glass jar. They don't know any better.

I walk over to where my mother and sister are lying on the lawn. "Shhh," my sister says. "She's asleep." And she is. In the midst of Helen's heaven, my mother sleeps.

When Megan was three and a half she woke up one morning pasty white and hot, with a temperature of 103.6 degrees. In Crane, Oregon, we were far from a doctor, and as always, my mother decided to play nurse. She held Megan naked in her arms, a towel underneath her, a cold washcloth on her forehead. We smashed ice with a hammer so Megan could suck on small pieces. Megan stayed hot. For two days she whimpered and cried. My father said we should take her to the hospital; my mother felt the fever would come down any minute. Megan wasn't throwing up, she was taking liquids, she would be fine. My mother hated doctors.

On the third morning, lying in my mother's lap, Megan made a strange gasping sound.

"Stuart!" My mother's voice was tense, just managing to hold in panic. I turned to look just as my sister's body stiffened, her legs kicking out across my mother's lap, her shoulders arching back, her head bent backwards against my mother's left arm. She began to jerk, like a little machine stuck in one motion. I would have laughed, it looked so odd, so absolutely funny, except it was, at the same time, the most frightening thing I have ever seen.

"Get your father," my mother said. "Get your father," she repeated sharply, because apparently I didn't move. I ran, looking over my shoulder at my sister. My mother was holding Megan so she wouldn't spill out of her lap.

He was outside.

"Something's wrong with Megan!" I shouted. He dropped his brush and ran past me, into the house. I followed.

Megan was still having spasms, but now tiredly, with a few seconds in between each jerk. Then she shuddered to a stop, a dead stop.

With very little talk we got into the car and took Megan to the hospital. Robert and I were left in the waiting room as the doctor took Megan and my parents through a door and out of sight.

Sitting in the waiting room with a dozen other sad-looking people, I remembered my mother once telling me that devout Christians believe anyone who has not accepted Jesus Christ as their savior would go to hell. "Imagine that," my mother said. "A God that would burn babies in hell for the crime of being born in a place that never heard of Him, not, mind you, that I believe in hell. But such a God, who would believe?" I apologized to God for my mother, telling Him He could do whatever He pleased about all those faraway children, but to please, please, not let my sister die and burn in hell.

Robert and I sat in the waiting room for more than a half hour. Just seven, Robert was all hunched up in his chair, knees bent, head tucked down, arms folded over his head so no one would see him cry. I didn't want to cry, although somehow my face was wet. I was so scared, fear was a live thing inside me, like a rat gnawing at my insides. I held my arms across my stomach, it hurt so much.

My father returned to the waiting room. Megan's temperature had been over a 106 degrees, he told us. They had to put her into a tub of cold water, and then they added ice. We would have to wait. My father asked me to move over so he could sit between Robert and me. Then he took my hand in his and squeezed it. We just sat there, holding hands. It was the last time I can remember holding my father's hand.

I knew Megan would die. I imagined her casket, with a pink satin interior and brass handles. I imagined the funeral, everyone crying. I imagined packing up Megan's clothes and her toys, my mother asking me if I wanted Megan's teddy bear. I wanted to say *yes, please,* but instead I said no. I said it out loud, then I repeated it, because I felt I would burst if I didn't. "No. No. No. No. No. No."

"Tamara?" my father said. "Tamara?"

"No, no, no, no, no, no." I was crying, unable to stop. I was causing a scene. People stared at me. I hated crying. I hated not being able to stop. I hated my sister for dying. My brother stared at me with big wide eyes. I wanted to smash his face. "No, no, no, no, no," I said. I banged my fists on my thighs. My father tried to grab my hands.

A nurse came over. "Can I help?"

"No!" I shouted. "Go away."

"She's upset about her sister," he said. I hated the apology in his voice. He should be apologizing for himself, for following my mother into atheism, for letting my sister die.

"Could you see how she's doing?" my father asked.

"Certainly," she said. She looked at me with such pity, I knew it was because Megan was already dead.

The nurse came back quickly. "Your sister's doing much better. Her temperature is down. She's going to spend the night here, but she'll probably be able to go home tomorrow. Really." She put her hand on my shoulder. I moved my shoulder away and her hand came off. "Really, she'll be fine. There's no reason to be scared, honey."

Megan came home the next day, just as the nurse said, but I didn't feel happy or relieved. I was furious at her for making me so scared, for making me feel stupid. My parents treated her like a little princess for months. If she sneezed, they held her in their laps, a palm on her forehead, or read her stories, whispering in her ear, asking me to run for her teddy. "Please find Teddy," they said, as if he were alive. "Please look all over for Teddy and bring him to your sister."

I really can't stand her, my sister. If she had died, I would have loved her.

My father drives my mother to her doctor's appointment, leaving us behind. She waves from the car, a scanty wave, mostly fingers.

The hospital is in Westfield, a forty-minute drive. The doctor in Mayville works out of his house and my mother says she wouldn't trust him to stitch a cut.

Today Rusty wants to show me his fort.

I follow him into the woods. The ground is covered with undergrowth, brambles, and fallen trees. Tall thin poplars with white speckled bark stretch up to the sky, vying for light; their round leaves make a *shhh* sound in the light summer wind. Rusty leads me to the right, past a stand of old pines with broken limbs and through a flat, almost treeless space where mayapples cover the ground like a thick green carpet. There is a well-worn path straight through the center of the mayapples, where they have learned their lesson from Rusty's feet. Gradually the earth rises

and the trees are mostly maple, some ancient, with branches
thicker than my waist. Saplings and younger trees grow between
the older trees, like thin children. We can see through the woods
now, to the top of the hill, where Rusty's fort is. We make
rustling, papery sounds as our feet swish through the covering of
last fall's leaves.

Rusty's fort is made from a conglomeration of old junk:
two wooden doors, a sheet of corrugated metal, a wide piece
of knotty plywood, several branches, random boards, and a
pale-manganese-blue shower curtain for a door. It's not round
and it's not square. Maybe octagonal. I don't think he was trying
for a specific shape, just trying to fit it in between some of the
trees. Rusty lifts up the shower curtain and we duck inside.

The ceiling is about six feet high, made out of chicken wire,
with a shower curtain lying on top of the wire. The shower curtain is clear with bright tropical fish painted on it, and it's very
dirty. Still, some light comes through. It feels a bit like we're
under water.

Inside there are two metal folding chairs, the legs bent at
angles that chair legs are not meant to go. I doubt you could sit
in them. There is also a beige sleeping bag on a piece of black
plastic, a lantern on a wooden box, a cardboard box with
kitchen things like cups and bowls, and in one corner is a metal
box with a lock on it.

"Neat," I say. He positively beams with pride.

We sit down on the tattered sleeping bag. Rusty absently
runs his fingers along the dirt floor.

"I don't bring no one out here," he says.

"Anyone," I say.

He nods, missing my point. "Yeah, you're the first."

This worries me. Doesn't he have any friends? Which makes
me wonder. "Did you know him?" I ask.

He blinks, confused. I've thrown him off track.

"The Burns' kid? The one who died?"

"Oh." He nods, taking some time to switch gears. His whole face twitches as he thinks. "Well, sure."

"Was he your friend? What was he like?"

Rusty looks around his fort, sure something went wrong somewhere, then he shrugs. "Well, he was smart, like you, and he was in tenth grade. He liked making stuff, science projects with knobs and batteries and stuff. He said he was going to be a rocket scientist and I sure think he would have. If he hadn'ta died first."

"Were you two good friends?" I want to know all about the dead boy. I wouldn't have dared asking these questions in the house, or anywhere within sight of the house, but it feels safe in Rusty's fort.

"Yeah, well, I've known him my whole life. And he was friendly. He liked to show me stuff. We shared comics and stuff. He gave me the idea for this fort when I was complaining about having nothing but sisters driving me crazy. We talked about . . . things. He never got to come in the fort though. He got too sick to walk this far. You woulda liked him."

I think I would have. It's his ghost I worry about.

Rusty continues talking, as if I opened up a drain that had been all clogged. "Timothy was sick for a long time. Didn't go to school for like half the year. He had leukemia. Cancer in his blood, just poisoning him. It made the Burns get so sad, like they got old real quick. Nobody laughed over there. The Burns used to be real fun, before he got sick. Mr. Burns got drunk on Saint Patrick's Day and painted the bull's horns green and stuck apples on them. It was great. Pissed that bull off real bad, but we couldn't help laughing." Rusty laughs, then just stops.

"I saw Timothy the day he died. I saw him dead."

For a quick second I think I'll say to Rusty that he doesn't have to tell me any more, but then I know I want to hear this stuff, and that Rusty wants to tell me. I nod.

"Well, I went up to his room, your room now I guess, and he was all white and his eyes were sunk into his head, like his sockets got big and swallowed them. You could see all the bones on his face. The Burns told me when I was about to go up to his room that they were taking him into Westfield soon, like in an hour, but Timothy didn't want to go and Mrs. Burns was all red-eyed 'cause she wanted to do what Timothy asked, since you want to do what your kid asks when he's sick. While I was upstairs you could hear Mr. and Mrs. Burns talking about it. They both knew they had to go. They'd been there a lot recently and just gotten back a few days ago. Timothy just shook his head when I asked him how he was, and rolled his eyes, which was real gross to watch 'cause they got all white and I thought for a second they wouldn't come back normal. I tried telling him my fort had all the walls up, and that I'd take him when he got back from the hospital next time, but he didn't seem to really care, you could tell." Rusty pauses and bites at a fingernail, working it off with his teeth, then he spits it on the ground and scratches his nose.

"So I sat there and felt stupid, and he kept closing his eyes, so I figured he needed sleep. I told him I was going to go and I'd see him in a couple days when he got back. When I went downstairs, you could tell they decided they were going to take him back, so I asked if I could help some way. Like helping carry Timothy downstairs or something. Mr. Burns said no, Timothy was pretty light now and he was just going to drive the car right up to the door, so I followed him out. Mrs. Burns was packing some sandwiches to eat at the hospital. So I went home.

"But I didn't go inside, I just sat on the swing waiting to watch Timothy get carried out, just in case they really did need me. But after Mr. Burns backed the car up to the door, he went inside and no one came out. Not for at least a half hour. So I got worried.

"No one ever told me he was going to die. No one said anything about it. We just put him in our prayers, asking God to help him get better, so I figured he would, or maybe if not better, he'd just go on being sick forever. But the Burns must have known. My parents too. They just didn't warn me.

"So, when I went back over and knocked on the door and asked if I should help, I didn't believe it when they told me he was dead. I thought maybe they just made a mistake. An ambulance came to get him and I was sure the guy driving it would say, 'What do you mean? He's fine,' but he didn't. They covered up his face with a sheet when they brought him out, so I guess I didn't really see him dead, but it feels like I did. I didn't believe it really until the funeral. Sometimes I still don't believe it."

"He's still there," I say, not knowing I'm going to say it until it comes out, wishing right away I hadn't said it.

Rusty squints his eyes at me. "What?"

He's looking at me like I'm crazy, which makes me mad. "His ghost is stuck in the attic," I say, a little too loudly for the cramped inside of the fort. It sounds like I'm yelling when I'm not.

"Shit, Tamara, you're nuts." He leans back, away from me. He actually looks a little scared.

"I am not nuts! I hear him. I can feel him."

He folds his arms across his chest, almost like he's protecting himself from me. "Well, I say you're nuts. Timothy is in heaven. Helen says so. The minister says so."

"Yeah, well," I say, wishing I never started this. I don't want to fight with Rusty. I want to get kissed, and maybe more. I want to get started on that whole bunch of stuff in the middle. He's the only boy around, so I don't want to get him mad at me. "So," I say, "now you think I'm nuts and you don't want to kiss me anymore?"

This stops him dead. Now we're back to where he wanted to be the whole time, but he's not sure how we got there. Neither am I.

He swallows. I can see his Adam's apple bob down and up. "I do want to kiss you," he says.

"So, go ahead," I say.

I don't have to say it twice.

We kiss for a long time, trying it different ways. Heads sideways. Heads straight, noses bumping. Mouths a bit open. Hard. Soft. Moving our lips slowly. Hard again. Finally we get tired of it and he figures out a way to make it new again. His hand slides down to my left breast, cupping it real softly as if he's afraid it might hurt me, or maybe that it might burn his hand. I have conveniently forgotten to wear a bra. I can feel him carefully move his hand around, discovering just that.

All on their own, my breasts kind of arch toward him. I'm embarrassed by this forward motion of my body, but I can't stop myself. His hand clamps a bit tighter and I moan, right through my lips that are pressed to his, although I can't really feel my lips anymore; my whole brain has slipped down into my left breast.

Now we kiss, both knowing that the kissing is just a good excuse for him to be feeling me up. We are trying to not move much, because if we do, we could knock a wall down. Still he finds ways to experiment, by squeezing my breast, then letting go, kind of kneading it like warm bread. It's getting hot inside the fort. I'm sweating and Rusty smells warm, he even tastes a little salty. Then he gently pinches my nipple right through my cotton shirt, and my nipple gets tight and hard and stays that way, and he can tell, because then he concentrates on just the nipple for a while and I know I'm making noises I never made before, except for the time my mother made chocolate truffles. And even then it was just one moan and this is a bunch of them all tied together in what seems to be one long breath, because I can hardly breathe and my heart is banging so hard I think it's going to burst. I really, really like this, but then I think of God.

I don't know where the thought comes from, but suddenly I think God is looking right down at me through the dirty shower curtain. He's got one eye on me and one eye on the rest of the world. He's shaking His head. I stop kissing Rusty and pull back. His hand tries to stay on my breasts, but I turn slightly away, and he gets the hint.

"Uhhh," he says. His hand is still in the cupped shape of my breast and his fingers still pulse in little flexes. "What?" he says. "Did I do something wrong?"

It can't be wrong, I think. It feels too good. But now I'm afraid. I can't make any mistakes right now, not with my mother on her way to the hospital. Maybe I shouldn't even be here. But for the life of me, I can't figure out why God would care. I remember my mother saying that if there was a God who cared if you ate fish on Friday, He must be insane and she wouldn't worship Him anyway. I wish I could ask Helen if God cared about me making out with Rusty, or him feeling me up, but I figure Rusty wouldn't appreciate that.

"I think we should stop. Before, you know," I say.

"I wasn't going to do nothing you didn't want."

"Anything," I say.

"Anything?" he asks, his mouth hanging open.

"No, I mean . . . Oh, forget it. It was good, Rusty. I have to say I liked it. But I should be watching my sister. I better get back."

"Oh, okay." He's still breathing heavy, still stuck on *anything*. "Can I just look? Would you? Would you mind?"

I wouldn't mind at all. I'd like him to. I think about God looking too, but just then a cloud must come across the sun because it gets darker in the fort. I figure God must be shutting one eye for a minute, or turning it somewhere else to where someone's doing something more wrong than this. I lift up my shirt.

"Don't touch," I say, because if I let him touch them now I'll never get home. Rusty's looking at my breasts like there's no tomorrow.

I lower my shirt. "Let's go."

"Hot dog! They sure are big!" he says, and rubs his hands together. I laugh. He's a funny kid. I kind of like him.

Seven

I pick at the peeling wood on the front steps. The dog, Kip, watches me as he lies on the grass a few feet away. He's always scrutinizing me with a half-wary, half-hopeful look, never getting too close. He'll let me pet him if I move real slow. Usually I don't bother.

My father drives up our pebbled drive, braking at the last minute before the driveway ends and the lawn begins. I don't see my mother. She must be lying down in the back seat, sleeping.

He gets out of the car, closes the door, and just stands there. His face is blank. His lips turn neither up nor down. His eyes look straight ahead. He starts to walk toward the house where I'm sitting on the top step, but I don't think he sees me. I don't think he sees anything.

"Where's Mom?" I ask. A quick shot of fear hits me hard. She isn't in the car. I know it without asking.

At the sound of my voice, he trips, startling himself. He throws out his arms in a swimming motion and manages to straighten up. He turns his head toward the barn, as if he thinks my mother might be there, as if she might come walking out with a big smile and he won't have to answer my question. My fear turns into a sharp anger.

"Where is she!"

Robert and Megan come out of the house and stand behind me on the porch. The sound of the screen door opening and closing makes him turn. He looks right through us. As angry as I am, I have a very coherent thought: it is amazing he made it back home without having an accident. With my image of him smashed to pieces, anger jumps back and fear jumps forward again. I think I'm going to throw up. I feel like I'm on a teeter-totter and I'm up too high to get off. I'm going back and forth but never down.

"Where's Mommy?" Megan asks. Her soft little voice just floats in the air; I can hear her words spread out and cover us.

My father nods. He takes a deep breath and nods again, at us as a whole. We are too many to ignore. "Well," he says. "She didn't come back with me."

"What?" I don't know who says this. Maybe we all do.

"For our own protection." He closes his eyes and presses his large hands flat against his cheeks, covering his eyes, and he stands like this for a minute or more. We don't say anything. We are too confused to speak. When he takes his hands down, his eyes are focused. He looks at me, at Robert, at Megan. "Let's go inside and sit down. I need to sit down." He is older right now than he was just this morning. His eyes are gray with webs of fine lines underneath and he moves awkwardly, his stride shorter than usual, as if it takes some thought to walk and he has to be very careful. We part to let him open the door and go inside, then we follow him in.

He lowers himself onto the faded stuffed chair in the living room, and the three of us sit on the couch. At least he doesn't pull the easel over. I couldn't stand the easel right now.

Robert is crying quietly. Megan sits on the edge of the couch, hands gripped in her lap. My fists and throat are so tight they hurt. "Where is she?" Megan asks.

"All right," he says. "Now listen closely. Your mother has tuberculosis. TB. You've heard of it, I know."

We have. My grandfather died of it, before we were born. My mother's father. It's one of the few things I know about him, except that I have his big cheekbones.

"It's very contagious, which means she can pass it on to us, to you kids. It's in her lungs. It may have spread. They don't know how she got it, or why. Maybe from her father. Maybe she caught it as a child but didn't know it, or it lay dormant and now it's come back, it's active. They just don't know."

"When will she come back?" Megan asks. I let her do the asking, since she's doing pretty well at it.

"They don't know. She's in a special wing in the hospital, but it's a small hospital. They want to transfer her to a sanitarium, a place just for tuberculosis patients. There's one a little over an hour away. There aren't many sanitariums left, so we're lucky it's close. The doctor says they may not take her. They're not taking new people anymore, but he says someone owes him a favor, and he's going to try. He liked your mother. Likes. Likes your mother. They could keep her in the hospital, but it would be better for her at the sanitarium."

"I want her to come home now," Megan says. "Now!" She says this so firmly, like an adult commanding a small child to sit, that for a moment I think it might work. *I'd* listen to her.

My father shakes his head. "I want her home too, Megan. But we will have to wait."

My brother's crying grows loud. He sniffles and sobs and whimpers all at once. My teeth tighten at the sight of him. "I want to go see her," Robert says through gasps for air.

"We can't."

"I don't understand," I say. "Can't they just give her a shot?"

"Not really. They have medicine. There *is* a cure. It's not like in your grandfather's age. There is a *cure*." He says this obviously trying to convince himself. He's not convincing me at all.

"You *let* them take her?" I say.

He shakes his head back and forth before speaking. "No. I wouldn't let them. I told them they couldn't keep her. I said it was against the law to . . . It didn't matter, what I said, because she wouldn't . . . She wouldn't come back with me. She said it was for us . . . for our protection. She wouldn't come home." He rubs at his eyes with the back of his hands. "She said to give you all a kiss."

I don't want his kiss. He could have made her come back. How could she not come back, just long enough to say good-bye? How could she let them keep her there? I am never going to see her again, and she thinks sending us a kiss will help? I hate them both so much I'm shaking.

"It's all your fault!" I say, thinking it's all my fault. Because I got her upset by going to church, or maybe God really didn't want me to show Rusty my breasts. "If you had eyes, you'd have seen she was sick long ago and she'd be better by now. It's all your fault. All you care about is painting!" I get up and stomp up to my room. But I want to hear what's happening downstairs, so I turn around and sit on the top step.

"I want to see her," my sister says.

"Me too," Robert whimpers.

"Oh Jesus," my father says. "I wish you could."

Not me. She can go rot. She didn't even try to come home first. She will never come back. She's gone. We never come back to places we leave.

"The cow," my father says. "What will I do about the cow? Who will milk the cow?"

"Fuck the cow," I say, just loud enough for me to hear the word come out of my mouth. It makes me feel better. "Fuck the damn cow," I say a bit louder.

"I'll try," my sister says.

"Thanks," my father says.

I laugh into my hands. I laugh so hard my stomach hurts. I laugh so hard I can no longer hear my brother crying.

Just after a dinner of boiled potatoes and grilled cheese sandwiches, which I had to make because my mother isn't here, I walk to the crossroads and up to the top of Valley View Hill. I don't tell anyone where I'm going. It's a stunning day. High-rising clouds with impossibly flat bottoms drift across the sky. Red-winged blackbirds skirt from bush to bush, warning each other that I am here. The air is crisp and thin and easy to breathe, a relief from the air inside our house, which is heavy and damp from the puddles of my brother's tears. He is such a sissy.

I don't go over into the grassy field; I stay on the road. Where is my mother now? How is she going to protect us? Whose job is that now? Who's going to stop my brother from crying? My father only knows how to paint. He's not even a very successful painter. He's going to make a terrible mother. I'm next in line, but I don't want the job.

I take a gulp of air and spread out my arms. I run down the hill, right in the middle of the road. As my feet begin to stumble, I launch myself into flight.

With bloody bits of gravel embedded in my skin, I wobble home, numb, and then not numb, to the pain. I have scraped the skin off my chin, my arms, my palms, and from my knees to my ankles. I don't think I have broken anything, but my skin is on fire.

"Oh my God, what have you done?" my father says as I walk into the kitchen, where they have just finished doing the dishes. His face goes pale.

"I tried to fly," I say. "I didn't make it."

He tells Megan to run across the road for Helen, and for a minute I think, *Yes. I need Helen now,* but when she comes she's not carrying a Bible, but iodine and clean cloths. She is followed by Rusty and Brenda. Brenda shrieks when she sees me, and Rusty pales, just like my father. Rusty asks me if I'm okay and I say sure.

Helen tells everyone to leave us alone, go outside. They all file out, looking backwards at me, nearly tripping over themselves. I can hear Brenda asking my father what happened. Then Helen turns on the kitchen faucet.

She fills a metal bowl with warm water. "Just stand there," she says. "Don't sit. Can you do that?"

"Uh-huh," I say.

"This will hurt," she says.

I think it can't hurt more than I already do, but I'm wrong. Helen washes my exposed skin, first just squeezing the water over me, then getting the rag wet again and gently wiping me down. I don't yell out, but I keep gasping for air that doesn't seem to ever reach my lungs. When I'm mostly clean, she lightly pats me dry, then anoints me with the iodine, which stings like fire ants, then fades to a dull throb. When Helen is done with me, I look like a bad joke, half orange, half white. Maybe mostly orange. I see my father's face peering at me through the mesh of screen.

"Can I come in?" he asks.

Helen says yes. He is followed by Megan, Robert, Rusty, and Brenda. He didn't know they were going to follow him in, and he looks at them with a frown. I figure he imagined a nice little father-daughter talk, with Helen as a wise and patient buffer. But he doesn't know how to send everyone back out, so they stand around in the kitchen. There's not much room, but everyone gives me plenty of space, as if my wounds might be contagious.

"You look goofy," Robert says, and he grins and almost giggles, even though his eyes are still red. I step forward and punch him in the stomach.

Robert yells as if he's been shot. Helen gasps. Brenda snickers.

"Go right up to your room, young lady," my father says.

"I'll go with her," Helen says.

My father looks like he wants to say no, that he is mad enough at me for my foolishness and my slugging Robert to not allow me even the slight comfort of Helen, but he lost control of everything this morning when my mother decided to stay somewhere else, and he hasn't found a way back. Besides, there is no denying Helen. He nods.

Rusty looks at me, a sad, scared look, and I know he feels terrible for me. It helps a little and I try to smile at him. Then I head upstairs.

In my room, Helen tells me to kneel by the side of my bed. This is a mistake, because when my knees hit the floor I holler and straighten back up. Even for God, I can't do this.

"Just sit on your bed then, Tamara. I'll kneel for both of us." She does, then bends her head. "We will pray for your mother first, that God will heal her, both physically and spiritually. Then we will pray for you, to heal you inside and out, just like your mother. You must also ask forgiveness for hitting your brother, and for purposely hurting yourself and your family."

"I thought I could fly," I say.

"You know better than that, Tamara. God did not give us wings. Now pray, and open your heart to Our Lord. Maybe you will find Jesus today."

But I don't pray. I bend my head and think that maybe I *can* fly. Maybe I just did it wrong. Maybe I have to start higher up, to catch the breeze. I am also thinking I didn't hit my brother hard enough by half.

The next day my father gives us the rest of the news.

"Let's get in the car," he says, right after the breakfast of cornflakes.

"Why?" my sister asks. She's getting good at asking questions. Before, she was a dormouse, and now she's like the squirrels—chatter, chatter, chatter. It's putting my father off balance; when Megan speaks I can see his body tense up as he braces himself against the kitchen chair.

"We have to go to the hospital."

"To get her back?" Megan asks. "Good." She walks to the front door.

"No, no," he says. "You all have to get tests."

Megan frowns. "For what?"

"For tuberculosis, stupid," I say.

Robert starts to sniffle. "I don't want to have a test."

"What happens if we have tuberculosis?" my sister says.

My father blinks, opens his mouth, and then closes it. He looks around the small kitchen, then toward the ceiling. "Well . . . Ahh . . . You would have to stay at the hospital too."

He's expecting a large protest, a slew of complaints, but instead my sister bounces up and down. "Oh, good!" Megan says. "I'll go pack." She skips out through the dining room arch and up the stairs.

My father wearily shakes his head. "Oh no." He looks to me for help. I shrug.

Now he slaps a hand against his forehead. "Oh Jesus, what are they going to think when they see you?"

I am a palette of bright colors: splotches of Windsor orange, permanent mauve, Prussian blue, magenta pink, and Indian red, covering all but a few spots of lightly tanned white, topped with a loose mop of dull brown hair which still retains tarred pebbles from the road. And I'm not quite ripe yet. I have a feeling there are a few more colors to arrive: purples and greens and dark black. I am a mess. Robert is blubbering by the sink.

"So, I won't go," I say. "I'll just stay here so I won't embarrass you."

"Just go pack some things for your mother," he says. "And be quick."

I kick Robert in the shin as I walk by.

As I pack my mother's things I think about the fact that my father has begun to say *Jesus*. He never said that when she was here. I wonder if we are already a bit less atheistic without her to make us "us."

In the car ride to the hospital I imagine I can't breathe. My lungs fill with thick, wet air. Sweat drips down from my armpits. I can feel my face flush. I tell myself I'm fine, but it reminds me exactly of how my father insisted there is a cure.

Robert has lost his voice from crying and has finally stopped whining that he doesn't want to go. Megan sits next to my brother in the back seat, her worn alligator suitcase at her feet.

No one speaks. We learned long ago that if my father *does* drive, it's best not to distract him.

I decide to pray.

As we drive into the hospital's parking lot, my father tells us that we will not be able to see our mother, even though she is right here. My sister doesn't say a word. She clutches her suitcase in a tight little fist as we get out of the car. My father doesn't have the energy to tell her to leave it behind.

I have my mother's things in a paper grocery bag. Her nightgown, slippers, a terry-cloth bathrobe, some underwear, socks, her cold cream, and a cross. I ran across the road to ask Helen for it right before we left. Helen beamed when I asked her and took the one right off her neck to give me. I bet she has a dozen more. I'm hoping my mother might take the hint.

Praying in the car helped me. I don't feel sick anymore. It was only panic. I'm strong as an ox. I could lift my brother and throw him into a tree.

My father knows where to go and we follow him down a long hall to a small waiting room, where he tells the receptionist our names. We sit in beige plastic chairs, all in a row like people waiting for a bus.

My father looks around the room with a sigh, and I know it is not because we are going to be tested by some doctor who might decide to take us away, but because the waiting room is so aesthetically displeasing to his eyes. The chairs are beige, the walls a faded dirty mint green, the woodwork dull off-white, and the carpet gray. The ceiling lights cast flat puddles of shadows on the floor, taking away any hope of dimensions. He leans his head back and closes his eyes.

Another family is waiting in this small room, all thin, blond, and sad-looking; a mother and a father, each holding a daughter, the girls so alike I think they are twins. No one says a word. I can hear the clock tick on the wall, a *thuck, thuck, thuck* sound, as if each second is an effort.

There are only two doors, the one we came through and the one next to the receptionist's frosted window. The window is closed. Blurry beige forms move behind the opaque window, seemingly unconcerned that everyone out here in this room is scared to death.

There are posters on the wall. An enormous set of lungs, with red and blue veins like a road map. Brought to us by the American Lung Association. Several posters are "a service of the U.S. Public Health Service," which recommends tuberculosis testing. I guess I'll follow that advice. There is a poster by the National Tuberculosis Association that says it is "fighting for the complete eradication of this disease from the face of the earth." They are taking the "zero tolerance approach." I picture well-groomed blue-eyed men in white coats herding everyone with TB together and dropping the H-bomb on them.

A nurse calls in the other family. They all look at each other when their names are called, as if they aren't sure she means them, then slowly they stand, lowering the twin girls to the floor, who grab their parents' hands and follow them through the door. Robert has brought his copy of *Haunt of Fear*. It's open on his lap to a picture of a man with his skull split in two by an ax, his eyeballs popping out of his head, but Robert seems to have forgotten how to read. He doesn't turn a single page for the next ten minutes. Finally the same nurse, a very short, heavy woman who is somewhere between twenty-five and fifty, calls our names.

"Tamara, Robert, and Megan Anderson?" she says. Of course she pronounces my name wrong. I correct her.

"Yes, yes, here," my father says.

She opens the door a little wider and waves us in. The other family hasn't come back out. I wonder where they've gone.

We are led into a lab with a wooden chair that has a flat wooden platform where your right arm goes. There are test tubes and syringes and big wide rubber bands on a cabinet nearby.

"You're the Andersons? For a tuberculosis test?"

"Yes, we are," my father says. The nurse writes our names down on the test tubes.

"Me first," Megan says, going straight to the chair and sitting down. She lays out her thin arm, wrist turned up.

The nurse gives a questioning look to my father. He spreads out his hands in a gesture of surrender. "Why not?" he says.

"You're a brave girl," the nurse says, dabbing at the inside of her elbow with a cotton ball.

"I have tuberculosis," Megan says.

"Oh my. I hope not," the nurse says.

"But I do," Megan says.

The nurse once again looks to my father, who merely shrugs.

"Well, let's just see. We're going to do a few tests. First a blood test. Have you ever had your blood drawn?"

"Uh-huh," Megan says. "When I almost died."

"Oh." She doesn't look to my father, obviously knowing there is no help there. She wraps a rubber band around Megan's upper arm. "Well, you must have survived. So you know what I'm going to do. Do you want to watch or turn your head away?"

"I'll watch."

The nurse picks up a syringe. My brother cries out and turns away. I watch, even though I want to turn away. The nurse sticks the needle into Megan's skin. Blood rises into the syringe. The room wobbles and I wish I were sitting down. This is completely different from sticking myself with a pin. It's slow, and the needle goes deep inside. When she pulls it back out, a tiny drop of blood forms on Megan's pale skin, and the nurse presses a cotton ball to it and covers it with a Band-Aid.

"Now just a TB skin test. This won't hurt much at all." Once again she wipes Megan's arm with a cotton ball dipped in alcohol, but this time lower down, between her wrist and elbow, where Megan's skin is soft and white. She puts a little gunlike thing on Megan's arm and then pushes a button. Megan doesn't even blink. "All done," the nurse says. "Who's next?"

"Me," I say, mostly because if I don't sit down, I'll fall.

"Okay." She looks at me funny. "What happened to you?" she asks.

"I tried to fly," I say.

"Well, that would do it," she says. Carefully she finds a place where there is no iodine or scraped skin to tie on the rubber band, so it doesn't hurt at first, but by the time she carries the needle over I think my veins will burst. The needle stings more than I expect and I let out a little *ohhh,* but then it's over. She explains to me all over again about the TB skin test, shoots me with the little gun, then washes her hands in the sink.

"And now you, young man," she says to Robert. He darts behind my father.

"No, no, no, no, no." His voice is high-pitched and somehow ghostly.

"But your sisters have been so brave. I know you can too."

"No, I can't."

"It's a very important test," she says. "And very quick. Just come on over and sit down and it will be over in a flash."

"No."

"Can you help me?" the nurse asks my father.

He looks around the room as if she might be talking to someone else. "What?" he says.

"If we can't talk your son into doing this voluntarily, we will have to call someone in to hold him down."

"Now, Robert . . ." my father says, turning his head to where Robert hides behind him.

"No, I won't, I won't, I won't!"

My father tries to talk him into it several more times. He grabs him but Robert kicks him in the shin. In the end, two more nurses are called in and they, and my father, hold Robert down. He screams his head off, the sound echoing off the tile floor and puke-green walls. My father bats me on the back of my head when I stick my tongue out at Robert.

Next, we need X rays.

"What's that?" Robert howls.

"Like in the H-bomb," I say. "X rays. Radiation. Get the picture?"

Robert gasps.

"Oh, heavens," the heavy nurse says. "They don't hurt at all." She looks at me sharply, as if I deserve all the scrapes and bruises I have. She kneels down and takes Robert's hand. "I don't know why your sister said that. I can't imagine she would want to scare you, especially since this is such a serious business, with your mother sick and all. Now you listen to me, Robert. It's just like taking a picture, except you have to hold very still, that's the only difference. But I'll tell you what. We'll have your sister go first, your *older* sister, and you can watch through a window. Okay?"

He likes this idea and nods. The nurse completely ignores me as she asks us to follow her. She keeps Robert's hand in hers. My father trails behind.

I have never had an X ray. I was exaggerating when I said they are like an H-bomb, but not by much. Every school I've been in has had stern talks about fallout and radiation. Radiation will make your hair fall out, your skin pucker up and die. I am not looking forward to this.

I take off my clothes and put on a light-blue hospital gown, open in the back. They have let me keep on my underwear. Holding the gown closed behind me as best I can, I'm led into a large dark room with a bunch of huge machines. The same nurse leads me to a large black pole that runs from the floor to the ceiling. There is a flat square of black metal attached to it, about two feet square. The nurse slides it down a few inches then looks at me, sizing me up.

"This is our chest X-ray unit, and I want you to pay close attention. Stand here." She maneuvers me like I'm a toy truck she's wheeling around, until I'm flat up against the thick cold whatever-it-is, my breasts pressed against it like flattened Silly Putty. She places my chin on a curved rubber rest that's on top of the X-ray unit, then she raises the whole thing by adjusting the pole on the side. I go up on my toes. "Too high," she says, then lowers it a millimeter. "Put your hands on your hips," she says. No "please" for me. She grabs my elbows and pulls them back, so I'm all on one flat plane, then puts her hands on my shoulders and shifts me around for a minute, her own private mannequin. Directly behind me is this thick black tube, coming down from the ceiling. I turn to look at it, and the nurse, with a slight rolling of her eyes, cups my head in her hands, turns me around, and snuggles my chin back into the chin rest. "Please don't move." I get a "please" this time, but it's like my father using my whole name. It's not meant as a kindness.

"Be very still now. Don't move. When I tell you to, you will take a deep breath, blow it out, then take another deep breath and hold it until I tell you to let it out. Do you understand?" I nod. I'm willing to bet she's going to make me hold my breath longer than most people.

Somewhere in this hospital is my mother, lying down on crisp white sheets, someone cooking for her, bringing her magazines. It is my mother's fault I'm here now with this sadistic nurse. And all this time Megan is playing her little angel role, with her stupid suitcase by her feet. I want to throw that suitcase out the window. Then Megan, then Robert, and then my father.

The nurse leaves the room. Through a speaker in the wall I hear her tinny voice say, "Take a deep breath, blow it out, now another deep breath and hold it." I am expecting a flash of bright light. I am expecting to blow up. Even though I can't see my family because the nurse has turned me away from the thick glass window that separates us, I know they are watching me. I think of screaming out in great agony, grabbing my chest, and falling to the floor. I can imagine the look of horror on my brother's face. I can imagine how mad I could get that nurse. But then I hear her say "Breathe," and the chance is gone.

Robert and Megan get their X rays taken. No one blows up. Our nurse leads each of us into separate rooms, where we will be examined by a doctor. They don't test my father. He went through all this yesterday, he just neglected to tell us until now. He goes in a room with Megan.

The doctor asks me a million questions.

"Do you cough at night?"

"No."

"Good, very good. Do you sleep well?"

"Yes."

"Good, very good. Do you eat well? Have a good appetite?"

"Yes.

"Good, very good. Do you tire easily?"

"No.

"Good, very good . . ." This goes on for a long time. I feel like a winning contestant on *Twenty-one,* because I know all the right answers. Finally he looks in my mouth, my nose, and my ears, thumps me all over with a rubber hammer, and listens to my chest.

"You seem fine to me, but we have to look at those X rays before you go. So you just wait here."

I wonder if my mother sat in this room. I wonder if she knew just by the thumps on her back that she would never get out of here. I wonder if she knew her answers to the questions were the wrong ones, if she even thought about lying. I wonder if she began to miss us from the moment that he closed the door and told her to wait.

I say a little prayer. *God, please don't let me be sick.* I say it like it's just a small favor, casually, so He doesn't think I'm asking for a lot. I hope He's in a good mood, that Jesus didn't do anything to get Him angry, like I did to my dad. I start thinking how tough it must be to be God's son. You couldn't get away with anything. A nurse knocks and sticks her head in. "Would you like a magazine?"

Finally, it's all over. We are declared fine. The bad news is that we have to get a shot anyway, just in case we have been very recently infected.

Megan won't let them give her a shot. She says she won't leave either. She crosses her arms, sits on the floor next to her suitcase, and closes her eyes. They have to call in one of the larger nurses that held down my brother to give her the shot.

My brother just sticks out his arm. He has survived the X ray and now feels indestructible. There is an ear-piercing shriek when the needle goes in. I'd snicker, but my father is looking at me with one of those looks that says *Don't you dare.*

But Megan still won't move.

His jaw clamped shut, my father picks her up off the floor. Her feet stay crossed beneath her, so it's very hard for him to get her out the door. Robert carries her suitcase. I open the doors. The nurses wave good-bye to us. We are to come back in three days for another booster shot and to have our skin tests read. I'm sure they are looking forward to seeing us again.

It's not easy getting Megan in the car. My father has to turn her sideways and shove. "Please," he says. "Please . . ." He doesn't finish. Whatever it is that he wants, he gives up before he can even ask, knowing it's more than he can expect.

That night, as the sun begins to set, during the time we would have, as a family, walked up the hill, my father holds a frying pan, looking at it intently, as if trying to imagine food inside its hollow shape.

I grab the pan. "Go paint something," I say. "Go paint something pretty." His head snaps up and his eyes blaze, like the eyes of the bull; they have a liquid hate. For a moment I am very afraid of him, and then he shakes it off, blinks, and he is just my father again, lost and guilty. "It's not my fault," he says.

He walks into the living room and stands in front of the naked picture of my mother. "It's not my fault," he says to the picture.

But we all feel guilty, and that, as much as my mother's absence, is what's making us tense. So we stay away from each other. My father should have known. We should have said something. And it's my mother's fault as well. She should have asked for help earlier. I think maybe she got so tired of moving around she found her own way of staying by leaving us.

I break eggs, grate cheese, chop a green pepper, mix it together, then cut up an onion, which nobody likes but me. My eyes burn. I picture my mother coming in the kitchen, seeing my tears, and trying to comfort me. Then I will tell her I'm not really crying, it's just the onion.

No one likes the eggs. They all complain about the onion. I tell them they can cook for themselves from now on and I open the door to call Kip inside. He looks hesitant, but a plate of eggs does the trick. *He* doesn't mind the onions. Afterwards, I let him stay inside. He curls up in a corner of the living room, his tail thumping lightly against the wood floor. The house sounds like it has a heartbeat.

In the morning, Helen comes to our door and knocks. I open up the screen, but she doesn't come in, so I keep it propped open with my body. She's holding a pie, a pretty pie with crimped edges and symmetric slashes in the crust to let the steam out. None of the top crust has separated from the bottom. My mother has never been able to do this, although I know she's tried.

"It's apple," Helen says. She stands on the top step. Brenda and Rusty stand a few yards back, on the grass. Robert comes up behind me and just watches. Megan is in her room, sulking, and won't come out. My father has walked up to the top of the hill to paint. My mother is gone. No one moves. I am suddenly wary of the way Brenda and Rusty stand so far away, of the fact that Helen doesn't come in. I don't want to accept this pie. I have a choice. The pie or the pretense that my mother will walk into this room. There is still the chance that the last two days have been a bad dream. The pie in Helen's hands says it's no dream. It says, *Sorry about your mother.* I can smell it.

No one says a word. We all look at the pie because it is easier to look at the pie than at each other. No one would understand it if I told Helen to take the pie back.

"Thanks," I say. "Come on in."

Helen looks down at her feet, then turns slightly and looks back toward her house. Then she looks at me. Then back at her feet. She is sometimes slow in answering, like my father, but there is something more going on. I wait.

"We can't," she says. "Mother and Father think we should stay out of this house. Because of germs. Outside is okay, though."

"What?" I say.

"Your house is bad luck!" Brenda shouts. "I wouldn't go in if you paid me."

"Brenda!" Helen says. "That's not true!"

But it might be. It's worth thinking about. But I can't let her say that. "The house is not bad luck. That's stupid!"

"Well, I ain't going in it ever again," says Brenda, her hands on her hips.

"No one's asking you to," I say.

Helen moves the pie closer to my hands. "It's warm right now. Just right for eating."

"Fine, we'll have it for breakfast." I take the pie from Helen. It's a very heavy pie. "Thanks." I go inside, leaving her on the porch. I watch as they walk off across the road.

"A pie for breakfast!" Robert says. "Oh boy!"

He thinks we've won something.

Eight

Robert is doing a thousand-piece jigsaw puzzle of a field of orange poppies, and he spends his days arched over the dining room table. He says when he finishes it, our mother will come home. I saw Kip eat a puzzle piece that fell on the floor. When he licked it, the puzzle piece stuck to the surface of his wide wet tongue and then disappeared into his mouth. Kip looked surprised when he began to chew, but he didn't spit it out.

It's hot. There is a slow warm breeze like a dog's breath. I go outside.

"Hey! Tamara!" I hear from across the road. Rusty waves me over. I start to cross the road but I have forgotten I'm barefoot and when my feet hit the melted hot asphalt I yell out. "Oh shit!" I turn and jump back to our grass, now facing my father, who has just come around the house.

"Come here," he says. The wrinkles on his forehead deepen. Glancing behind me I see Rusty disappear behind his house.

"You can't talk like that, Tamara. I won't allow it."

"You and who else?" I say, shocked at the words that come out of my mouth. My father's face goes limp, as if it has just forgotten its own shape. His lips move about, looking for a word, a reaction, something significant to say. Then his mouth snaps shut and he just stands there, his nostrils flaring in and out. He looks at me closely, squinting, as if he is trying to figure out who I am.

I squirm under that look. I want him to stop looking at me that way. "I'm sorry," I say.

Finally he nods. "Why don't you go to your room now. Write a letter to your mother. Ask her how she's feeling. Tell her what you're doing with your time."

No, I think. "Fine," I say. "But you can't read it. It's private." I shove my hands in my pockets, tight fists against the fabric.

"All right," he says. "I'm going to talk to her tonight on the phone, before they move her. I won't waste her time with reports of your language, or your attitude. Besides, I'm sure this is only temporary, a reaction to too much too fast. If you feel the need to let off steam, go back by the pond and scream your bloody lungs out. No one will hear you. It might even do some good. But no more profanity. Do you understand?"

"Yes, sir."

"Good then. Go write your mother."

An hour later I hand him an envelope with two sheets of paper inside. The envelope is sealed. The pages are blank.

A hard rain pelts my window with a bright loud noise and a wail of sad wind. I think I will never sleep for the racket, but that thought is my last before the dream of God comes. He's very angry at me, shaking a large knuckly fist. The sound in my dream is turned off, or there is static, like crinkling tinfoil, so I don't hear what God says but I get the message anyway. "Write your mother, you heartless child, you despicable daughter. Write!"

The dream, my room, and my heart explode in a shock of light and a crack of thunder that is so loud it rattles the glass in my window. A deep, earth-shaking crash follows. Then it is darker than black ink, darker than is possible, and there is only one explanation. I am dead. But I can hear the rain pounding on my window. I don't think it rains in hell, or is this dark in heaven. I tell God I will write my mother right now if He will turn on a light.

The whole outside lights up again, a light so bright I can see every detail in my room for a brief second, then it's gone. But I saw where my notebook lay, and the pen, and I understand. I start to write, in the dark, knowing it will be illegible in the morning. But only with my pen moving across the page do I feel safe.

Megan and Robert yell. "What happened?" "Daddy!" "Mommy!" "Where are you?" "What happened to the lights?" I write. "Dear Mother, I am so sorry about . . ."

In the morning, we find that the maple tree ten feet from our house has been split in two, half still standing, half lying on the lawn; not even a twig touches the house. Of course, God is not mad at the Burns. He just wanted to scare me. My letter to my mother is four pages long.

My mother writes back.

Dear Tamara,

I was so happy to receive your letter today, especially after the confusion of opening your letter of yesterday. I understand how angry you are. There is no need for dramatics.

I am not allowed to do much of anything, only lie in bed or sit in bed, but at least I don't feel trapped inside, since the windows are large and always open. They are big believers in fresh air. It is absurd, of course, that they have taken me from where I got plenty of fresh air, but the nurses just smile and nod if I mention this fact. They treat us like children, not very bright children at that.

They take my temperature every hour and give me two shots, twice a day, every day. Streptomycin and isoniazid. I must admit, I am a big coward about it. This is the price I must pay to be cured, so I grit my teeth and pretend I am somewhere else. The important fact is that these medicines are new, and now tuberculosis is curable, you must believe this. We are living in a modern age. I will get better and come home. Just tell your father not to move away until I do.

It is a war, they say, a war against tuberculosis, and they will wipe out this horrible disease from the face of the earth by rounding up everyone who has it, now that there is a cure. I am a private in this war and must do as I'm told. I am also a prisoner. I miss you terribly, but I must do my part. If I came home, I could spread this to you (I am thrilled to hear you have passed the test), and you in turn would pass it on to your friends. The word tuberculosis *sends shivers up my spine, since it is exactly this disease that stole my father from me. But I, and my fellow inmates, will be the last to suffer. When you are my age, tuberculosis will be all but forgotten.*

My time is up. I get five minutes to write twice each day, following my shot. They won't allow us phone calls. They say it makes us too emotional, and we must rest, rest, rest. I must admit, I am very tired. I love you. Say hello to the Murphys and the Burns. Give Edith a hug and a kiss for me.

Mother

For a moment I believe she will come back. My throat is tight and I can't swallow. I tell myself not to be stupid. Preparing for the worst is easier than hope.

• • •

Megan stays in her room, coming out only to go to the bathroom. She refuses to speak to anyone. My father carries her dinner upstairs, and the clean plate down. My father says she will come out when she gets good and bored, and I think he really doesn't know her very well. My bet is she'll stay there for a month or more, until we have forgotten all about her.

In the middle of dinner, just the three of us sitting around the big dining room table, Robert throws a fit, demanding to call our mother on the phone. "I have to tell her something!" he shrieks. "I have to! Right now! I have to talk to Mommy. Right! Now! Right! Now! Right! Now!" He is choking on his tears and can only get one word out at a time. It is pretty pitiful to watch and makes me want to scream, but maybe not at him. My father puts down his fork and says, "If you do, it will upset her and make her sicker. Is that what you want?" It is a pretty mean thing to say and I almost go over to Robert to put my arm around him, but I don't. The idea of my doing this makes me so sad that my eyes burn. It's more than cooking a meal or folding laundry. If I comfort Robert in my mother's place, who will comfort me?

Robert doesn't answer. There is no answer. No one wants my mother to get sicker, but I bet he wants to call her all the same. He doesn't eat anything else, not even dessert. He goes to bed early and so do I.

Every morning at seven my father goes outside to paint, then he comes in for lunch, takes a twenty-minute nap, then paints his couch picture: right now it is of a bouquet of yellow roses in a Ming vase. A lady sent a photograph of the Ming vase from some museum. Then he rests his eyes again for twenty minutes before he goes outside to paint until dusk. There is a perplexed look on his face whenever he looks at Robert or me, as if he has forgotten our names. It has made it easier on him that Megan stays in her room.

Today, when Rusty waves me over, I have on my shoes. I'm more than ready.

"Want to go to my fort?" he asks. His face is pink from the sun, and from a blush that spreads from his cheeks to his ears, and, I imagine, from his forehead to his toes.

It's mid-July. The day is hot and clammy and only slightly cooler in the fort. It's still morning; by afternoon the fort will be unbearable. It smells like mint, like I'm inside a mint candy. On the upside-down wooden crate there is a jelly jar with a fistful of cut mint and wild daisies. I'm touched at this effort, which makes me feel uneasy.

"It's pretty hot," he says. "Gonna be a real hot day."

"You could take off your shirt," I say.

"Uh, okay," he says, as if this never occurred to him, as if he wasn't thinking the same thing I am. He peels the white T-shirt off over his head slowly, since there's not a lot of room in here. With *his* shirt off, I am warmer than I was a minute ago. I can feel my breath kind of hitch in my chest. His skin is as pale as my father's canvas. I think of finger-painting his chest and laugh, a nervous laugh, a stupid giggle.

"What?" he says, sounding offended.

I wave a hand. "Nothing." We are sitting on his sleeping bag, turned awkwardly toward each other. His nipples are the same pale brown of his lips, and there is absolutely no hair on his chest. His eyes look at my face, then uncontrollably downwards, then away, then back to my face. There is something so honest about him, like all of him is right here, on the surface of his pale skin; not that he is empty, but that he's exposed, like a walking-around X ray, and I feel sorry for him and jealous of him at the same time.

I don't know if I want to touch him or pinch him. "You know, it's not fair guys can take off their shirts and girls can't." I say this as if I'm really mad, as if it were a debate in school, but he knows there's only one correct answer.

"Well," he says, shrugging with his bony shoulders, as if he really doesn't care, as if he's not trying so hard not to jump right out of his skin, "I'm not the law or nothing. You can take your shirt off. I won't tell no one."

"It *is* hot," I say, just to keep this moment going a little longer; we're both having fun. There's a part of me that's a bit worried about what's going to happen next.

"Yeah, it's hot. Go ahead."

"Really?"

His reply seems to get stuck in his throat and finally he just nods.

"Well, okay." I'm wearing a light-yellow blouse with mother-of-pearl buttons. I unbutton the buttons from the top, letting the blouse fall open bit by bit. I can see his chest go in and out with each breath. Trying not to bump anything, I shrug off my blouse as gracefully as I can. I am naked to the waist. This is completely different from when I used to go walking around naked in my house. My nipples get hard as he stares. I watch as they get pointy and pucker. I had no idea this would happen.

We look at each other. Now we have to pretend this is no big deal. He presses his mouth together as if he's tasting his words. "Want a Twinkie?" he says.

I shake my head no. I feel like I have no time, like it's already tomorrow, or next month, or my father is painting that last picture. As I look at Rusty, I can see my car driving away. I want desperately to be *in* this moment. I want him to touch me so I know it's now.

"Do you want to touch them?" I ask, kindly, not a challenge, maybe a little bit desperate. I swallow. Trying to hold something down that wants to take off.

"Oh, yeah," he says. "I do."

"Okay," I say, moving closer to him.

With his right hand he reaches out and holds on to my left breast, then squeezes it lightly, like checking to see if a pear is ripe. His other hand comes up and he cups both my breasts. If they made bras like his hands, they'd make a million dollars.

Then we're kissing and he's rubbing my breasts, and my hands are on his back, his sides, in his hair. There's a lot of moving around, until we're lying down on our sides facing each other. We've stopped kissing, just so we can breathe. I feel like I'm swimming in mint tea, the smell is so strong and the air so thick. Rusty kisses my lips once, then my neck, which is the nicest feeling in the world, and then he moves lower and kisses my breasts. He presses his mouth to my nipple and sucks on it. I think I'll die right now, then I feel his hand, warm and firm on my crotch, and it's all I can do not to moan out loud. It's more than I can bear.

"Stop," I say.

His hand comes away from my crotch and he looks up at me.

"I guess we better not do that yet," I say.

"Not yet? Okay. Sometime, though?"

"Maybe," I say. I want to, but I know what's stopping me. It's that my mother's gone. If she were home, I'd keep going; I'd let Rusty do even more. She'd be washing the dishes, or milking the cow, and she wouldn't suspect a thing. I could eat dinner with the memory of Rusty's hand on my crotch, and I'd grin and answer my parents' questions and feel I'd gotten away with something. But when I go home now, she won't be there, and I'll feel guilty.

"Let's just take a nap," I say, which is absurd, it's only noon, but Rusty says okay. We shuffle around a little until we find a position that's comfortable, both on our backs, my head on his shoulder. Then we both pretend to sleep.

About ten minutes later, when I begin to suspect Rusty doesn't understand, he whispers my name so softly that it's like a leaf falling. I pretend I didn't hear it. He shifts slightly, waiting to see my response. I keep breathing slowly and steadily. Finally he moves his hand, as if he is just getting more comfortable. It finds that same bumplike resting spot on my crotch and settles in with just a slight pressure, just the right pressure.

This is okay, I think. If I were really sleeping, like I *could* be, I wouldn't know he was doing this. It's a small excuse, but it will do.

Dear Mother,

I hope you're feeling better. Everything is fine here. The Murphys say hello. It's very hot and muggy. I water the garden every day. Robert is doing a puzzle and Megan is reading a lot of books. I am doing the cooking. I tried making your meat loaf but I couldn't make the gravy right and we threw it away. The gravy. The meat loaf was okay. I just had a meat-loaf sandwich with ketchup. What do you eat?

I finished the crossword puzzle book and Daddy says he'll take me to get a new one when we go to the store. I am going to make tuna noodle casserole tonight. There is a hummingbird that comes to the garden for the petunias every morning at ten. You would like to see it.

The Murphys are going to take us to church again tomorrow. I will pray for you, even though you don't want me to. It can't hurt and it might help. Helen says it will help, she is sure. She says she includes you in her prayers every night, which I'm sure does a lot more good than mine. Brenda has only two more weeks in summer school and she says she's going to get a C in math, all because of me. She gave me the green plastic necklace she won at a fair. The one she always wears. So now I have to wear it. She says we're blood sisters.

I miss you very much and hope you come home soon.

Love,
Tamara

I don't tell her I have scabs on my arms and legs that look like the bumpy growths on trees. I don't tell her that Megan hasn't said a word in weeks, or that Brenda wanted to prick fingers and trade blood, but got scared I might have tuberculosis even though my test was negative, and I called her stupid and we're not talking right now. I don't tell her I knocked over her vase when I was sweeping, and that it broke into a thousand slivers. I don't tell her that sometimes I imagine crawling out the attic window, naked, and standing on the sloped roof.

On Sunday, the Burns come to visit their farm. My father has gone out to the pasture to paint, even though he knew they were coming. My sister is in her room. My brother hovers around the dining room table like a moth afraid to land. The border and a small corner of the puzzle are finished. He doesn't even attempt to put pieces together right now; he just stares at the pieces as if they are ancient hieroglyphics with a message just for him. He won't let me touch the puzzle. Somehow he has lost the top of the box. It's under my bed.

I am left alone with the Burns, to play my mother.

"Hello, Tamara," Mrs. Burns says. Her skin is tan and wrinkled. She's so eager to get into the garden her eyes flick over that way, then back to me, as if the garden might run off before she gets there.

"Hey, sweetheart!" Mr. Burns says, slamming his car door. Then his smile fades. "Oh," he says, in a quieter voice, "I'm sorry about your mom. How's she doing?"

"Okay," I say.

"Well, well," he says. "Good. You give her our regards, will you?" Kip rushes out from under the hydrangea bush, his feet slipping on the driveway's pebbles. His tail wags fast but low, like a broom. "Oh, Kip, you rascal you," Mr. Burns says, squatting down over his large belly to give Kip a bunch of rough buffs on his head, then a few solid pats to the old dog's rear. "You being a good dog? Hey, Kip? He's being a good dog?" Mr. Burns asks me. "Not causing you no trouble, is he?"

"No, no trouble."

"He's a good dog," Mr. Burns says. There's a moment of quiet now, while Kip just stands there waiting for God knows what and Mr. Burns looks at him, taking something in I imagine, some moment he can carry back with him that will assure him he's doing the right thing by leaving Kip here. It takes a while, then Mr. Burns stands up and looks around. Kip figures that's all he's going to get and walks over to Mrs. Burns and sits by her feet, patiently, but not with hope.

"Where's your dad?" Mr. Burns asks.

"Painting." I shrug and smile, trying to look apologetic.

"Well, well," he says. "I guess I'll just get my chores done. Who's milking the cow, now your mom's . . . not here?"

"My sister," I say, then remember she's been in her room for days. Oh Jesus, I think. Edith will have exploded by now.

"Your sister?" he says, squinting his eyes, then looking over at Mrs. Burns. I can tell they are both thinking we are a bit strange, but I'm used to that. "I better go look and see."

He heads up to the barn and I want to call him back I'm so scared what he might find. "Would you like some lemonade?" I yell, running up and cutting him off.

He just moves around me, patting me on the head. "No thanks. Don't you bother none."

"Mind if I look at the garden?" Mrs. Burns says.

I turn to look at her. "No, fine," I say. When I turn back to the barn, Mr. Burns is gone. I tense, waiting for a shout.

Nothing happens, then I see him coming out of the barn. "Must be in the back pasture. I'm going to walk on up. You tell Mrs. Burns for me?"

"Sure," I say. I quickly try to remember when I saw the cow last. I can't.

"Oh, Tamara," I hear from the garden. "Can you bring me a pot? These beans need to be picked."

"Sure," I say. I go in the house and get a pot. I don't have to go through the dining room, but I do anyhow, just to swat my brother on the top of his head. "Get out there," I hiss.

"Leave me alone, boogerhead," he says.

"Did you milk the cow?" I ask.

"No way," he says.

"Oh hell," I say. I go back outside and up to the garden.

Mrs. Burns is on her knees, bent over the beans. "They should have been tied up," she says, "but I guess you all have had your hands full. Think you could get me some stakes and twine?"

I do. We spend the next half hour tying up the beans, just motions, no words. We work well together, not like when I try to help my mother, who tells me what to do, then sighs when I don't do it exactly as she would. When the beans are all picked, the pot is half full, and it's a big pot.

"Boil the beans just for five minutes, then dump out the water and mix in some cream of mushroom soup," Mrs. Burns says. "Cover it with some bread crumbs, then bake it for a half hour at 350 degrees. You getting along all right?"

"Yeah, sure," I say.

"Shoot, I don't think so," she says. She looks at me and brushes her hands together to get off the dirt. "You must be scared, with your mother gone. The Bible says the Lord won't give us more than we can bear, but I don't know. I just don't know about that anymore. Still, you are a young girl, and you're tough, I can tell. You doing the cooking?"

I nod.

"Well, I'll bring over a few easy recipes, and we can go over them." She looks up at the house, her house. "I guess it's stupid, me not wanting to go in there, but I don't."

We both stand there looking at the house as if it might do something. It's kind of creepy. Finally, we turn away, and glance right into each other's eyes. Somehow, that's just as scary as thinking the house might shout "Boo!" I'm not sure if she likes me. I never cared much about an adult liking me before. I wish I could think of something nice to say. But she does.

"I'll tell you what, I'll come by and pick you up some afternoon and we'll go to my sister's, and we'll bake all day, then you can bring the food back here and stick it in the freezer. Would you like that?"

Once again, I nod. I would like to go there, not that I want to cook really, but I guess I'd like her to like me. Then I remember Edith and I think when Mr. Burns finds her up in the pasture, dead or bloated in horrible pain, they will never speak to us again. I swear to myself that if Edith is still alive I'll milk her every day myself.

Pressing against her thighs with her hands, Mrs. Burns stands up slowly. "You're a quiet girl. I was too. You'll get your voice soon enough. Mr. Burns and I, we can talk up a storm sometimes, though you wouldn't know it to look at us. I don't know why I tell you, but you look like someone who needs to hear something. I just don't know what." She dusts off her pants. "Just let me know if I hit the right thing, will you?" She smiles at me and I smile right back. I want to thank her. I want to warn her about the cow, so it won't come as a shock. I want to ask her about her son, if she thinks his ghost is somehow stuck here, like the things I've left behind. She heads back down to the car.

Still no sign of Mr. Burns. I ask Mrs. Burns if she'd like some tea or something. I see her thinking about it, like there's a lot of thought to go into this question. "No," she finally says. "Let's sit in the barn."

We go in the barn and sit on hay bales. I've got on shorts and the hay scratches my legs. A bird chirps once in the rafters, then it's quiet. It's so much cooler in here; the air feels lighter, crisper. I shiver, then rub my arms.

"You know when I decided to move out?" Mrs. Burns asks me. "I picked up a glass, just for some water. What could be more simple than that. But I knew, with that glass in my hand, that it was the very same one that Timothy drank his last glass of water out of. I remember taking it down to the kitchen a few days after the ambulance came. I washed it and put it back on the shelf. I was taught never to throw anything away, and I hadn't learned then, like I have now, that I could change. So when I took that glass, to fill it up, it was the same one, because none of my glasses match, you might have noticed that. Well it was the straw that broke the camel's back. Still, I couldn't throw it away, and I couldn't drink from it, and I couldn't put it back in the cupboard, 'cause Mr. Burns might use it and if I saw him do that it would spook me just the same, so I packed it up in a box. That's when I packed up all Timothy's things. Took me a few hours. Then when Mr. Burns came down from the pasture—he can always find something to do back there that sure takes him a long time— well, I told him we had to move out. And we did. Luckily my sister had just left her place. She had everything we needed, so we just took our clothes. It made it easier. We could pretend we were coming back.

"Mr. Burns never argued about us leaving, although I can tell you we argued about a million things before Timothy died. But not since, not one argument. It isn't worth it, not now. I don't have anything against a good old-fashioned argument, at least not one that's not mean and nasty."

She takes a breath and wipes at her eyes, although she's not crying or anything.

"I don't think we'll be coming back, Tamara. I really don't think so. Not that we've mentioned it yet. I just don't think I can." She shuffles her feet against the hay bale, like a kid might, just to hear the noise and knock a little hay loose. She looks like a kid, she's so small, and it's dim in here, you can hardly see her wrinkles.

"Your son," I say, "he's kind of *in* the stuff in your house, isn't he? In that glass and the chairs and the steps and my . . . his bed." I'm surprised I'm saying this but I go on. "And there must be a whole lot of him in those boxes in the attic. I can see how it might scare you."

She shakes her head before saying a thing. "I don't think it scares me, Tamara, not like you mean. It just makes me so sad. There are things I wanted to do with Timothy, lots of things, if I start to think about it. And things I wish I said. We weren't brought up to say the things I should have said, not in ordinary life. We just say, 'Go to bed' or 'Are you warm enough?' or 'Wipe up that spill you made.' I can remember saying a lot of that stuff, but even when he was dying I don't remember telling him he was sweet and thoughtful, or that he had the most beautiful eyes. You would think that house would comfort me, with his memories, but it just reminds me of the things I wanted to do differently. Like the wallpaper in his room. That's not paper for a boy. I could have done something with soldiers, or ships, but I never did."

I have all sorts of things rumbling around in my head now. Like the idea of a room papered just for me. But the one thing that really keeps sticking in my head is that the Burns might not ever move back here. The house would be for sale then. This connects to something my mother said in her letter. *Tell your father not to move before I come home.* We might be here awhile. Then a quick thought goes through me: that I don't want to move anymore and if my mother doesn't come home for a long time, *we'll have to stay.* It's an awful thought, but I can't make it go away now that I've thought it.

Mrs. Burns and I sit on the hay bales, while dust motes float around in the sunbeams. I could sit here forever, I think. If not forever, at least for a long time.

"My brother had TB," she says. Her hands are folded in her lap. She's just as comfortable as I am.

"Did he die?" I ask.

"Well, yes," she says.

"I knew it," I say.

"Well, now," she says. "He died, but not from TB. He flew a helicopter. Crop dusting. He got better and went back to work. A blade came loose and the helicopter, it turned right upside down. It wasn't TB that got him, and it won't get your mom, but that's no reason not to tell her you love her. It will make you and her feel a lot better. You know what, I'm damn sick of people dying. I'm going next." Then she laughs. "My goodness, the things I say when I get going."

A shadow appears in the sun-filled doorway. It's Mr. Burns. "Well, what are you two ladies doing in here?"

"Oh, nothing much," Mrs. Burns says.

"Well, the cow's fine, and I checked the fences and the cattle have more than enough to eat. Your sister must be doing just fine. Give her my thanks. We better go. You coming, Mrs. Burns?"

"I am."

"You take good care of yourself and your family, Tamara," Mr. Burns says as we follow him back out into the sunshine.

"I will," I say.

"I'll call you about that cooking date, dear," Mrs. Burns says.

"Thanks," I say. But I wonder if she will. I think Mr. Burns gave us the time she needed, and she got everything said she wanted to. The cooking was just an excuse we don't need anymore. Still, I will go, if she calls. I'm even a bit hungry now. After they leave, I cook the beans like she suggested. My brother and I eat them for lunch, and he says they are really good. I leave the casserole dish on the stove for my father, and go upstairs to write to my mother.

That night, I ask my father who has been milking the cow. "Helen," he says, as if I should have known. I should have.

Nine

In the early morning, dew sticks to the tips of grass, winking and glittering like diamonds. If you stand in the right spot, you can find a dewdrop that captures the sun. It can blind you; a tiny miniature sun in a drop of water. It is the most beautiful sight I have ever seen.

The trick is finding the right spot, the right dewdrop, the right time of day. It takes so much for things to work out perfectly, and so little for them to go wrong.

Dear Tamara,

How are you? Are you still tutoring Brenda? Bought any new records? How are Edith and Kip? I miss you so much. I love getting your letters. They mean so much to me. I am feeling better bit by bit.

There are so many rules here. Specific times to eat, to lie down, to sit in the sun, to get shots, to swallow pills, even to go to the bathroom. I am not one for rules, but they have put the fear in me: they say I will not get well if I am not very good, which means to do nothing, nothing, nothing. Even eating is to be done slowly, without emotion. Fifty years ago the cure was vigorous outside exercise, even in the winter. At the moment, that sounds like a luxury I can't possibly imagine; that is, my body actually keeping up with a routine like that. Thank goodness I didn't get this just ten years ago. They were puncturing lungs and removing ribs! I guess I can't complain.

They are talking about shutting down this place because tuberculosis is on the decline. I feel like an anachronism.

Yesterday a new patient came. They say she will be the very last, that her family bribed someone, but she certainly doesn't want to be here. She sobbed all through the night. Today she is still completely inconsolable. The nurses scold her, and there are rumors she will be moved to an empty wing by herself so she can't upset us. I recognize some of myself in her sad, pale features. She makes me wonder if I didn't protest enough. I simply came in and lay down. It's something to reflect on. I have much time for reflection.

I am allowed to write for ten minutes twice a day, if my temperature is close to normal. Unfortunately, that isn't very often. I would protest so much resting and quiet, at least I hope I would, if only I weren't so tired.

I hope you are doing well, and helping your father take care of Megan and Robert. It is much to ask, but there it is. I have no choice but to rely on you. I will get better. I will come home.

Love,
Mother

There is another letter from my mother, for my father. He is out in the pasture. I steam open his letter with the teakettle, like I read in a Nancy Drew novel. It actually works, even though the envelope gets damp and wrinkled.

Dear Stuart,

I'm sorry I haven't written for a while, but today is the first time in five days my temperature is close to normal. They are such sticklers for rules. But it works. I tried hard not to do anything stressful, just so I could get well enough to write. (They consider rolling over in bed a stressful activity.) I will write this quickly, so I can write a letter to each of the children. I don't want to send one letter to you all. I want each letter to be a private hug. I am afraid I am waxing on sentimentality, but I write these letters in my head for days before putting them to paper, and they metamorphose from chatty hellos to raw emotions. At this very moment I feel as if my heart will burst open with my need for each of you. I miss your touch. I miss Tamara's smirk and her offhanded love. I miss Robert's soft hands and his wide-eyed looks. I miss Megan's simple need for me, the way she will crawl into my lap like a cat and I don't dare move for fear of disturbing her comfort. I miss you wholly and completely.

The nurse has threatened not to give me your letters because I get so visibly upset. Your words seem to bleed onto the page. I know you are lost without me, and it should be comforting that you love me so, but it's not. You must find a way of living without me for a while longer.

It's strange, but I'm more tired now than I was on the farm. I wonder if it's just the knowledge that I have TB. It's an exhausting thought. I cough constantly, and can't sleep, just doze fitfully in a semi-state of wakefulness and delirium. They say the streptomycin could make me go deaf. There are two patients right now that are actually losing some of their hearing. In my dreams, people's mouths move but I don't hear a word. The dreams are worse than the reality of what's around me, so much so

*that I relish even the sound of a cough or the nurse telling
me it's time for a shot. I have no choice. I follow the rules
so I can come back to you.*

*Here comes the nurse to take away my letter. It is my
own fault for crying as I write. Tell Robert and Megan I
will write tomorrow.*

I love you,
Me

My mother's letters take two days to travel fifty miles. They
are like the light we see from distant stars. By the time her letters
reach me, she could be dead.

I get my curse. I'm hanging the wash up, pinning pants upside
down, when a thick warm wetness oozes out into my underwear. It always starts like this, a flood out of nowhere like a dam
bursting. Legs slightly apart I walk inside to go upstairs to the
bathroom.

"What's the matter with you, beanbreath?" Robert says as I
amble awkwardly through the dining room.

"Shut up, buttface," I say, walking past my father, who is
painting a couch picture.

"Tamara! Watch your mouth!" my father says.

"What, beanbreath is okay but buttface's not?" I mutter as I
hobble up the stairs, trying not to let my thighs touch each other.
It's dripping down my legs now. I hate being a girl. I'd do anything to be a boy. Then I think of Rusty touching me, and I
waver on this thought.

There are no napkins in the bathroom cupboard where they're
supposed to be. I look in my room. Under my bed. In my mother's
room. Under her bed. Nothing. Nowhere. I begin to panic.

I go back to the bathroom, pee, and try to clean myself up.
With a towel wrapped around me I go to my room, get clean

underwear and clean shorts, and go back to the bathroom, where I wad up some toilet paper and stick it in my underwear like a napkin. Then I wash out my underwear and shorts and hang them over the bathtub.

I'm going to cry if I don't scream. So I scream. "Shit, shit, and shit!"

This, I guess, is definitely worse than buttface.

"Tamara Anderson, get down here right now!"

I stomp down the stairs, which is not a good idea, since it seems to shake more blood out of me. The toilet paper is falling apart.

"Tamara," my father says, "I have had quite enough of your foul mouth. This time you've gone too . . ." He stops, looks at me, tilts his head. Robert is standing in the passage between the dining room and the living room, eyes big, like we're performing some horror show for him. I feel something running down my legs, out from under my shorts.

"I have my curse. I need napkins," I say through clenched teeth.

"Oh. Don't we have any?"

"No, obviously." My eyes burn. I'm right between furious and tears. I concentrate on furious.

"Can you go across the road and ask Brenda or Helen?"

"No way. Not like this." Anyway, I wouldn't. Rusty might come to the door, or their father, and then what would I say? I'm here for some feminine napkins please? I'd rather die.

My father looks at Robert, who furiously shakes his head. "I'm not going. No way I'm asking for that stuff."

"Are you sure we don't have any?" my father asks.

"Yes. Unless *you* have some."

He doesn't get mad back, he just nods.

"Okay. Then I'll drive to town and get some." He starts cleaning his brush with a cloth. "Do they come in sizes?"

Now my eyes fill up with tears, but I blink them back. I'm standing here with blood dripping down my legs, my brother staring with a smirk across his whole face, and my father asking me about napkin sizes. I don't know if I'm about to cry because I'm embarrassed, or because I miss my mother, or because I'm so relieved my father is going to go get me some napkins and he's treating the whole thing so calmly, as if he's going into town to buy toothpaste.

"Junior," I say.

"Okay. One box? Maybe I should get a few, for next time." He doesn't wait for me to answer. "That's what I'll do, I'll get two boxes. Why don't you go take a bath while I'm gone."

"Okay," I say. "Thanks."

"Nothing to it but to do it." He smiles at me. "See. We'll survive."

I nod, but think to myself that he isn't the one with blood running down his legs.

It is so hot that even with the windows open, I am suffocating. I kept a frog in a box once. The box had a lid so he wouldn't jump out. It was during a summer like this, when everyone moves slowly because the air is too thick to breathe. I forgot about the frog for a few days. It was dead by the time I remembered.

Tonight, as I lie in bed, I start to cry because I once killed a frog. It's just a little cry, and I stop myself quickly.

Megan still won't come out of her room. I imagine she's molding in there. My father got her books from the library, and bought her a radio, but she didn't even say thanks. He tried to starve her out one day, refusing to bring her food, but his conscience got to him, and as it got dark he took up a tuna sandwich, fried eggs, a

pitcher of milk, and an apple. She wrote him a note asking for
cookies, and he brought them up too. I think she sneaks downstairs when we're outside. My mother's box of lined paper is
missing, and the deck of cards from the dining room cabinet. I
bang on her door with my shoe when I wake up in the morning.
Just a friendly hello. She's so stubborn she makes me want to
spit.

Robert and I go to church with the Murphys. We missed the
Sunday after my mother went to the hospital, but last week I
made Robert come with me by telling him God would make our
mother sicker if he didn't. This Sunday he just gets dressed. I
don't even bother asking Megan.

   At church, people talk to me, asking how my mother is, saying
they hope she feels better soon. The parents of Cindy, Brenda's
cousin who got killed in the car accident, tell me to be brave and I
mumble thanks. They were here last week and everyone greeted
them in soft voices, touching their shoulders and hands. I can't
believe they come to church. Aren't they mad at God? I head
down the aisle to our pew, relieved when the services start. We
sing songs that sound just like the songs we sang last time.
Browsing through the hymnal, I see they are all very similar. At
church the same things happen each week, in the same order,
almost the same words. No big changes. It grows on you.

   The minister's story is about loving God. He reads from the
Bible. "Thou shalt love the Lord thy God with all thy heart, and
with all thy soul, and with all thy mind. This is the first and
great commandment. And the second is like unto it, Thou shalt
love thy neighbor as thyself." I look over at Brenda with her
short hair, which she curled by rolling it in rags last night, and at
Rusty, who looks at me and can't help grinning, and at Helen,
who sits up straight, her eyes bright with belief and attention.

Then I look at their parents, in their Sunday clothes. They have changed, the Murphys, since we moved in. We seem to have had a good effect on them.

Next, the minister tells a story about a man from his hometown who became a missionary in Africa, spending the rest of his life in poverty and filth. He says this man understood that the colored people in Africa were the very neighbors God was speaking about. He says God has a mission for each of us, and as varied as those missions are, they all stem from the love-thy-neighbor message. "If we love our neighbors as ourselves, then we will want them to believe and know the risen Christ our Lord, and find salvation in baptism, no matter their color or race. Sometimes, our missions will carry us far from home, but home is in Jesus' arms, which is anywhere and everywhere in this vast and magnificent world we live in." Helen is leaning so far forward in her seat I think she might fall right off the pew.

I feel like telling them they don't have to go to Africa to find colored people, and I wonder how they would feel if colored people moved into this town. This makes me think about my mother. Since I'm in church, I close my eyes and ask God to cure her. I wonder if praying in church is better than at home, or if all the prayers here get jumbled together into one big prayer. I guess if He can create the world, He can get the prayers all sorted out. I still don't believe He made the world though, at least not in seven days. I don't even think the Bible mentions dinosaurs. I'll have to ask Helen.

I try to sing the last song, "God Bless America," because I want to be part of what's happening in this church, I want to enter into this knowledge that they have, but my voice is flat, even to my ears, so I stop singing and just listen. Robert is singing. His voice is flat too, but he doesn't seem to mind.

After church, on the way to the car, a girl from my class, but not one of the popular ones, pulls Brenda's hand, and they whisper to each other until Mr. Murphy calls to Brenda to get a move on. In the car, Brenda is unusually quiet, and I wonder what the girl said, and if it was about me.

Back at the house I change out of my dress and into my blue-jean shorts and a red-checkered blouse. I put on my bra too, because I'm not going to go to Rusty's fort today, not that I don't want to, but because of my curse. I wouldn't want him to try anything with that. When the Burns come and Mrs. Burns asks me to help her in the garden, I say sure.

She never called me about the recipes, but she smiles at me like she really means it. I still don't know if she's just being nice because my mother's sick, or if she likes me. Her eyes don't cloud up anymore when she looks at me, so maybe she's seeing me, and not just someone who is her son's age, a reminder, of sorts. Her really seeing me is a bit scary. I wonder what she sees.

The tomatoes have finished blossoming and are beginning to grow and turn red. We stake the plants and tie them up with coarse rope.

"Where do the tomatoes come from?" I ask Mrs. Burns as she ties a knot. "I mean, plants absorb water and minerals out of the dirt, but it doesn't seem like enough to make tomatoes, or zucchini, or cauliflower. If all the vegetables growing eat the dirt, then you'd expect the dirt to get used up, but it stays there. I don't understand."

Mrs. Burns wipes a hand across her forehead. "The Lord only knows because I sure don't."

I am strangely satisfied with this answer. I don't think I was asking the question for an answer, really, it was more a test, to see if she answered like my mother would have, with every ounce of information she possessed, followed by the suggestion we look it up at the library. Mrs. Burns' answer is the one I want, not because it involves God but because it's the answer I imagine

most moms give. "Well, I bet they'll be good tomatoes, anyway," I say.

"I'm sure they will." Mrs. Burns looks around the garden. It
looked like nothing before, but now, even though it's not nearly
full, it has some promise. "Come August, you will have more
tomatoes than you can eat. Which reminds me." She rolls the
rope up into a ball, tucking the end into the hollow center. "I
want to show you something."

Before she does, we put all the tools away in the barn. She
wipes off the cutters and oils them, washes and dries the trowels,
stores the extra stakes by size, and puts everything away in a
thick wooden box.

"Okay, follow me." She leads me to the back of the house, to
the back door that no one ever uses because it leads only down
dank steps to the basement. When any of us go to the basement
we just walk through the mudroom behind the kitchen, then
down the steps. Not this way.

Mrs. Burns runs her fingers through her tight curls and then
straightens up as much as she can. "Okay," she says to herself.
"Okay now." She puts a hand out to hold the door handle, then
twitches, like Kip does when a fly lands on his ear. She opens the
door and we go down.

I've been down here plenty, to do the wash. There is a big
black furnace, and the washer and wringer. There are also shelves
with tools and boxes of nuts and bolts, and an old generator on
the floor. A door opens into a room with canned stuff, which I
looked at once but my mother said to leave alone. Mrs. Burns
leads me to the room with the dozens of shelves and the hundreds
of canned fruits and vegetables. Along one side is store-bought
stuff, like nuts and Spam and miniature hot dogs. The other side
is home-canned stuff, with labels on the top of the jars.

"That row is strawberry and raspberry jam, some peach too.
The next is apple butter, blueberry jam, and rhubarb jam. Then
there is applesauce and tomato sauce. Now, these are beans, and

those are baby onions, and all that is pickled tomatoes and peppers. The bottom row is pickles. I want you to eat them."

"Well, my mother said not to."

"I'm sure she did. And that was just right, but you know what, there is just too much here. It will go to waste. You will be doing me a big favor. I'd hate to think of all that labor going to waste. You know, I think I'll take some jam." She goes into the main part of the basement and gets a basket, then fills it up. Even though she's taken over a dozen jars, the shelves still look full.

"Why did you make so much?" I ask.

"Something to do, I guess. And we had Timothy to feed. He was thin, but he loved pickles." She looks at the row of pickles. "Please, Tamara, eat as much as you can. All of it," she says, meaning the store-bought cans too. "It won't last forever."

"You did this because of the bomb?" I ask, noticing that there is a row of canned milk too.

"Well, some. I always canned fruits and vegetables, but, yes, I thought we should be prepared. It seems pretty silly now. That bomb shelter is a sad sight. If they do bomb us, Tamara, I just hope Mr. Burns and I go to the Lord quickly. I don't want to be one of the people left to clean things up. You can. I'll leave that to you young-uns. Maybe you won't make any more bombs after you have to clean up that mess." She shrugs. "But tell you what, even if you make yourself sick on pickles and jams, there will be enough for when the bomb does fall, because come September, you and I will be canning, I'll guarantee it."

"Do you want to take some of this other stuff?" I ask, pointing to the store-bought cans. "You paid for it."

Mrs. Burns shakes her head and moves toward the basement stairs. "To tell the truth, my sister's basement looks pretty much like this. I just don't like her peach jam and pickled tomatoes as much as I like my own. She has raspberry jam though that will knock your socks off."

We go back the way we came in. When she gets out in the sun she puts the basket down and kind of shudders, like a dog shaking water off. It's not because of the cobwebs though, it's the smell of the house she doesn't want left on her clothes.

Mr. Burns is coming down the hill and he waves to us, a big wave. We both wave back.

"Can you believe it?" Brenda says with a grin.

I can believe it, but still it amazes me. We are sitting at her picnic table, supposedly doing math. Brenda has just told me the girl she was talking to outside church today is pregnant. She's fifteen. Just like me.

I swat at a fly on my leg. There are way too many flies, big stupid black flies that circle and land, circle and land, no matter how many times I swipe at them. Then there are horseflies, bigger than the black flies and smarter; they hide under benches, and when I'm not paying attention, they land on my thigh and bite. They're slow though, and can be killed, although it leaves a mess of blood and squashed fly. Finally there are the deer flies, with their triangular-shaped wings, who buzz in tight circles right above my head until the drone drives me crazy. Then they pretend they have gone away by suddenly becoming quiet. That's when you know they have landed in your hair. I'd go inside, but Brenda can't come in my house and I don't want to go in hers. If we go in the barn, Brenda will jump around on the hay bales. The picnic bench seems to hold her relatively still.

"What is she going to do?" I ask.

"What do you mean?" Brenda says, frowning at me. "Get married."

"At fifteen?"

"She's pregnant," Brenda says, as if I didn't understand her the first time.

"Yeah, but . . ." I don't bother finishing, because it is obvious. That's what she'll have to do. "What's he like? The father?"

"A stupid idiot. Lindy has no taste. It's Kevin Hooper. He's in the grade above you, but he should be going into twelfth grade this year. They flunked him when he was in fifth. He shot his baby-sitter with his dad's rifle when he was seven. Shot her in the shoulder. Can you believe it?"

Now this I can't believe. "No. How could he do that?"

"With the *rifle*," Brenda says.

"So when will she get married?"

"Pretty soon. She's due in November."

"Where will they live?"

"With his parents. Her dad said even if Kevin does marry her, he'll kill him if he sees him."

"How can he not see him? What about at the wedding?"

"Well, that would be in the church, so he wouldn't kill him in a church, not on her wedding day."

"Will she go to school?"

Brenda shakes her head. "I doubt it. Kevin's mom is a little funny in the head, I don't think she could take care of the baby."

"What about the girl's mom?"

"She's dead," Brenda says with a shrug.

This I don't want to hear. I don't want to hear about dead moms. "So, do you understand what a variable is?"

Brenda pinches up her mouth and sucks on her bottom lip, rubbing on her chin until there's a red mark. I let her think, if that's what she's doing. "Nope."

I have been explaining variables to Brenda for the last hour, but she refuses to learn. I want to strangle her.

"Okay, last time. It's a letter representing a number. There will be enough clues in the problem to figure out what it is."

"Why not just tell us the number in the first place?"

"It's a way to make you think, Brenda, to move the numbers around until things balance out."

She rolls her eyes. "I don't want to think about moving numbers around. What the hell good is it going to do me?"

"You'll pass eighth grade."

"Oh. Okay. But it still stinks."

"Now look." I write a problem. A + B = C.

"There are no numbers!" Brenda says. "How the hell am I supposed to figure it out?"

"It's not a real math problem. It's just something to give you an idea of what a variable is. Now look, I'll give you some clues. A equals Lindsay. B equals Kevin. So C is what?"

"The kid!" Brenda yells, proud of her fine deduction.

"Right. Now three times C is what?"

"Three kids."

"And a ton of diapers!" I say.

"Stinky, shitty diapers!" Brenda shouts.

"So, you see, a letter just stands for something. Here, look at this problem in your book." I point out a simple algebra problem. Her eyes glaze over.

If Brenda passes her math test next week, it will definitely be a miracle. On the scale of one to ten, I'll give it an eight. I'm going to add them all up. When they hit a hundred, I'll believe in God. But I'm going to deduct some points for making my mom sick, so it won't be so easy. I figure if there is a God, He's got the advantage. If He's real, He'll prove Himself, even if I stack the deck.

During the last week in July it's over ninety every day. It's so humid the clothes never dry on the line. At night, the heat makes it hard to sleep; the sheets stick to my skin, and even with the window open my room feels small and airless. Above me, boards creak. My mother would say they are swelling with humidity. I think Timothy is pacing, restless, bored, and hot. I know I am.

Rusty and I go to his fort, but the heat of our bodies in that shower-curtain-capped place becomes sickening and after only minutes we pull apart and decide to leave. Also, Robert has begun to follow us around. Twice, Rusty and I had to stop making out when we heard my brother trying to sneak up on us, his footsteps crackling on the layers of old dry leaves. The first time I chased Robert all the way back to the house and beat him up on the lawn. The second time he got away from me and hid in the pine trees for hours. When it gets cooler, I'll beat him up, just for reminders. It's too hot right now.

Mosquitoes are everywhere. They love the raw edge between the fresh new skin and my old broken and peeling scabs. So I stay in our house and listen to my records or the radio. I do everything slowly, like sad music. I sweep the floors, vacuum, and dust, pretending to be an old lady, an ancient servant who works for a reclusive millionaire. I cook dinners, making a small dent in the canned food, mostly the store-bought ones. I know how to make a good grocery list now, because if I forget something my father won't drive me back. "Make do," he says. He doesn't care what we eat.

I hate doing the wash the most, so I leave it until there is nothing left to wear, then do it all day long. Robert helps, but he complains so much I always end up hitting him and he cries and I get sent to my room.

Wednesday my father surprises us by saying he will take us into Westfield for a movie. The last movie I saw was *Stalag 17,* over a year ago. But my sister will not leave her room, and my father will not leave her alone for that long. I open her door and tell her I will kill her if she doesn't leave her stinking room, but she doesn't even look up from her book. I tell my father to stop getting her books from the library and bore her to death, but he just sighs.

I think about Timothy more and more. Whenever I open my bedroom door the curtains move. I think he sneaks down from the attic to his old room when I'm not around—like my sister sneaks downstairs when we're out—just to keep in touch with what used to be. I think he wants to be caught, wants to be seen. Wants someone to talk to him. Sometimes, when I've been sent to my room for hitting Robert, I tell him how awful my father is. I tell him how unfair everything is. I don't tell him about Rusty and me. It would be like teasing him to tell him good things about life.

There is another letter from my mother.

> Dear Tamara, Robert, and Megan,
>   I have done something rather bold. I told the doctor if he didn't allow me to read I would refuse to eat. I have lost a bit of weight, so he agreed, on one condition: I eat more than I have been. I requested books about TB, and found some fascinating information I want to share with you. Some very famous and talented people had TB. (And died from it, since they weren't lucky enough to live in this time of modern medicine.) Keats, Chopin, Chekhov, Dostoevsky, D. H. Lawrence, Eugene O'Neill, Robert Louis Stevenson, Ralph Waldo Emerson, Edgar Allan Poe, and many others. They say that TB affected their minds, causing them to become more creative as they got sicker; some of their most exciting and imaginative works were written in the last years of their lives. Apparently, because of the disease, there is an actual change in the brain that causes it to be greatly stimulated. I think it would be interesting if you did some reading on the subject. It's best to understand the things that affect our lives. (Rather than turn to the crutch of religion for support.) Yes, your father tells me you are still going to church, and I must admit it worries me. (I never commented on the cross you sent me, Tamara, and I know you meant well, but I gave it away.)
>   Tell Helen I think of her, and the conversations we had, and that what bothers me is her superiority, and her belief

that having religion makes her moral, and just, and good.
That is a choice each human on this earth has, regardless
of religion. You, my children, are examples of that. You
are good, moral, decent, loving, and thoughtful. I don't
have to thank a god for that. But I want to thank you.

I am doing well. There are moments, as now, when
everything seems bright and clear, more clear than ever
before. I suppose it is a possibility that these moments are
the effect of the TB, but I must admit I relish them. There
are other times when I am morose and slow and miss you
all so terribly I can't think straight.

> *Time's up. Miss you. Love you,*
> *Mother*

I can't believe she is so eloquent and so sick, so much the
same and so different. She writes with more love than I can ever
remember. It's like a letter from someone who is saying the right
things because they are really saying good-bye. I give the letter
to Robert. When he's done reading it he goes upstairs and gives
it to my sister. He doesn't come back down. The house is so
quiet I can hear the heat rise. It must be very hot in the attic. I
think about dead people all day.

The next day, a letter comes for my father. I steam it open again.
He never noticed the first time, even though the envelope was
funny-looking from the steam and the rubber cement I glued it
back together with. It looked like it fell in a puddle.

Dear Stuart,
My mind races, questions torment me. I sweat at night
with worry. The nurse says if I don't stop being so restless,
she will take away the books. I'm afraid I burst into tears
when she said this. It didn't help. I am writing this note

while the nurses have a meeting. My temperature is high today, but one of the other patients gave me her pen and paper. I will owe her something. That's the way it works.

During my first week here, I felt like an utter failure, as a mother and a wife. For giving in to TB. For leaving you all so easily. But from the moment I heard the doctor's diagnosis, I have become a coward, meek as a lamb. I have been afraid of TB my whole life. I watched my father cough blood and become flesh and bones. He, too, refused to go to the doctor until it was too late. The sanitarium he died in was not a good sanitarium, not like this one. More than half the people died.

But lately, I have moments when I come out of the fog of depression and fear, and see life as this glorious thing I need to fight to keep. The fight is not easy. The way to fight it, they say, is to do nothing, to take my shots and rest, and I do believe they know what they are doing, but I lose a little of me, or a lot of me, by this constant inactivity. Without stimulus, I am atrophying, dying inside. I am terrified now of what I am becoming. But in the bright moments, when my brain works, I see possibilities I have never seen before. I have begun to think about my mother. She and my father, like you and I, were devoted to each other. From the moment he died, until her car accident four months later, she was like a hollow shell. Could she have really driven into that tree on purpose? The idea haunts me. You must promise me, that if I die, you will keep me alive in your heart, but move past my death, find the joys in life that we have already known, the joys that are out of my reach right now, but still sharp in my memory. You must live on, positively, not just for the children, but for yourself. Promise me.

I am very, very tired right now, and I should put this down, but I want to tell you that I love you a million

times more than you will ever know. My joy is knowing
you love me in the same way. I am a lucky woman. TB
has taught me how lucky I have been.

Me.

After I glue the letter closed and flatten it as well as I can by
pressing against it with an encyclopedia, I leave it on the dining
room table. Then I sit on the wood floor in the corner of the dining room, where the air is slightly cooler. Kip comes over and
rests his head on my leg. I scratch his head. He must miss the
Burns. He must wonder what he did wrong to be left behind.

Ten

The first Tuesday in August it starts to rain. The temperature drops into the seventies. It rains all week, never stopping. The bomb shelter becomes a swimming pool. It is finally useful.

It is late afternoon, and rain falls outside, so much rain that it bands together like thick ribbons unspooling from the sky. I am melancholy, listening to Teresa Brewer sing "Till I Waltz Again with You," wishing I could sing like that.

The phone rings and I jump. It also startles my father, who is painting a couch picture of a summer cottage, dogwood trees blooming at the edge of an English garden; a photograph of this scene is clipped to the top of the easel like a price tag. Both of us look at the phone as if a lion has appeared indoors. It rings again, and he nods at it. "Okay, I'm coming," he says to the phone. He carries a paintbrush over with him, pointed up like a dagger, tipped in cadmium red from painting the brick path that winds through the English garden.

"Yes, hello," he says gently, thinking, as I do, that maybe this is a doctor. So few people ever call us. Then he listens for a long time, his lips tightening together, his eyebrows almost folding down into his eyes. He shakes his head back and forth in small rhythmic motions. My hands sweat. My brother comes in from the dining room, standing in the archway. Robert and I hold perfectly still, as if any movement might bring bad luck.

"No," my father says. "I'll do it. Please wait until I get there."

Then he listens for a while.

"Yes, I could get there by then. It's important to me to do it myself."

Silence.

"I could, if you think . . ."

Silence as he listens and nods. I want to suck my thumb, a habit I gave up at six. I can almost feel the round pad of my thumb pressing the roof of my mouth. My tongue curls around nothing.

"I have two, but they're not . . ."

The person on the other end cuts him off again. Is my father talking about us? Has he forgotten Megan already? And what are we *not*? Not ready to face a corpse? I look up at the painting of my mother on the wall; she smiles with a closed mouth, she looks relaxed, as if she could sit there naked forever, even with her arm folded over her head. The picture changes as I look at it, from being a picture of my mother to something cold and scary; it feels like an heirloom of a distant dead relative. She has been gone only a month and already I have forgotten what she looks like except for in this pose. Tears fall down my face. I brush them away with my sleeve.

"Fine. I know. Thank you for calling. I'll bring them with me."

He hangs up, bites his upper lip, and stares at us. "I have to go to New York."

I look at Robert, who looks at me. We both understand now. It is his art, not our mother, and more than feeling relief, we are furious. Robert turns and walks from the room.

"What?" I say, not that I misunderstood a word he just said, but that I am daring him to repeat it.

"I have to," he says. "The pictures, the new ones, have turned out to be quite popular. They want to set them up in the new gallery now, and they want whatever else I have. Apparently Renny showed a sketch to someone who loved it. They'll pay good money for more sketches. I need to be there to hang the show."

I say nothing.

"We need the money, Tamara. The sanitarium isn't cheap."

"Then mail him the sketches and don't waste money on an airplane trip." I know he'll fly. He would never make it if he drove for eight hours. I can just imagine the scene of the accident. Crushed canvases littering the highway, bright with blood.

"I have to go," he says. "Please understand. I have to." He waves his hands as if he's surrendering, but he's still holding the brush and it looks more like a man trying to wave a flagless flag. He looks like an idiot. He is an idiot. And a fool. And heartless. I want to run away from home. If I had one.

"You'll be okay for a couple of days," he says. "I'll get Helen to come over. She could sleep here at night. I'm sure she wouldn't mind. You like her."

I don't answer him. My arms are folded across my chest, holding hard against a scream, a *Fuck you and I hope you go to hell* scream, that I would shout, except for the picture of my mother on the wall.

"I better tell Megan," he says, with a look toward the stairs. He walks over to the easel and cleans the brush, then places it carefully with the other brushes. He looks back at the stairs again. "Maybe I should ask Helen first." He goes back to the phone, picks it up, listens a second, then puts it down. "I don't know their number. I'll just go over there." He goes out to the kitchen, taking a jacket from the coatrack. He doesn't even know that they aren't allowed in our house. I'll let him find that out for himself.

My father comes back fifteen minutes later, taking off his wet shoes as soon as he comes in the door. Still, his socks leave puddles of water on the kitchen floor. "I'm going to change. I'll be down in a minute. Wait right here for me."

Robert and I look at each other. Where would we go?

We can hear him changing, throwing things around, then yelling through the door to Megan to get out of her room and come downstairs. He comes down alone.

He waves us to the couch, then paces back and forth in the tight space between his easel and the floral chair.

"Well, there was a problem with my plan," he says. I grin. "But I've worked out an alternative. You will stay at the Murphys'."

I gasp, loud and clear, like someone just jumped out of nowhere and scared the bejesus out of me. I can feel my heart race. "No," I say. "I won't." I have that same panicked sound to my voice that Robert had when he said no to his shot.

Robert doesn't say a thing. He doesn't look scared at all.

"We don't have a choice," my father says. "They think this house has germs. I convinced them you kids don't, but I couldn't change their minds about the house."

"I won't stay there," I say.

"I don't care," says my brother. "It's okay with me."

My father smiles kindly at him. "That's my boy. The problem is going to be Megan. But I figure she'll go over there when she finds out she will be alone in the house at night. Helen says she'll carry Megan over if she has to. Mr. Murphy says she can come in to do that if she covers her mouth with a handkerchief. They're very adamant about this germ thing."

"Your problem is going to be me," I say, standing and trying to look firm, although the idea of sleeping in this house, with Timothy's ghost and the noises it makes, without either parent, does not sound too exciting.

"Tamara, you will be no problem at all. Your mother relies on you. Do you want to disappoint her? Besides, we're only talking about a few nights. You can stay here during the day. It's not that I don't trust you alone, it's just that it would be unsafe at night in the country like this. There have been some awful things happening . . ." He doesn't have to finish this sentence to scare the bejesus out of Robert.

"I'm not staying here alone at night. Tamara can, but I'm not. Would I be sleeping in Rusty's room?"

"Yes. On the floor though. They have a sleeping bag for you."

"Cool," Robert says. And now I see his ulterior motive. He's always trying to follow Rusty around, get in with him. This is like a dream come true.

"Helen and Brenda share a room, but Helen says she'll sleep on the couch and Megan can have her bed. You'll get the floor, Tamara. They have a sleeping bag for you too."

"I'm not sleeping there!" I say. "I'll get cockroaches in my ears at night."

"Tamara Anderson, I can't believe you said that. The Murphys are fine people and it's very good of them to let you sleep there for a few days."

"If they're such fine people, how come you and Mother never even invited them over here once!"

He stops pacing. He actually looks ashamed. "We should have," he says. "It's our loss that we have been so solitary." He looks out the window, although you can hardly see the Murphys' house because of the rain. "We'll invite them over when I get back."

"They won't even come in our house!" I shout. "We have the cooties!" I stomp upstairs to my room and slam my door. I don't think I slammed it hard enough, so I open it up and slam it again.

I pick up the mirror on my bureau and look at myself. I'm not pretty in the least. I have big features and mud-colored hair and no mother and now I have to go sleep in a tar-papered house because my father wants to fly off to New York City. I notice he didn't offer to take us with him. That would never have occurred to him.

I slam the mirror down on my bureau. It is a miracle it doesn't break. I give God ten points for not breaking the mirror, and subtract thirty for making us stay at the Murphys'. He's back to ground zero.

Saturday morning, my father drives away, taking an overwide turn out of the driveway because he glances back at us for one final look. The front left tire goes off the paved road, almost into the ditch, then he overcorrects, zigzagging the car down the country road like a drunk. One hand reaches out through the open car window; a quick, haphazard wave, then he is gone.

I can't believe he's left us, I tell myself, full of indignation, but of course I do believe it, with no trouble at all. Helen stands between Robert and Megan—who has come downstairs *and* outside. I'm a few feet away, but we are all in a straight line if you connect the dots. Across the road is the rest of the Murphy family, watching my father leave. It's early enough in the morning that Mrs. Murphy hasn't left for work. For a moment, after my father is gone, no one moves and I feel like I'm in a painting titled *The Day Their Father Left*. The sun is low in the sky and shadows lie sharp on the ground like slashes. The dog sits on the porch, waiting to be fed.

Megan breaks the silence by turning, stomping up the steps, then slamming the front porch screen door, which is too light to slam properly, but she does a good job of it anyway.

"Jeez Louise," Robert says.

"He's the worst damn driver in the world," I say, not caring that Helen can hear me, not caring about much, I tell myself. "He'll probably crash the car on the way to the airport and die."

Robert slugs me in the arm. I didn't see it coming and it surprises and hurts me. "Take that back," he yells at me.

I give him a good shove with both my palms on his chest and knock him to the ground.

"Now, now, please," Helen says. She bends down over Robert to help him up, but he slides away on the wet grass and stands, putting up his fists.

"Come on and fight like a man," I say, waving my fingers, gesturing for him to come at me. "Sissy!"

"Hey, Robert!" Rusty's voice from across the road stops us all. "Come on over! I got to show you something!" Rusty's mother stands next to him and nods to Rusty like he's done a good thing.

With an evil glance at me, eyes squinted like a beady little rat's eyes, Robert swaggers over toward Rusty. My teeth tighten against each other and my eyes get hot. I bend over and pick up a handful of pebbles from the driveway, and throw them at my brother. They fall short, bouncing on the road like the faint echoes of distant rain.

"I'm going to the pond," I say to Helen, who looks bewildered, her mouth slightly open as if she has something to say but has forgotten what it was. I don't wait for her to remember.

At the pond, I take off all my clothes and lay them on the ground as if they are another person, then I lie down on them, my face to the sky, my breasts rising and lowering with each breath. I imagine myself a virgin sacrifice. Brave and too proud to cry.

About an hour later, my stomach rumbles, but I refuse to go back. No one has come looking for me. No one needs me.

Everything is dense with color; the deep green of rain-soaked grass, the black of wet bark, the rich brown of cattails, the golden yellow of wild yarrow, the warm orange of Indian paintbrush, the tiny explosions of purple clover. I know why my father wants to paint. I just don't understand anything else about him.

I have a thought that keeps rising up and I keep trying to push back down, but now it's stuck in my head, even though I don't want it there: I want my mother to stay sick, so I don't have to move again. I am afraid God will hear me, and think I am really asking for this to happen, but no matter what I do I can't stop myself from thinking about it.

I want to believe in God, but I'm scared. I'm afraid of getting what I want, and afraid of losing what I have. I'm scared that if He comes to me and I know He is real, my mother won't love me anymore. I'm scared my father doesn't love me at all. I can't move. I close my eyes and listen for a voice that isn't mine to tell me what to do, but even the birds are quiet in the noonday sun.

I go back to the house when I can't stand the hunger any longer. Across the road, Robert, Brenda, and Rusty are building a bonfire, dragging logs and sticks out of the woods and piling them up like a tepee. I can hear my brother shout Rusty's name. "Like this, Rusty? Should I put it here, Rusty? Do you want more sticks, Rusty?"

I go inside.

At dinnertime, Helen comes to the door to fetch me. Megan stands behind her. We are all going to eat outside at the Murphys' picnic table. Reluctantly, I go over. I have been smelling barbecued chicken for the last half hour.

Megan follows Helen around like a baby duck. It makes me sad to watch. Megan needs a mother, and chose Helen, not me. Megan still isn't speaking, but she does whatever Helen asks her to do.

For dinner there is barbecued chicken, baked potatoes, green beans, and applesauce. Robert picks up a drumstick, but Rusty stops Robert's hand before he can get it to his mouth.

"We say grace first," Mrs. Murphy says. Robert looks at the drumstick, then Rusty, then bows his head.

After grace, there is no talking because everyone is too busy eating. The chicken falls right off the bone when I bite into it. Megan puts fresh-cut chives on her potato, just because Helen does, even though I know she hates chives. I can see her face trying so hard not to grimace with each bite, but she eats the whole thing. Rusty nudges me with his foot under the table but I ignore him. Robert is the first one to speak.

"Can I light the bonfire? Rusty said I could."

Mr. Murphy laughs. He has a deep laugh for such a thin man. "Sure, Robert, as soon as we're done eating and the table's cleared."

Robert eats twice as fast as normal, which is almost impossible. When his plate is cleared he watches everyone else eat, willing them to finish.

"Should we clear the table now?" he asks.

"Pretty soon, Robert." Mr. Murphy winks at him.

When everyone is done, Rusty slaps Robert on the back. "Let's take in the plates and get some matches." Robert tries to get up too fast and falls off the bench. Rusty helps him up.

Brenda, Helen, and Mrs. Murphy get up to carry in plates also. Megan silently does the same. I am stuck between staying here with Mr. Murphy and going in the house. I stay.

"We sure were lucky to have such a nice day," Mr. Murphy says, smiling at me. He has a piece of barbecued chicken stuck on his tooth, and it looks just like his tooth is missing.

I nod. I guess it was a pretty day. I wouldn't call it nice.

"So you're staying with us, huh? I think Brenda's pretty excited about it, having you sleep over. You've been very kind, helping her with her math. She was proud as a peacock, getting a C+ on that big test. Thank you."

Brenda never even told me. I give God an eight, like I promised, but take it away for making me stay here. He's got nowhere near a hundred points yet. I give Mr. Murphy a half-smile and say, "It's okay, I don't mind helping her." When I look away, I see the tar-paper house. I want to shudder. It reminds me of a picture my mother showed me of a model of a human body with no skin. "How come there's no wood on the outside?" I ask, right away ashamed I said it, but I can't take it back.

Mr. Murphy looks at me and doesn't say a thing. He isn't smiling now, but he doesn't look mad, just thoughtful, like he has all the time in the world to answer my question. Finally he just shrugs. "You know, Tamara, siding costs a lot. More than I have at the moment. And the rain stays outside, and we stay dry, so I guess we just have to thank God for that much. Sometimes it's just a waste of energy to be cross about the things you can't do anything about." He pauses for a bit, then kind of chuckles to himself, like he just heard a good joke. "Someday I'll fix it up," he says. "Mrs. Murphy will sure be glad when that day comes, I can tell you that."

I look down at the table. I don't know what to say. Luckily I hear the screen door bang shut. Robert comes running out. "Can I light the fire now, Mr. Murphy, can I?" Brenda is right behind him with a bag of marshmallows.

"Okay, let's do her. You ever light matches before?" Mr. Murphy asks, as he gets up and limps over to the tepee of old limbs and broken-up kindling that's been built up even taller than his head. He douses the whole thing with lighter fluid.

"Oh sure! I lit matches before!" Robert says. He burns his fingers on the first two tries, but insists on going for the third. Mr. Murphy cups his hands around the wooden match as soon as Robert lights it, and together they travel the few yards to a loose wad of newspaper stuffed into the bottom of the pile. The paper catches with a whoosh, and the flame spreads, following a trail of lighter fluid. In seconds, the kindling is crackling and popping, fire snaking along the old logs and broken branches. Robert whoops like an Indian. Brenda is already stuffing lines of marshmallows on the sticks Mr. Murphy cut off baby maple trees right before dinner. I watch the fire. I can't take my eyes off of it. It's a great and wonderful bonfire. The biggest I've ever seen. Suddenly there is something moving behind me. Mr. Murphy has brought me over a folding chair that has bright-green plastic strips. Some of the strips are missing, or dangling down to the ground. I say, "Thanks," and sit down.

The flames twist and turn, racing along dry twigs, hovering tightly to thick logs, heating my face, relaxing everything inside me that is tightly knotted. Rusty comes over and offers me a marshmallow on a stick, but I tell him no thanks. I must say it just the right way, because he nods and leaves me alone. I have wanted so much today, but right now all I want is to watch this fire, and it's so easy to do. I'm not mad at anyone. I'm not even mad at me. I just sit and stare. It is better than church.

I don't move again until most of the logs have fallen, and the ashes are a city of blistering reds and oranges, alive and breathing. Sparks spit and fly up, becoming stars. Above me the Milky Way is a soft haze of starlight. The Big Dipper rises over the tree line and I can make out Orion's Belt and the Archer among the millions of other stars. When I do move, it is only to pull the chair closer. I like the hot, burning feeling on my cheeks and knees. I watch the fire burn down as marshmallows are roasted and jokes told and people go back and forth, their shadows flickering against the trees. I give God a ten for this moment.

I am breathing so slow I don't know I have fallen asleep until my head bobs and jerks me back awake. For a moment, I wonder where I am, but then Helen is leading me into her house and up the stairs to the bedroom, where a sleeping bag and pillow are already on the floor. As my head sinks into the pillow, I fall sound asleep, just across the road from the pretty little farmhouse I pretend is my own.

Eleven

"Wake up, Tamara," Helen says, gently nudging my shoulder. "Time for church." I can smell bacon and eggs. Blinking, I sit up and look around. I'm in Brenda and Helen's room. It is the strangest bedroom I've ever seen. One side is neat to the point of frugality. A bed with a plain white cover, smooth as icing, a small bureau with a Bible and a brush. A few pairs of shoes lined up under the window. That's it. The other half of the room is papered with torn-out pages from magazines. Pictures of James Dean dominate the others, but Audrey Hepburn is up there, along with Grace Kelly, Marilyn Monroe, and Rita Moreno. These pictures also cover the closet door, the sides of Brenda's bureau, and the headboard on her bed. The bed is a lumpy mess of blankets and clothes. Shoes poke out from under the bed, along with more clothes, pieces of paper, combs, notebooks, and stuffed animals. I couldn't live on either side of this room, and they live in both.

I notice that my good peach-colored dress with the white-trim collar is hanging from a hook on the closet door. My black patent-leather shoes wait underneath.

"I sent Megan over to your house to get your dress," Helen says. "We thought we'd let you sleep in, since you seemed so tired last night. Breakfast is almost ready, and everyone else is awake, so please get dressed and come down as quickly as you can."

I almost say, *Yes, Mother.*

By the time I come down, everyone is sitting around the table, stools and chairs tight together so everyone can fit. Megan is wearing her yellow dress and Robert his suit jacket.

The food is on the table but no one is eating.

"Good morning, Tamara," Mrs. Murphy says. "Please sit down and join us. We're ready to say grace."

I sit on a stool between Brenda and my brother. I feel like I'm dreaming. Everyone is dressed nicely, with their hands folded in their laps, hot food steaming from platters. My brother's head is bowed. We are about to say grace and go to church. This would make my mother really sick, I think. Sicker, I correct myself.

"Bless us O Lord and these Thy gifts which we are about to receive. Amen." Everyone says Amen. Helen nods to us. Platters are passed. We eat.

I look around, expecting to see cracks in the walls and junk all over, maybe even a car bumper. But the inside doesn't look anything like the outside. It's neat, dustless, everything in its place. The floors are covered with oval rugs made out of tightly rolled rags of different colors, mostly reds, oranges, and golds. The curtains are homemade, light blue with gold swirls, and the same material has been made into pillows and table covers. The gold color is picked up by small brass pieces: candlesticks and bowls and small vases without flowers. There is a picture of Jesus on the wall in the dining room. No other pictures at all. I'm glad now that Mr. and Mrs. Murphy never came in our house. What would they think of my nude mother, with her wide dark nipples and excessive pubic hair, on a two-and-a-half-by-six-foot canvas? I wonder what Helen thinks of us? I bet she believes we will be going to the deepest darkest regions of hell when we die, and to save us will be the greatest miracle she could ever perform.

After breakfast, Mrs. Murphy says, "Why don't you boys go listen to the radio while we clean up. We'll be ready to go to church soon."

Rusty, Robert, and Mr. Murphy go in the living room. Mrs. Murphy and Helen put on aprons to wash and dry the dishes while Brenda, Megan, and I clear the table. Mrs. Murphy washes dishes like a machine; she could do this blind. There is not a motion of her hands that is wasted. Nothing clinks or bangs. She is so fast Helen is still drying dishes as Mrs. Murphy shakes the cloth place mats out into the garbage, wipes every counter spotlessly clean, and polishes the dining room table. Megan, Brenda, and I have to stand up against one of the walls just to get out of her way.

"Okay, gentlemen, we're ready," she says. Outside, I look behind me. It is the same house I have been looking at from across the street for the past few months, with the clutter, and the junk cars, and the forgotten toys in the high grass. The inside and the outside are so different, just like the two sides of Helen and Brenda's room. We have never had a house that becomes like us. We have to fit into other people's shoes. I understand now why my mother has to hang up my father's paintings so quickly, the same ones every time, his oldest paintings. To remind us of who we are.

As I get in their car and we drive away I want my mom back so much it hurts. We hit a pothole and something rattles and clangs underneath our feet. I imagine my family falling apart like the Murphys' car, losing pieces bit by bit. Robert is sitting next to me and I put an arm around him. He flinches and looks at me as if I might slug him next. That look makes me want to, but I don't.

This is my eighth visit to church and I know what to do. I take the hymnal out of its wooden pocket and I am ready to open it to the right page number. We stand to sing, and I mouth the words, then sit to listen to the announcements, then pray, then sing some more, then pray.

Today, when we bow our heads to pray, I pray hard. I say, *Dear God, you probably know this, but my mother was taken away to a sanitarium because she has TB, and I think she's very sick. I'm worried she's going to die and my father's going to drive into a tree. I'm scared we are going to be left orphans and I'm going to have to take care of my brother and sister or end up living forever with the Murphys. I've been doing the cooking and cleaning, and I'm not very good at it, and the garden's not weeded, and my sister won't talk. I guess I'm pretty angry at my mother, and my dad, and I know I shouldn't be. I really need some help. I am praying to ask you, first, to make my mother better. Just in case you heard me thinking about her staying sick, I didn't mean it. If you are punishing her for not believing in you, can't you just make her believe? If it's impossible to make someone believe who really doesn't want to, then you could make me believe, because I'm at least trying, and if you make me believe, I promise to work real hard on my mother. But I need to really believe, to convince her, because she is a good arguer. So, I am praying to you, asking you to show me that you are real and to make my mother better, and I know it's a lot to ask, but I would think you would want me to believe, so I'm not asking you to do something wrong. So, please, help me. Thank you.*

When I open my eyes, everyone is rising to sing. We sing "Jesus Is All the World to Me," and this time I sing the words softly. No one can hear me, but I can. It's a wonderful feeling, to be singing with the people in the church. As always, when I am here, listening to the voices, I feel this rush of hope that I might fit in.

The minister reads something from Luke 24, about Christ dying for our sins, and how we must all accept Him as our savior, which is the same thing the minister always talks about. But the people here are the ones who believe this. Why keep repeating it? I imagine that the minister's words are like nail polish; with each coat we get stronger and stronger so we don't chip, so our belief is harder to break. I will have to write to my mother about this idea. She'll appreciate the humor, if not the sentiment.

I wonder if she misses me right now. What is she doing? What would she be doing if she were home? She'd probably be with Edith, or at the pond. She must miss those things. I grin, thinking about what I could send her to remind her of Edith. I wonder if God minds a sense of humor, or me thinking about cow manure in His church. I cover my mouth with my hand, in case He's watching.

We sing "God Bless America," and I know this is the end. I stand at the same time everyone else does, not after. I think God might have started helping me already.

In the Murphys' car, I still have the hopeful feeling that I did in the church. This time it has followed me out. I am sure that God will do something amazing when I get back to the house.

I spend the rest of the day weeding the garden with Mrs. Burns, waiting for a sign, looking up into the sky as much as I can without Mrs. Burns noticing. It's pretty cloudy, but I figure if God is going to show Himself to me, He can make the clouds go away. When the Burns leave, I sit on the front steps, humming bits of hymns I remember from church, but I hum softly, my ears listening for God to call my name. I tell Rusty I don't want to go to the fort, that I need to be alone. The feeling from church, that I belong to something, is fading. My butt gets sore. By dinnertime, my jaw is tight and now I'm not only angry at my parents, but I'm getting angry at God. Why make me wait? What's the point? If He's there, why not do this *now*? Doesn't He want to save me?

Sunday night is Mrs. Murphy's night off from the dishes, so she can spend the evening reading the Bible. I help Helen clean up. I wash and she dries, because she knows where to put the stuff away. Megan scrapes the food into the compost bucket and helps Helen put away the silverware.

"I don't get it, Helen," I say. "I don't know why God won't let me know He's real. You say you *know*. How do you know? Did He *talk* to you?"

Helen rubs at a plate until it's more than dry. "He's in my heart, Tamara. It's like knowing that I have a hand, or a nose on my face. I don't question it, because He's right there inside me and I can feel Him. And He talks to me, but not with words. He leads me. Everything I do is because Jesus lives in me."

"But I need to *know*, Helen, and I keep asking Him to let me know, but nothing happens. I'm feeling pretty stupid just staring into the air."

"Well," Helen says. "There's only one thing I can say. You must trust in Him. He is there. You have to act on that trust, you have to believe *before* He does something for you. You have to do something for Him first. You have to accept Jesus as your savior. Trust in Him and you will find Him. Let me tell you a story."

I scrub pots as Helen tells me a story about some kid named Lazarus, who, if I understand it right, died, and then Jesus brought him back to life. He was a friend of Jesus'. I point out to Helen that Jesus did special favors for friends, and since she's so close to Him, maybe He would save me for Helen's sake. Helen says that's not the point of the story. I never get the point, even after she tells me the story twice. I wonder if I will ever understand any of this, if religion is like a foreign language that I would have understood a lot better if I had started earlier. These Jesus stories are so impossible to believe. If Jesus can do this stuff, why won't He do other miracles, like helping that kid whose parents kept him in a cage for three years, or not letting Siamese twins get born? And if God is Jesus' father, and more powerful, why doesn't He end hunger or stop wars? It seems to me that God's and Jesus' miracles are getting smaller and smaller by the century. I don't think He can help my mother get better. Helping Brenda get a C+ in math might be all He can handle these days.

That night, when we go to bed, Brenda kneels to pray, looking at me over her shoulder. I kneel down beside her. I'm going to try one more time. I pray to God. And to Jesus. I get confused who I'm supposed to have in my heart. I tell Him I need Him. I would like Him to be my friend. It would be nice to have a friend who I wouldn't lose every time I moved. I tell Him to please, however He wants, let me *know*. While I'm sleeping will be fine. No signs. Just let me wake up knowing. He doesn't even have to raise me from the dead.

In the morning, I'm just the same. Rusty asks me if I want to go to the fort. I say sure. I tell Robert if he follows us, I'll burn his comics in the Murphys' trash can. He looks at Rusty with the same big eyes Kip looks at Mr. Burns with, all wet and hopeful. Rusty tells him he better stay behind and Robert runs across the street to our house.

On the way through the woods, Rusty points out an area of fallen trees, mostly beech, lying across the forest floor like a for-gotten game of giant pick-up-sticks. They're on the side of a hill to our left. I've noticed them before, but never thought much about it. "Why are they all fallen down?" I ask.

He walks off the path and toward the trees. "A tornado. The summer before last summer. It came right over the hill from behind the Burns' house, jumped over their house and our house, and came back down right here, less than a quarter mile from our house. We were in the basement. My dad knew it was coming 'cause the sky turned yellow. Holy moly, I was scared. The walls shook. We could feel the trees falling, right through the floor." Rusty weaves around a patch of thornbushes and under some low branches. I follow right behind him, wondering why we're not going to the fort. Doesn't he want to kiss me?

"A real tornado?" I say. It sounds lame, but it was what he was hoping I'd say, I guess, 'cause he turns and grins.

"Yeah. Huge. It picked up the Griffins' trailer and dumped it upside down in their pond and Mrs. Griffin's aunt died." It's an odd thing to say with a grin, but I know what he means.

This was real-life stuff, and it happened right here. Nothing happens here.

Rusty walks along a fallen tree, his arms spread out like wings. He's going on about the tornado, the damage it did, how branches were scattered all over his roof, how the cattle got so scared they stuck together in a tight pack for days.

"The weirdest thing was Kip. He just disappeared. The Burns went crazy about it, then some farmer they know found Kip a mile away and drove him home. I think he got caught in the tornado. Can you believe it?"

"He could have just gone for a long walk," I say.

Rusty's face loses some of its sparkle. "I suppose—"

"And then again, it probably was the tornado," I say. "Maybe it dropped him in a pond and he just swam out." I climb up on a fallen tree parallel to Rusty's and try to balance myself.

He nods, his grin back. "I bet that's what happened. That dog hasn't been the same since."

Maybe Kip is different because his boy died and never came back to call his name or pet him, but I don't mention it. We wobble around on the trees for a while, trying to jump from one fallen tree to another, pinwheeling our arms and laughing when we fall. "The tornado scared the shit out of me," Rusty says. "But what I'm saying is, I liked that. It's a funny feeling, getting scared and then being okay." He holds on to a branch sticking up from the tree and spins around. "I'm going to join the Air Force. My dad says it's a good idea."

"Why?" It's all I can say. I'm trying hard to balance *and* think about Rusty leaving. My foot slips off the log and I have to start all over again.

"My dad was in the armed forces, in the war. That's how he got hurt. He really loved it, but he wishes he joined the Air Force. He says I could learn a lot of stuff in the Air Force, a vocation, and I could see a lot of places. I'd like to learn to fly an airplane. That would be so neat."

I have to stop moving. I sit down on the tree I'm standing on, straddling it like a horse, not that I've ever ridden a horse. "You could get killed. There's going to be a war with Russia."

"Well, sure, but I won't get killed. You should see my dad's medals. They are so cool. Did you know he's got a Purple Heart?"

I have no idea what he's talking about. How could he get a purple heart? "Is that some disease he got from the war?"

Rusty stops in mid-step on a log and stares at me. "What? Are you kidding me? Shit. You got to be kidding me. You don't know what a Purple Heart is?"

I shake my head.

"Shit. It's a medal. For getting wounded in the war, for being brave. He's got a Distinguished Service Cross too. Don't your dad have any medals?"

"He wasn't in the war. He had a punctured eardrum."

"What?" Rusty's looking at me with his eyes all narrow, his feathery eyelashes bunched up together. "What are you talking about?" This subject is embarrassing me. It's just another way I don't fit in. I remember all those blue stars on the windows. I told my mom I wanted a blue star on our window, and she got mad. She said not to mention it again. It was a sore subject. It made my dad feel bad. I told her I didn't care, I still wanted a blue star. I was five years old and I made one with my crayons and taped it to our window, and my mother tore it down and spanked me. It was the only time she spanked me. "His eardrum, in his left ear, has got a hole in it, so he couldn't join the Army," I tell Rusty. "And he was too old. He was too young for World War I."

Rusty nods, like now I'm making sense. "Yeah, he's a pretty old guy. I thought he was your grandpa or something. But still—Well, I guess he missed out. But I'm not gonna. I got to get out of here. I got to get away. I want to see places. I want to see Hawaii, and Africa, and shit, the whole world. I tell you, I'm gonna be a pilot. You'll see." He jumps down off the log he's standing on and then jumps right back up. "I'll come back and visit my parents, it's not like I'm never coming back, it's not like I *hate* this place. I just ain't gonna get stuck here." He looks up at the sky, for his plane. "The sky gets yellow before a tornado. My dad told me about that, and when I saw it really happen that day, I yelled for him, and he made us get in the basement. He's pretty smart. It's a good thing he told me. It sure is a strange color. A yellow sky." He's still looking up, and now I know he's trying to imagine the sky that way, kind of hoping it might happen again.

"So," he says. "You want to go to the fort?"

I think about it. I don't want to be in the fort now. Talking feels good. I'm glad he's telling me what he wants to do, even though I don't want him to go. "Not now," I say.

"Yeah, okay." He snaps a long twig off a limb and waves it around like a sword. I get this tight feeling, right in my throat, and it's because Rusty is just like me. We think we're so grown-up, but I bet he'd be scared if he were in a war right now, just like I'm scared trying to be my mother.

"I could show you a beaver pond," he says.

"Okay."

Rusty leads me away from the fallen trees, through more brambles, then down a hill. Trees are gnawed off knee-high into sharp points. The land becomes swampy and we have to curve around the side of the hill. Rusty tells me to take off my shoes: if we want to see the beavers we have to walk like Indians and not talk at all. It's fine with me. I'm busy thinking. My mother would love to see the trees chewed off like that. I wonder if she ever hated trees because of her mother driving into one. I wonder if living surrounded by trees is a test of her strength. I wonder what it would be like to believe in God and then stop believing, rather than not to believe and then to believe. Do you ever really get rid of the not believing or the believing? I believed I could fly. Then I tried to fly, and I couldn't. Maybe I just didn't believe enough. Maybe I have to give Him another chance, even though I don't want to anymore, because it hurts when He doesn't show up, just as much as falling down Valley View Hill.

Suddenly, we are there, on the edge of the pond. I can see the dam, built from logs and twigs, so tightly woven together it holds in all the water. There is a mound of more twigs and logs, the beavers' den, with grass growing right on the top. The swampy pond is huge, a whole acre or more. We can't see any beavers. They must be hiding. Rusty straddles a log and there is enough room for me to sit right in front of him. He wraps his arms around my waist and I lean back against his warm body. We sit quietly, waiting to spot a beaver. They never come out, but it's so nice to be held, I don't care.

After we come back from the walk, I go over to our house to get some clothes for tomorrow. Robert's there. He glares at me from behind his comic. Just as I'm going up the stairs, the phone rings. Robert picks it up.

"Hello," Robert says, without any of that wavering his voice has been doing for the past year, that jumping around from squeaky to hoarse, even inside a word, as if the word had an extra syllable. "Yeah, hi, Dad," he says. He nods, pressing his lips together, listening carefully to what my father is saying.

"Okay," Robert says. "Yeah, that's okay. We'll be fine." I can imagine what he's agreeing to. My father isn't coming home tomorrow.

"Yeah, I'm okay," Robert says. "I got to light the bonfire." A pause. "Yeah, pretty good. Okay. See you when you get home." He holds the phone out to me. "He wants to talk to you."

I walk over slowly. "Hi, Dad," I say, trying to sound very casual.

"Hi, honey," he says. "How are you doing?"

"Fine," I say. "When are you coming home?"

"I don't know. Maybe Wednesday." He pauses. "Today's Monday, right?" he says, obviously not so sure.

"Yeah." He does this, forgets what day it is. Just now I figure out why, as if someone near whispers it in my ear. It's because he doesn't go to work. Or church. All the days are the same to him. It hits me hard just how different he is from other people's dads. It makes me pretty angry. "How come you can't come home?" I ask.

"My show starts tomorrow. Tuesday evening is opening night." He pauses again. "So, I'll try to come home Wednesday." He coughs, a bunch of coughs all together, with different sounds to them.

"Daddy," I say, "are you okay?"

"I was just eating something. Got stuck in my throat. Sorry."

It scared me, to hear him cough. I can't believe he is eating and talking to me, as if they are both just as important, as if he couldn't have waited to take that bite later, when he is done talking to me. He's trying to kill two birds with one stone.

"I'm going to get baptized next Sunday," I say, not that I am, but now I might.

"Tamara," he says wearily, "let's not do this."

"Would you be mad?" I ask.

"We'll discuss this later. Let me talk with Megan now."

"Oh, so you believe in miracles?"

"Tamara, please."

"Well, you don't think she's going to break her vow of silence just to say hi to you on the phone, do you? Jesus, Dad, she hasn't talked for almost a month. Not one word. Don't you think that's strange, even for her?"

"Just tell her I asked about her, and that I love her, will you?"

"Sure. Bye." I slam down the phone.

"Is Rusty back?" Robert asks me.

I almost say no. I almost tell him Rusty went to a friend's house for the rest of the week. But Robert looks so miserable. "He's back. He wants you to come over."

Robert throws his comic up in the air and is out of the house before it hits the ground. I go into the kitchen to get some chips or something. There's nothing to eat. Just the canned food in the basement. Waiting for the war.

Twelve

Tuesday it rains again, a misty rain we can hardly see but that soaks into our clothes just as fast as regular rain. Rusty and Brenda have to clean their rooms and do some wash, and Helen is teaching Megan how to sew, so Robert and I go over to our house for a while. My father has been gone for four days. The house smells empty.

I go up to my parents' bedroom and try on some of my mother's clothes. I like her yellow cashmere sweater best and when I hold it up to my nose it smells like she does when we sit on the couch to listen to the radio. I wonder if people smell different at different times, so I sniff the rest of her shirts. They just smell clean. Wearing my mother's sweater, her blue cotton skirt, and her black high heels, which fit me perfectly, I wobble over to my father's bureau. I open the small top drawer on the left and find it crammed full of junk, which surprises me because his paints and art things are so well organized. It's like finding another part of him, in a little drawer. It smells of leather and paint. Everything of my father's smells like paint. There are handkerchiefs I've never seen him use, and one of them is a lady's, with pink embroidery on a scalloped edge. I smell it, and my eyes close and something flutters in my stomach. It is my mother's handkerchief. I lay it on top of the bureau. Next I take out a pipe. My father doesn't smoke, but in the one picture I have seen of my grandfather, he is holding a pipe. This must be his. Also in the drawer is a folding knife, a fountain pen, a billfold with one dollar, several small round stones, a bunch of loose change, and a picture of Robert and me at some beach, both knee-high in water, squinting at the camera. In the back of the drawer is a stack of letters, the ones my mother has sent him from the sanitarium, and, under them, three letters on yellow legal paper. They are letters from my father to my mother. I wonder why he didn't send these ones. I sit on the bed and read them.

July 12, 1954

Liz,

Love you. I need to say that first, in case I can't say anything else. I have never written you a letter. I think I sent you a postcard from New York once. It had a picture of Central Park.

I have started this letter six times. I always get this far and then I find I have stared at the paper for a long time. I see us walking around the pond in Central Park, you taking those big steps and waving your arms, furious with someone you have just had an argument with about minimum wages for women (see, I do remember some details about way back then, even though you think I don't), and I said, "Hold on, let me get you a podium," and you said, "Screw you," and I was so afraid I made a big mistake, and you let me think I had until I apologized at least forty times. I'm sorry, again. For everything and for absolutely nothing, because, given the chance, I wouldn't change a thing, because it would change you, and even a fraction of a difference would be too much. Have I ever told you you're perfect?

I wish you could hold

The letter ends here, with words scratched out after the word *hold* and I can't make any of them out. I read the next letter.

July 22, 1954

Liz,

I just mailed you a letter. I said all the right things and I meant them, but now I have to tell you the truth. I'll save this letter so when you get back you'll know what it was really like without you. It stinks.

Megan won't come out of her room. I don't know how she does it. I would go insane inside that long. It smells terrible in there, but she looks healthy. I try to talk her into coming out, but she just stares at me. She is so stubborn. What makes the women in this family so stubborn? Robert is miserable and shows it. He'll burst out in tears at the slightest thing. I would too, but I promised you I wouldn't cry in front of the children, and I never have. I have begun to paint in the pasture. It gives me some freedom to sulk and weep. I do weep. I am an old man who needs you.

Tamara has cloaked herself in anger. She sees everything in black and white. I want to tell her to look at the shades between, how they soften the world so we can love it even when it hurts. Sometimes I want to grab her and shake her, tell her no one is to blame, but I am afraid to say the things she needs to hear because she thinks everything I say is wrong. She is like the paintings I wish I could paint but can't. I am afraid she is beyond my ability to raise. She needs you. You are her reds and yellows and greens, her indigo, emerald, and ultramarine. I am only black.

Robert will do okay. I suppose they all will, but at least he lets himself feel sorrow, although Tamara still teases him about it and I have to send her to her room.

Robert is like a rubber ball. He's bouncing between places right now, strength and fear, loss and discovery, certainty and confusion. He'll land in the right place. When you come home. *I say that to myself a hundred times a day.* When Liz comes home.

My paintings have changed. I still find the flying girl takes me someplace new, but it's more than that. Sometimes I look up from the canvas, startled to see the world plain and simple. The paintings are now complex. They speak of loss, and need. They have come alive, as if the trees and hills and sky in my painting want something, lack something, and they don't know what it might be, only that they need. I actually think as I paint, What? What do you want? *My paintings now are like nothing I have ever done before, and I know why. It's because you eased the demons from me each night just by listening to me talk, by holding me in bed, and now no one listens to me at all and my fears and desires come out through my fingertips, finding their way onto the canvas. I must admit, I love it. I am afraid to tell you, because it means I have profited from your illness, but I suppose I have profited by you in every way, and this is no different. You are my compass. I need you.*

And Love you,
Stuart

I read this letter twice without wanting to; my eyes just do it although I can feel my whole body shouting to put it down. When I'm done I breathe through my mouth because my nose is stuffed up. I bet he left this letter for me to find so I will feel sorry for him. I fold it up so I can put all the letters back just as I found them. I'll never mention them to him. I won't even read the third one.

But I have to.

July 27, 1954

Liz,

You have been gone three weeks and I can't take it. I'm sorry I wrote that last letter telling you I will die without you. It was stupid to mail it. I thought you should know how much I missed you, but you haven't written for a while and when I called Dr. Henderson, he said you had taken a turn for the worse. I blame myself. I hate myself for what I have let happen to you. I wait each day to hear from you. I wait each day to know it's a day less before you come back. Please come back. Don't give up on me.

This letter is unsigned and crumpled worse than the rest. My hand shakes as I try to fold it. When I put the letters away I am still shaking, so I hit the wall as hard as I can. The plaster beneath the wallpaper dents. It hardly hurts at all. I take off my mother's sweater and skirt. The shoes have already fallen off my feet. I feel sick knowing I was wearing her clothes as I read those letters. On the way out of the room I slam my fist into the wood around the door, and that hurts. I do it again.

I have to pretend I didn't read those letters. I have to forget them. I don't want them inside me.

I will act as if nothing has happened. My mother says you can trick yourself into being happy by smiling. I grin stupidly and decide I will go paint my nails. The back of my hand is already swelling.

I paint my nails downstairs in the living room while Robert does his puzzle—which is almost finished. There is a small section of green leaves left to do, and one piece missing on the petal of an orange poppy. The petal looks wounded by that empty space, like a tooth knocked out. We are both quiet but tense, especially Robert, who instead of being excited about finishing his puzzle looks like he might explode. He's developed a twitch; a blink, blink, blink, then a pause, then it starts again. I grin at him and he sticks his tongue out at me. The phone rings and I flinch, spilling orange nail polish all over my left thumb.

Robert looks at me but doesn't move. I stick the brush back in the bottle and answer the phone on the fourth ring.

"Hello?"

"Is Mr. Anderson home?" a cool, smooth voice asks.

"No, he's not. Can I help you?"

"When might he be home?"

"I don't know," I say, trying to guess who this is. It wouldn't be someone from New York, since my father's there. It could be a doctor from the sanitarium. "He might not be home for a couple days," I say. "Is this about my mother?"

"In a way," he says. "Who am I speaking to?"

"I'm Tamara Anderson. Who is this please?"

Robert is looking at me with a worried expression on his face, chewing on a fingernail.

"My name is Dr. Ostrum. Is there an adult I can speak to?"

"No, there's not," I say. "But you can tell me and I'll tell my father."

"How old are you, Tamara?"

"Fifteen."

"Oh." He pauses and I can almost hear him thinking, wondering if I'm old enough to hear whatever he has to say. I'm holding the phone so tight it hurts my hand.

"Might your father be home tomorrow?"

"No, he won't," I say. "Maybe not for a week. But I'll be talking to him."

"Can I reach him someplace?"

"No." I am close to begging him to tell me what it is all about, how my mother is, but I don't because I worry he might think me immature. It must work. He clears his throat.

"Okay, Tamara, here's why I'm calling. I'm a federal veterinarian and I work with the U.S. Department of Agriculture, in
the Bureau of Animal Industry. We've received a report from the
county health commissioner about your mother's tuberculosis.
They contact us when someone diagnosed with, or testing positive for, tuberculosis has been working with farm animals. We
need to come out and test your cows for tuberculosis. Your
mother mentioned a milk cow to the Health Department case-
worker. A milk cow and several beef cattle. So I need to set up an
appointment, the sooner the better. Do you understand?"

"No," I say. I don't understand why he's calling about the
cow. "Why the cow?" I say. Robert comes right up next to me
and tries to listen into the phone. I turn my back to him so I can't
see all the questions he's mouthing.

"Well, cows can carry tuberculosis. It might be how your
mother contracted the disease. Do you drink the milk too?"

I take a deep breath, getting scared. "We don't. She did."

"Well. You see then. It is possible your cow has tuberculosis."

"It's not our cow," I say, wanting nothing to do with having
a sick cow.

"Whose cow is it?" He sounds confused.

"They are the Burns' cows. We rent their farm."

"Oh," he says. "Can I have their phone number?"

"Sure." I give it to him.

"Thank you, Tamara. You've been a big help. I imagine I'll
be coming up there tomorrow. Who milks the cow now that
your mother's not there?"

"Helen."

"Who's Helen?" the man asks.

"Our neighbor."

"Well, will you tell Helen to wear rubber gloves, and throw
away the milk. She'll need a tuberculosis test too. She should go to
her doctor as soon as possible. But, like I said, I'll be out. We'll get

the milk cow tested. She might be fine. It's more than likely. Don't you worry. I'll talk to Mr. Burns and we'll get it straightened out. You *will* tell your father all this when he calls, won't you?"

"Yes," I say.

"Thank you again, Tamara. Good-bye."

"What the heck was that about?" Robert says.

I roll my eyes because I still can't believe it. "It's a guy who says Edith might have TB and he has to come give her a test."

"No."

"Yeah."

"No, you're kidding me."

"Really, Robert, that's what he said. And he said to tell Helen she has to be tested too."

"No."

"Yeah."

"Jeepers creepers." Robert's eyes are as big as saucers. He's forgotten all about the last ten pieces in his puzzle. "Let's go tell her," he says. So we do.

Helen's in the kitchen as always. She throws a fit. She doesn't even let me finish telling her half of it before she starts asking questions and jumping to conclusions.

"I have TB? From that cow? How could that happen? What am I going to do?" Her hands fly about like trapped birds. She touches her face, her neck, her chest, as if she's afraid they might not be there anymore. She walks into the living room and looks at her face in the mirror on the wall. Robert and I follow.

"You just have to get tested, Helen. It's not that bad," I say.

"Not bad? I could be dying right now. I have to devote my life to God. I can't die!"

You'd think the way she loves God so much she wouldn't mind dying at all because she'd be with Him, but she's talking so fast her lips flutter; it's like she's a different person. I guess she's really scared.

"I'm sure glad I didn't drink that milk," Robert says. "Boy oh boy am I glad about that." I shove him. "What?" he says.

By now everyone is coming into the living room. Brenda and Rusty and Mr. Murphy. Mrs. Murphy's at work. They're all asking what's wrong and I try telling the story again, but everyone interrupts until Mr. Murphy tells everyone to be quiet.

"This vet, he said Helen should get a test?"

"Yes. And she should use rubber gloves when she milks the cow."

"I'm not milking that cow anymore!" Helen shouts. "I will not milk that cow!"

"Well, no, of course not," Mr. Murphy says.

"I'm going to church!" Helen says. "I have to pray."

"Your mother's gone to work, Helen," Mr. Murphy says.

"Then I'll walk!" She stomps out of the house.

"It's a two-hour walk to church," Rusty says.

"It'll do her good," Mr. Murphy says. Then he turns to us. Robert, Megan, and I have all bunched up together. "Why don't you kids go home for a while. I need to call our doctor."

We all nod. Brenda starts to follow us out the door, but Mr. Murphy catches her by the back of her shirt. "You stay here," he says.

We go home.

As we cross the road, we can see Helen walking away, getting smaller in the distance.

"She didn't say good-bye," Megan says. For a moment, I think this is me thinking; I'm so sure it can't be Megan. Then, when I realize it is Megan, I wonder if she means our mother or Helen. Either way, Megan is crying, rivulets of tears running down her pale round cheeks. She has been abandoned too often.

"She'll be back," I say. "She's just gone to church."

"I don't think so," Megan says. "I don't think she'll come back."

The misty rain has stopped. Leaves drip soft exotic sounds on grass so green and wet it's like walking in a sea. The attic light catches the sun and winks brightly. I think about Timothy. I think maybe he's stuck in the attic because secretly he didn't believe in God either, and his soul got left behind. Maybe he just believed in regular people, like his mom and dad. Maybe there are some things parents just can't do, and he knows that now. And now we have abandoned him too. Lately there have been more noises in the attic. My mother would tell me a squirrel has gotten in through the rafters, but she's not here.

I pause before the steps to our house, not wanting to go inside, now that the rain has stopped. Megan stands one step behind me as Robert pushes past us. "I'm reading *The Vault Keeper* and nobody better bother me," Robert says, and disappears inside. I think this might be a good time to tell him about the ghost in the attic, just to give him a *real* thrill, but I don't want to go inside even to torture him. I sit on the steps and take off my shoes. Megan does the same.

Megan follows me to the unfinished bomb shelter, where there are three inches of warm standing water. There is no drain; the idea was to keep rain out, the rain of radiation. The bottom is slick with a slimy moss and the place smells of mold, but it's still fun to walk around in, slicing through the water with our bare feet, pretending to skate on the slick surface. The sun seems to blink and I look up to see a large blackish bird fly across the sky toward the stand of trees to our right. A moment later we hear the laughing cry of the pileated woodpecker, followed by the hollow echoing sound of him hammering the tree with his hard beak, marking out his territory, saying, this is my home, my home, my home.

I waste time just shuffling my feet, pacing back and forth in the water, until I decide to do what I knew I would do all along.

"Come on," I say to Megan, even though I don't need to tell her to follow me. She will anyway.

I go into the barn and out the back of it, and stand in the mud at the bottom of the hill. "Ally Ally In Free," I yell. "Come and get it! Yoo-hoo! Come on, come on, come on!" I don't think it matters what you yell, it's the tone, a high-pitched sound that carries through the air like a dinner bell. We wait. Edith comes loping over the hill and galloping down. Before she gets to the barn I turn and go inside to get the sweet oats she loves. Megan scoops out a handful too. Edith heads toward us and we back up until she is standing by her stool, then let her munch the oats out of our open palms, her thick warm lips spilling very little onto the ground. Then, while Megan rubs Edith between the eyes, I pull over the metal pail and begin to milk her. I know I should get some gloves, but I don't. I'm going to do this just like my mother did.

Edith's udders are huge and swollen-looking and her teats dry and warm and rubbery. I have tried this only once and stopped quickly, but now I concentrate on the task, closing my thumb and finger around her teat, then pulling just a little as I close the rest of my fingers from the top to the bottom. A spray of milk comes out and misses the pail. I get hold of another teat with my other hand and do the same thing, aiming more carefully. The milk makes a light rattling noise as it hits the inside of the pail. I go back and forth from one hand to the other, finding a rhythm, getting most of the milk into the pail, which fills so slowly I think my arms will fall off before I get an inch of milk in there. Edith is a big animal, and at first I keep glancing at her legs and hooves, thinking she might try to kick me, but she seems to like what I'm doing, and I rest my head against her side, like my mother did. This gives me more leverage and I increase my rhythm.

Milking a cow is a good place to think. I wonder if my mother did a lot of thinking here. I wonder if she worried about dying and decided she didn't want to, and why. Was it us? Was it Daddy? Was it this place? We are closer to a town than we have been in a long time. Maybe it was like eating something sweet. Maybe she realized that something she was avoiding was really something she wanted. Maybe she decided it was the time to get her strength back, so she could be strong enough to fight to stay here. That's what I think. But then I worry she just left us, plain and simple. Left me. And I get mad again.

I think about Helen walking off to go to church, and it reminds me of my sister going to her room. Helen's not going to church to pray, but to hide. But Megan came out of her room and Helen will have to come home, and I—what? Something nags at me, like I am supposed to do something I have forgotten. Or stop doing something. I feel, like I do in church, that I almost have it, some answer. The sound of the milk splashing into the pan becomes a what? what? what? what? There doesn't seem to be an answer.

When I'm done, Megan follows me to the ditch, where we dump out the milk. As I turn with the bucket, I notice the red flag is up on the mailbox. The mail has come while we were in the barn.

There is a letter for my father. I tell myself I will not read it. I don't want to read it. I think these things as I tear it open just as if it were addressed to me. Megan doesn't protest. She lowers my hand so she can read it too.

Dear Stuart,

I miss you. I am very tired, more so than when I first came. I know the doctors must be giving you reports, so you know more about how I am doing than I do. They don't tell us anything. They treat us like little children. The frightening thing is that sometimes I enjoy it. I am so weary it feels good to be told to lie still. My cough has come back worse than ever. I have lost a few more pounds and my temperature stays high. I have heard the nurses say the medicine doesn't help me as it should. They act as if I have committed a crime and don't even allow me to get up to go to the bathroom. I am once again writing this letter on the sly. Don't tell the children I'm worse. I tell you only because you must plan on me being here the full six months at least—except there is talk of closing the place down and sending us all to different county sanitariums, or county hospitals. I would like to stay here. I am tired of moving about.

There is a bit of a community here, by which I mean the patients have formed social groups, with structures. Those here the longest are on the top of the ladder. It is much like New York. I even found myself jealous, actually wishing I had been here longer so I could be in that group. I thought I escaped all that when we left the city, but maybe I am still a city girl at heart. Maybe when I get out of here we might go back for a visit.

Some patients here have sex together. They call it cousining and they do it so boldly the staff must know. Personally, I can't imagine it, even with you.

Day and night I am grateful for just one thing. That you and the children didn't catch this. When I heard the diagnosis, I saw myself as something deadly to others, like a walking bomb. If you had caught this too—

My dreams are so strange. I dreamt I was riding on Edith. We were racing across a wide-open field. I could feel the breeze in my hair. Then suddenly, I was sitting on the porch at the house in Colorado, and the sky was so blue. There was something about bats flying in the daytime, and I was scared, and when I looked back at you, you were gone. Jane, the woman in the bed next to mine, who has given me this pen and paper, woke me up. I guess I was crying in my sleep. I have made friends here, although they

*baby me because I am so sick. One man got to go home
yesterday. It made me cry.*

*I had better stop writing. Jane will mail this for me. (I
am the only one at the moment who is not allowed out of
bed.) I miss you. I love you. Say hi to the children. It will
be a while before I can write again.*

Me

I refold the letter and put it back in the envelope. I wish I
hadn't read it. I wish Megan hadn't read it.

My mother isn't getting better there. She's getting worse. My
father should read this letter. Get her out of there. But he's in
New York City being honored for painting pictures of my sister
flying nude.

The phone rings two times, then stops. Robert must have
answered it. It will be the sanitarium saying my mother is dead.
She has given up. I shouldn't make Robert take this call. I go
inside. Megan follows.

Robert is explaining about the cow having TB. "And Tamara
says a vet is going to come here and . . . Okay. She's right here."
He hands the phone over to me. "It's Daddy." I roll my eyes. I
don't want to talk to him.

"What is Robert talking about?" my father asks without saying *Hello, how are you?* "The cow has tuberculosis?"

I tell him everything the doctor told me in as few words as I can.

"Well, that's just wonderful. A sick cow. She got TB from a
cow. What next?"

"Helen has to get tested and she's at church praying."

"What?" He sounds exasperated, as if all this were happening to him. "Well, I'll have to come home," he says.

"Why?" I ask.

"What do you mean, why? Because I should."

"We don't need you. The veterinarian doesn't need you. Mr.
Burns will come take care of the cow with the vet. We're staying

at the Murphys'. There are lots of other men here. We don't need an oil painter right now."

"Damn it, Tamara, give me a break."

"You're the one who always says to be practical. I am. You can stay there. We don't need you right now. Maybe later. Don't worry. We'll be fine."

"I'll be home tomorrow, Tamara. Tell Mr. Murphy that. You and I will have a little talk when I get there, about your attitude. I'll see you then."

"Fine, but you don't need to."

"Good-bye, Tamara."

I know when he says my name that many times I'm in big trouble, but I just don't care. I hang up, then remember the letter in my pocket. But he must know she's not getting better. He must.

Megan stands a foot away from me, watching me with big doe eyes. Her thumb is in her mouth. Robert is jammed into a corner of the room, sitting on the floor reading a comic. I want to crawl into my bed, stick my thumb in my mouth, and go to sleep.

"We're going swimming," I say.

Robert looks up. "Mommy says we have to have an adult with us."

"Do you see any around?"

He shakes his head no.

"You going to tell on me if we do?"

Another shake.

"Let's go get Rusty and Brenda," I say.

"I got to get my suit on."

"Who says you have to wear a suit?"

His mouth pops open. Thoughts cross his face like clouds in the sky, each a little different. He's thinking about being naked in the pond, which will scare him because he's already afraid of the fish. He's thinking I'll call him a sissy if he doesn't go skinny-dipping. He's thinking of seeing Brenda naked. The last thought is enough. "Okay." He stands up. I walk out of the house like the Pied Piper, innocent children in tow behind me.

Brenda's outside on the tire swing. I wave her across the road and tell her my plan and say we'll wait by the barn. She runs off to get Rusty. In a few minutes, we're all on the way to the pond, Kip tagging along, happy to be part of a group of kids. I wonder if he's forgotten Timothy yet. I wonder how long it takes to forget.

Brenda walks next to me. "I'll catch hell if my dad finds out we snuck out to go skinny-dipping."

"Scared?" I ask.

Brenda laughs. "Nah. This'll be fun. Hey, Rusty'll see you naked. Did you think about that?"

I grin. "No, *completely* forgot. Oh, well."

"He has a crush on you," Brenda says.

Something flutters inside me. It's a giddy feeling. I grab Brenda's hand. "Let's run!" We hop over cow pies and shriek when we barely miss one. Kip barks at our heels. It's a warm day full of blue. It's a day to keep, so I try to store in my mind the feeling of holding Brenda's hand, of the way the air smells crisp, the sound of our voices, then I hear Rusty laughing behind me and I decide without a moment's hesitation that I will get pregnant with Rusty and never move again.

At the pond we take off our clothes, pretending it's no big deal. We stand with our backs to each other, yards and yards apart, each one of us trying to figure which piece of clothing to take off first, which last. Rusty tries whistling something, then stops. I turn my head and catch a glimpse of Rusty's white butt, just as he's stepping out of his underwear. He sees me looking and does a little hop and a skip on one foot, to keep from falling over. When I pull off my shirt, I can see Brenda's eyes widen. Brenda has breasts like small measuring cups, not even whole cups. Maybe the one-half-cup size that I use to measure milk into pancakes. I like her breasts more than mine. They look like they don't get in the way.

Megan's the only one who really doesn't care about getting undressed. She's also the first one in the pond.

"Ohhhh! It's muddy between my toes. And it's really warm." It's only up to her waist. She plops into the water and splashes around. Rusty's trying real hard not to look at me, but he can't help it. He's a shade of hot pink, a blush from head to toe. His penis starts to lengthen and he runs into the water and out to the deep end, where it's just over his head. "It is really warm," he says. "Jesus, Brenda, you're skinny as a pole."

"Fuck you, Rusty." She goes in the water, walking in slowly. "Ugh! I don't remember it being so slimy." She runs and belly-slams in the water as soon as it's deep enough.

I take my time walking through the water to the deep end, even though I hate the soft muddy bottom of the pond. There are little baby leeches in here. I got some last time, in between my toes. They rub right off.

Robert's the last one in, which means he has to stand there naked, out of the water, while we tease him. His penis is a tiny thing, all shriveled up. Finally he gets in, and once he does, he loves it.

Kip sits by the edge of the pond, watching us carefully. He has a sense of responsibility. He's already lost one boy.

Brenda, Rusty, and I have races across the deep end. More than once I feel Rusty touch me under the water. Brenda wins every race. She has the body of an eel. And Rusty and I are a bit distracted. Robert can only do the doggy paddle and tread water. Megan has decided to cover herself in mud, and brings up hand-fuls of the stuff. I don't want to spoil it by mentioning the leeches, so I don't.

We see who can do a dead man's float the longest, and I win. Brenda helps Megan learn the doggy paddle, and soon Megan's out in the deep end with us all shouting to her to swim to us. Finally she gets tired and goes back to covering herself with mud in the shallow end. The pond is a murk of stirred-up mud by now, and you can't see more than a few inches under the surface. Rusty gets bolder and fondles anything he can touch. Robert obviously tries to touch Brenda because she shouts, "Hey! Get your paws off me!" but then she laughs so hard she swallows water and chokes, and we all laugh, including Robert. We are doing another dead man's float contest when Mr. Murphy finds us.

Brenda pushes me and I roll over in the water to yell at her.

"Oh, shit," she says under her breath, looking up the hill. I look in the same direction and see her father limping at a fast pace down the hill toward us. Robert and Rusty are already looking that way. We all tread water, afraid to get out. On the edge of the shore, Megan is covered from neck to toes in mud, looking like a child pagan ready for some sacrilegious ritual.

"Get out," Mr. Murphy says from between clenched teeth, as soon as he's near enough to be heard.

The pond is very muddy now, the water opaque. I don't know if he knows we're skinny-dipping, although our clothes are spread out all over the ground. Megan's the only one whose body is showing, and you can't really tell with all the mud.

We swim to where it's too shallow to swim anymore, then on some instinct, all stand at the same time. Mr. Murphy's jaw goes limp, then he shakes his head sadly and turns his back to us. "Get dressed," he says very softly, but we all hear. It takes a while to put on our clothes, since we have nothing to dry off with. Megan's the last one dressed because she has to keep dunking under the water to rinse off the mud.

Back at the farm, Mr. Murphy tells Robert, Megan, and me to go to our house and stay there. Brenda and Rusty follow him across the road. None of us has said a word. Kip goes under the hydrangea bush with his tail between his legs. He is sure he has done something terrible. I hold the door open and call him inside.

We go upstairs and I fill up the bath for Megan. She has more than two dozen leeches covering her body, like tadpole tongues. She doesn't mind finding them. "Here's another one, Tamara," she says, pointing to a spot on the inside curve of her elbow. I take a fresh wad of toilet paper and pinch it off. From the direction of Robert's room, I hear my brother scream.

Around four o'clock I make tomato soup and grilled cheese sandwiches for a late lunch.

"Jeepers creepers," Robert says, "can't you cook anything else?" He's got a wad of grilled cheese in his mouth, so I ignore him. There's not a lot of food left in the refrigerator, but the pantry in the basement is still almost full. But no milk.

After we eat, Robert finishes the puzzle, except for the missing piece. It's actually a boring-looking puzzle, all those poppies broken up by the wavy puzzle lines. An attempt at bright beauty, but it fails.

"Kip ate it," I tell him. "Right when you started it. Sorry." It's not like I ate it or anything, but maybe I should have told him.

Robert sucks on his bottom lip, thinking. "It's a stupid puzzle anyway," he says. He picks it up by a corner and shakes it. It breaks into three pieces. As Megan, Robert, and I pull apart the pieces and toss them into the box, we hear someone knocking on the front door.

It's Mrs. Murphy.

"Hello," I say. I open the screen door but she won't come in. Her face looks kind of tight, and she's staring at me steadily in a way that makes me realize she's pretty mad right now. I guess she heard we went skinny-dipping.

"We're going to church this evening and want you to come along." The stiff way she says this makes it obvious she won't take no for an answer.

"Our good clothes aren't washed." As a matter of fact, not much is.

"Well, wear something else." This is said directly at my clothes, not my face. She raises her eyes and gives me a stern look that changes into one of sadness. This tar-paper-house woman pities me. Her look has its intended effect. I feel shame. But not because I went skinny-dipping or am wearing dirty clothes, but for something that has to do with my missing parents, as if I personally have chased them away.

"Be ready by six please." She turns and walks away.

I tell my brother and sister what we have to do.

"It's Tuesday!" Robert says.

"I guess it's open anyway," I say.

"But why?"

I shrug. "Because we did something wrong, so we gotta ask God for forgiveness. Mrs. Murphy looked pretty mad."

"I don't want to go," Robert says.

This surprises me, because he's always liked church. Well, at least for the last few months. But we really don't have a choice, and by five minutes to six we are ready and standing in our driveway. All the Murphys come out of their house and get into the car, then they drive across the road and we climb in. No one says a word. Rusty doesn't even look me in the eye, but Brenda does. She winks at me when her parents aren't looking. I wink back.

There aren't many people in church on a Tuesday evening, just a few old ladies, and Helen in the front row, who glances back at us with red-rimmed eyes, frowns at me, and lowers her head again. There is no minister, no organ music, no singing. We are to sit and pray all on our own. But I can't.

It has been one long day. I just want to curl up and fall asleep. I close my eyes and I realize I am talking to my mother. I tell her I'm sorry I read the letters, that I get so mad at Daddy, and that I am mean to Robert and Megan sometimes. But when I try to apologize about swimming naked in the pond, she says I didn't do anything wrong. Actually, she says that *skinny-dipping* wasn't wrong, but we should have asked an adult to go along. I can't help grinning, even in church. It is nice to know she is still the same.

After we sit for a half hour, Mrs. Murphy stands, so we all do. But instead of leaving, she walks over to Helen and the two of them whisper while we all stand in the aisle. Finally, Mrs. Murphy kisses Helen on the forehead. We leave. Helen stays. Mrs. Murphy tells Mr. Murphy she will come back for Helen later.

No one talks during dinner. Mr. and Mrs. Murphy look at each other from across the table, and I can tell she's mad and she wants him to know it, and he knows it and wants her to know he knows it, but appreciates her not bringing it up while he eats. Every time Rusty looks at me he blushes, so he mostly looks at his plate. Brenda kicks me under the table at least a dozen times but I'm too nervous to kick her back. Robert rolls his eyes at me once, and I can't believe he did that. Megan just eats as if this whole silent movie is perfectly normal. When she asks what's for dessert, Mrs. Murphy actually flinches, at which Brenda kicks me again. Mrs. Murphy says there will be nothing for dessert tonight, and that after cleaning up we are all to go right to bed. It's still light outside, but I'm sure not going to argue with her.

Mrs. Murphy washes the dishes, but this time she bangs some of the pots.

When we go upstairs, Brenda closes her bedroom door and shows Megan and me the bruise forming on her butt. "Did you guys hear me screaming?" she asks.

"No," I tell her. "I'm sorry I got you in trouble."

"Shit, I'd do it again anytime," she says. "It was a lot of fun. Your brother tried to feel me up! Under the water! Can you fucking believe it?"

I can't. I laugh so hard I have to hold a pillow over my mouth.

Megan, Brenda, and I go through her magazines, until Mrs. Murphy comes in and makes us say our prayers. Kneeling at the side of Brenda's bed I close my eyes, bow my head, and remember Rusty's hand groping for my crotch under the warm muddy water of the pond.

Thirteen

In my dream I am on the roof, naked, arms spread out, ready to fly. The ground seems so far away. *Jump,* I think. A phone rings and rings again. I hear someone yell, "Your mother is dead." I wake up with a jerk. The phone is ringing. I hear footsteps on the stairs and then the murmur of a voice. Outside Brenda's window, the world is awash in white, an early morning fog as opaque as milk.

In my nightgown, I creep out of Brenda's room. Mrs. Murphy stands at the bottom of the steps holding a cup of coffee. "That was your father," she says with a trace of frustration in her voice. "He won't be coming back today. He says he'll fly in tomorrow."

I shrug. "I'm going home for a while."

Mrs. Murphy nods. She doesn't tell me to get dressed first. She isn't going to play mom. She isn't going to worry about our physical bodies, only our souls, and I'm betting she's just going through the motions. I don't think she has much hope for us.

Outside is the thickest fog I've ever seen. I can see only a few feet in front of me. If I stand in the middle of the road, my house is invisible. I stop and look behind me. The Murphys' house is gone. I turn in a circle. There is only me in this world, collecting dewdrops on my skin. There are no colors. No reds or greens or yellows, no indigos, emeralds, or ultramarines. No blacks. Only me. I walk up and down the road. As I move, the world moves with me. What I have just left is gone. If a car came I wouldn't see it until it was too late. But it is hard to believe in what you can't see. I feel both invincible and lonely, like Superman on an empty planet. I turn around and go back to the Murphys'.

"I forgot something," I say to Mrs. Murphy, and head upstairs. Megan is lying on her back, sleeping with her mouth open. I could drop a spider in there, but it's just a thought that passes. Brenda is curled up around her pillow. She seems kind of young, I think. Or I feel older.

I sit on the end of Megan's bed and watch her sleep.

A while later when Megan wakes up I whisper in her ear, "Let's free Edith."

Megan grins and says, "Okay." I thought she might argue with me, since Edith made our mother sick, but she understands. This is for our mother.

As Megan and I get dressed, Brenda wakes up. I tell her my plan. "After breakfast we'll say we're going to our house, then you and Rusty sneak out and meet us behind the barn."

She's all for it. She combs her hair with her fingers and throws on a pair of shorts. "I'm ready! Let's go eat!" Then she goes in Rusty's room and there's a lot of whispering.

Mrs. Murphy is dressed to go to work and has left us bowls for cereal on the table. Helen is dressed too. She doesn't say a word, just goes out to the car. "Be *good*," Mrs. Murphy says. It's not the kind of *Be good* my mother would say. There is an emphasis on the word *good* that makes it sound Godly. Mrs. Murphy is good at that. We all nod solemnly. We are good at *that*. Especially Brenda.

As Mrs. Murphy leaves, Mr. Murphy comes downstairs, holding on to the banister and kind of hopping down the steps.

"Good morning," he says. "Good morning," we chirp brightly. We say grace and eat quickly.

"We're going to go over to our house to clean it," I say to Mr. Murphy.

"All right," Mr. Murphy says.

"Hey, Brenda," Rusty says. "Want to see my fort?"

"Really?" Brenda says, her eyes lighting up. "Really?" I can tell she thinks this is for real. "Sure!"

I kick her under the table. I bet a lot of talking gets done this way.

"Well, see you later, Brenda," I say. "Thanks for breakfast, Mr. Murphy." We each carry our bowls to the sink and rinse them off before we go.

The fog has lifted, but everything is damp. The leaves drip, as if it's raining under the trees. We go in the house, down to the basement, and out the basement door. We run from the house to behind the barn like escaping convicts, one at a time. Brenda and Rusty show up about ten minutes later, coming across the street from a ways down the road so their dad can't see them. When they get close, I can hear Brenda and Rusty arguing.

"You can't do this," Rusty says.

"Screw you," Brenda says.

"We shouldn't," Rusty says.

Now Robert joins in. "Yeah, Rusty's right." He'd agree with anything Rusty says. I almost hit him.

"The vet's coming today, Tamara," Rusty says.

"Exactly," I say.

"I don't get it," Rusty says. "Why don't you want the vet to test the cow?"

"Because if Edith's sick, he'll kill her, stupid," I say.

"But if she's sick, isn't she gonna die anyway?"

"Maybe," I say. "But the vet will kill her for sure."

Rusty shrugs. "Why don't you wait to see what happens. Maybe she's not sick. The vet's not going to pull out a gun and shoot her right away. He's got to do the test first, then come back. You can do something then, if you still want."

"I have to do it now." And I do. I have to *do* something. My hand's too sore to hit another wall. This sounds more fun anyway.

Rusty scratches his chin and wrinkles his nose. A thought comes to him, you can see him discover it just as if he stepped on something sharp. "You can't let her loose, Tamara. If she wanders off and doesn't get milked, she'll get sick."

"We'll go get her after he leaves."

"She might get really lost," Rusty says.

"We could tie a rope around her neck, and tie her to a tree," I say.

"She'd bellow. The vet would hear her."

"We'll get in trouble," Robert adds.

"I don't care," I say.

"Me, neither," Megan says.

"Hell, let's do it," Brenda says. "You guys are damn sissies."

"Am not," Robert says.

"Am too," Brenda says. "So there. We just got to cut the fence and walk her into the woods a bit. Come on!" She goes into the back of the barn and comes out with an ax. "I can't find no cutters. This'll do."

As we head up the hill I look at the bull that nearly killed me. He's watching us with those red beady eyes. I bet if the vet has to test him, he'll have to shoot him first.

Edith's up on the first rise of the hill, eating clover. She's far from a fence. She raises her head and looks at us, still chewing. She's not thrilled to see us.

"I'll go cut up the fence and then you guys chase her through the open part." Brenda goes over to the fence, about a hundred yards away, and starts smacking at where the barbed wire is attached to a post. We surround Edith so she doesn't go the wrong way.

"Okay!" Brenda hollers. With a final chop, the barbed wire springs loose from the post. She hauls it to the side. "Make her run this way!"

"Jeepers creepers," Robert says.

"Okay, get on this side." I tell Rusty, Robert, and Megan to come around to where I am. Rusty and Robert come, but not too quickly.

"Okay! Go!"

Megan claps her hands and hollers, a whooping sound I never knew she could make. She jumps up and down, then waves her arms and charges toward Edith. Megan looks like an insane monkey. Edith twitches, her eyes widening. She looks like she might have a heart attack. She starts to stumble about, not in one direction but all over, one way, then another, then in a circle, then stops, then starts. Brenda calls, "Here, cow, here, cow," from her place by the fence.

"Get away from the fence!" I yell at Brenda. "You're scaring her." Brenda can't hear me because of the noise my sister's making. Robert and Rusty aren't doing anything much but staying where they are, which helps just because Edith doesn't run their way. But it's a big field, and there are a lot of other places to run.

Megan and I get as close to Edith as we can, which isn't too close, since Edith looks really panicked now and skittish. Her back feet stomp the earth. Her heavy head ducks down and jerks back up, turning back and forth, trying to see all of us at once. Brenda can tell we need help, so she circles around from her spot and joins us. We're waving our arms and yelling "Shoo. Shoo, cow, shoo!" Edith stops dead in her tracks, her eyes bulging, raises her tail, and craps.

We all laugh, except for Megan, who keeps up the whooping sound as if once her voice got out, it never wants to go back inside again. Rusty falls on the grass and slaps it with his hand, and Robert does the same, just to be like Rusty. Brenda hugs me, laughing on my shoulder, tears coming out of her eyes.

When we finally get ourselves under control, we see Edith has headed over to the hole in the fence. She's just a few yards away.

"Come on!" I yell. We all charge at Edith, shouting and clapping and waving our arms, and she takes off through the hole in the fence like a bullet, right into a dense patch of an old apple orchard. By the time we get to the fence, we can't see her anymore. But at that moment, we hear the blaring of a car horn.

"Damn," my sister says. We look at her in amazement.

"We better go," I say.

As we come around the side of the barn we see the Burns waiting by their car.

"Well, hello, the lot of you," Mr. Burns says. "You all out here to greet me, huh? Hey, where's the old man?" I think he means my father, but right away Mr. Burns slaps his thigh and whistles. "Here, Kip, here, boy. Come on over here, you old bum." Kip runs up to Mr. Burns, wagging his tail. Mr. Burns leans over as far as his belly will allow and scratches Kip's head. "You okay, boy?" he asks the dog. There is worry in his voice.

"You look okay. Yeah, you do." He nods to himself, as if he's trying hard to believe something, then he straightens up and looks at me. "I hear this vet thinks we might have a sick cow. He's meeting me here now, to give her some test. We'll see about this. I don't think that cow is sick at all. Never made us sick a day in our lives. They're all healthy, the cattle too, you'll see. Not one day were we sick. And you look healthy as beavers to me." He's trying to convince us, to convince himself.

From behind, Mrs. Burns puts her hand on Mr. Burns' shoulder and gives a squeeze. "Everything will be fine, Sam." She smiles at us all, the smile a bit weary, a bit of a show.

"You won't let him kill Edith, will you?" Megan asks, stepping forward.

Mr. Burns blinks. "Who?"

"The cow," I explain.

"Why, no, sweetheart, nobody wants to kill her. And I don't believe anybody's gonna want to either. But it's very nice of you to be concerned."

Mr. Murphy comes out of his house carrying his mug, and limps across the road. He nods at Mr. Burns and extends his thin hand. "Hello, Sam. Hi ya, Emily." Then he looks at us. "Hello. Something going on here?"

"Nothing," Brenda says.

Mr. Murphy tilts his head to the side, as if he's trying to see around us, see if we're hiding something behind our backs. He knows something's up. He rubs at his lips. "Uh-huh. Better not be."

"I'm meeting the vet here now," Mr. Burns says. "Your dad here?" he asks me.

"He's out of town," I say.

"Oh, yeah," Mr. Burns says. "The vet said he was gone. Gone a while, is he?"

I shrug. Who knows when he's coming home. Who cares?

"Well. Let's go look at the cow, shall we?" Mr. Burns says.

We all look at each other. I think Mr. Murphy catches our looks, but we are saved, momentarily, because the vet drives up.

The vet gets out of a mud-covered blue car, unfolding like a fan. He presses his hands to his lower back and bends backwards and forwards, letting loose a light groan. Then he stretches his hands up above his head and yawns. "Oh my," he says. "That was a long drive. Hello, everybody."

I'm completely speechless. He is as tall as my father and gorgeous. He's probably almost thirty, with jet-black hair, a square jaw, white teeth, and dark smoldering eyes right out of the movies. He's got on a white shirt and new blue jeans. "I'm Dr. Ostrum." He reaches out to shake Mr. Murphy's hand, since he is the nearest adult.

"I'm Mr. Murphy, sir. Just the neighbor. Mr. Burns owns this land."

Mr. Burns introduces himself and his wife, and all the adults shake hands. Then Dr. Ostrum looks at us kids.

"And who is Tamara?" he asks.

"I am."

He shakes my hand. "Glad to meet you. Sorry to scare you on the phone."

"You didn't scare me," I say. "But you sure scared Helen."

"Helen's the girl who milked the cow most recently? I should talk to her."

"She's my daughter," Mr. Murphy says, his tone both belligerent and apologetic. "She got that TB test yesterday. She goes back on Friday."

"Good. Do you mind if I call and see how that turns out?"

"No. That'd be fine. I better be getting back." Mr. Murphy looks over at his house as if it were calling him. "Good luck with the cattle, Sam. Good day, Emily. Why don't you kids come with me, get out of the doctor's way."

"Oh, they'll be no trouble," Dr. Ostrum says. "If they want to watch, it's fine with me."

I'm torn between wanting to leave before they find Edith is gone and staying near Dr. Ostrum. But I don't have to make the choice because Mr. Murphy does. "If they're any trouble, send them home," he says, then turns and walks back across the road. He must know this is the most interesting thing that's happened since Timothy died.

"So, where's the milk cow?" Dr. Ostrum asks, leaning in through the open window of his car to pull out a black doctor's bag.

Mr. Burns looks at me, and I shrug.

"Must be up in the pasture," he says. He walks over to the fence and opens the gate.

"Well, let's go get her," Dr. Ostrum says to me. Then he winks. He winks right at me. The wink almost makes me forget the hole in the fence.

With Mr. Burns in the lead, and Mrs. Burns at the tail end, we walk through the field, watching our steps. I'm embarrassed by the cow-manure piles, as if I had forgotten to pick up my dirty clothes. I want Dr. Ostrum to like this place because I do, and I know if I see him frown or shake his head in disgust, I will like this place a little less. Liking it is so new it's a fragile feeling that could be ruined by the disdain of a handsome man who winked at me. I want to point out the patch of wild foxglove along the edge of poplars, or tell him about the pileated wood-pecker. The woodpecker would be the best thing to mention I think, because he works with animals, but maybe they're not as rare as my mother says they are. Maybe it would be like point-ing out a crow to this man.

"So, Tamara," he says, turning his head toward me and grin-ning with his shining white teeth, "you have an unusual name. How did you get to be named Tamara?"

"My great-grandmother's name. I'm named after her." I wish desperately I had an interesting story about my name, but for the life of me I can't even think of one to invent.

"It must be tough, having your mom gone, huh?" He looks at me again, his eyes opening with the question, like he's really expecting an answer from me.

"Yeah, I guess." It's only the stupidest answer I could have come up with and I want to take it back. I'm watching him and not looking where I'm going. I step right in the middle of a cow pie.

He has to see me turn bright red, but he acts like nothing happened. "Tell the truth, we haven't seen people infected with bovine tuberculosis for a while," he says. "Oh, there she is. What happened to the fence?"

We're over the ridge. The stupid cow is standing *this* side of the hole in the fence, eating grass.

Mr. Burns stops, scratching his bald head. "What the heck happened to that fence? Looks like it's been torn down."

"I have a good idea," Mrs. Burns says.

He looks at her. "Huh?"

She looks at us.

"Really?" he says, the wrinkles on his forehead getting deeper, just like my dad's when he gets mad. "You kids did that?"

Rusty nods, and says, "Yes, sir." The rest of us just look down at the ground.

"You're damn lucky that cow's too stupid to run off," Mr. Burns says, shaking his head. "Rusty and Robert, you two are gonna help me fix that fence as soon as the doctor's gone. Am I right?"

"Yes, sir," they both say.

Mr. Burns turns away, dismissing us. "Now listen here, Doctor, I don't think that cow is sick. I said it before and I'll say it again, Mrs. Burns and I never got sick from that cow. I think this is all a big mistake."

"Maybe so, Mr. Burns. But it's my job to check things out. A man has to do his job."

"Well, sure. But I'm betting she's fine."

"I'm hoping you're right," the vet says. "Now maybe we should lead her down to the barn so we can contain her while I give her the test."

"All right. You kids stay back here now." Mr. Burns has brought a rope along. He and the vet walk over to Edith.

"Hey, hey, hey," Mr. Burns says. "Come here, sweetie." She doesn't run away, and Mr. Burns slips the rope around her neck. Then she gets scared and tries to pull away, but the rope is tight. Mr. Burns talks to Edith, rubbing her neck. She calms down and follows him reluctantly back to the barn.

"Stupid cow," Brenda says. I can tell she wishes the cow were gone, not because Edith wouldn't have to get the test but because it would have been much more fun, real entertainment. She probably doesn't even care she'd be grounded or worse.

Megan takes my hand as we walk down the hill.

Back at the barn Mr. Burns ties the rope to the barn post. Dr. Ostrum puts his bag down on a hay bale and opens it up. He pulls out something that kind of looks like a fat syringe.

"Now, this is called an intradermal test," he explains, in a tone that reminds me of my mother. She would have loved this, this kind of hands-on experience. "The fold of skin under the tail is where I'm first going to inject her. Then I'm going to give her another injection into the lip of the vulva."

I bet I'm the only one in the room who knows what *vulva* means. I try not to blush, but my face gets hot. "The trick is not getting kicked in the process," the vet says with a wink. "Want to help me out here, Mr. Burns?"

"Sure thing."

Dr. Ostrum tells Mr. Burns where to stand and how to hold a leg in place, then bends over and lifts the cow's tail. Mrs. Burns has her hands on Edith's head and says shhh, shhh, shhh as if calming a baby. We kids are all crowded around the vet, trying to see what he's doing.

"I need some light here, guys, you got to move back please." We do. He messes around down there in the private parts of the cow, who is not happy about it at all, bending and turning her head and mooing low guttural sounds. Then he's done and stands up. He goes over to his black bag and puts the syringe thing away.

"I'm going to give her a checkup too. Just give her a little looking over." He comes back and asks Mr. Burns to hold the cow's neck for him, then the vet opens Edith's mouth and shines in a flashlight. "Say ahhh." The cow moos and everyone starts laughing. A sparrow flutters around in the top of the barn, upset with all the commotion, then flies out the open door.

The vet rubs the cow all over, feeling for something. Then he checks her ears, which really makes her tail swish. Finally he listens to her lungs with a stethoscope. "Seems fine to me," he says. "I'll test the remaining cattle after I see how this turns out. I'll be back in three days to check on the injection sites. I'll be able to tell you more then. Can you meet me here, say ten?" He's talking to Mr. Burns, who agrees, mentioning once again he bets the cow is just fine and this is a waste of time.

The vet shakes Mr. Burns' hand and nods to Mrs. Burns. "Thanks for your help, kids," he says to us. I watch him from the barn door as he bends down and gets into his car. I wave good-bye, but he's already backing out. Just by being here, Dr. Ostrum made me feel more exciting, and now I'm not.

Fourteen

Thursday morning my father calls again with another excuse. Megan and Robert and I don't even blink when Mr. Murphy gives us the news, but I suppose our disappointment shows because Mr. Murphy asks us if we are all right. Mrs. Murphy doesn't say a thing, but she opens the refrigerator and shakes her head. From out of her big square uniform pocket she takes a sheet of paper and writes down a few words. I think about the loose change in my father's drawer. It's probably not more than a few dollars, but I'll bring it over and leave it on her kitchen counter. I'll ask Robert if he has any money. He eats the most.

When Mrs. Murphy leaves for work, Helen goes into town with her so she can spend the whole day praying at church again. It's humid and the air is so thick it sticks to our skins like cotton candy. I don't dare suggest we go to the pond. We sit around the Murphys' reading comics and listening to the radio. I fall asleep in a chair and wake up with my neck bent permanently to the right. Since Helen isn't here, Brenda has to cook dinner. I show her how to make the green bean casserole, and we also make a meat loaf. Brenda pats the meat loaf into a huge cone with a point on top. She says it's my boob. She says Rusty doesn't like meat loaf, but she bets he'll eat plenty this time. I flatten it with a quick smack and tell her now it's *her* chest. She tells me to fuck off and walks out of the kitchen. I form the meat loaf into a perfect oblong shape and draw lines across it with ketchup. Brenda won't speak to me all night. It's so quiet, I can hear my brother swallow.

Friday my father doesn't even call. Mrs. Murphy decides Rusty and Brenda should get tuberculosis tests when she takes Helen in to have her test read today. Helen stares at her arm all through breakfast. Doesn't she realize if God is going to save anyone, it'll be her? How much holier do you have to be?

It's a gray day, like there's a lid on the sky, a solid sheet of unpolished tin. Robert, Megan, and I go over to our house and I bring my record player downstairs. We listen to music and read comics we've already read a dozen times.

Around one o'clock, Mr. Murphy decides to check in on us. He knocks tentatively on the door and asks if he can come in. I can see him take a deep breath before entering, and then hold it as long as he can, which is pretty long. He's got a cup of coffee in one hand. His other hand is shoved in his pocket.

"Mind if I sit down?" he asks.

"Sure," I say, surprised and wary.

He sits in the floral chair, directly facing the nude painting of my mother. He can't help seeing it. I can tell exactly when he realizes it's my mother. He flushes just like Rusty, and shifts his position so he's not facing the picture, even though that means he's at a funny angle in the big stuffed chair, half in, half out, with his bad leg sticking straight out. Robert and Megan are both on the couch with comics in their laps, not reading because they are now too nervous. I sit in one of the high-backed wooden dining room chairs, which stays in the living room by the staircase.

"Just felt an adult should be here," Mr. Murphy says, obviously as uncomfortable as we are. "I told your dad I was watching over you, so . . ." His cheek twitches and he looks around the room. I think he's trying to see if there are any more strange things he might not want to look at.

"So, you travel a lot, huh?" he asks.

"Yes," I say. "We do."

He asks where we've lived. I recite the list.

"Boy," he says. "I've seen so little of this country. You're very lucky. Where's your favorite place?"

"Diamond, Georgia," Robert says. "We lived there last year and I had a friend named Benny who had a BB gun. He let me use it."

"Mom said you couldn't," Megan says.

"I did, though. A lot of times," Robert says.

"You like guns?" Mr. Murphy asks Robert.

Robert nods, looking quite serious, as if he's been around a whole lot of guns. "Sure do," he says.

"I have a few," Mr. Murphy says. "I hunt deer in the fall. We eat venison all winter. I'll show you how to hunt, if your dad says you can. Rusty's got a rifle might suit you."

Robert stares at Mr. Murphy like the man just blew up. His jaw drops open. He can't even talk. Robert looks so goofy Mr. Murphy starts to laugh. "Oh boy, look at you, you look like a rabbit caught in the headlights. Well, at least I know you can hold still and be quiet." He laughs some more.

"You shouldn't kill deer," Megan says.

"I know how you feel, child. Helen used to say the same thing. But it's God's way. We do what we need to survive, and He has provided much bounty for us in these woods. You eat chicken, don't you?"

"Sometimes," Megan says. She makes it sound like she's forced to eat chicken.

"Well, you should see those creatures run about with their heads cut off when they get killed. It'd put you off chicken I bet.

But we got to eat, so we have strength to do the Lord's work, and bring people into the arms of Jesus. So, you want to learn to hunt, Robert?"

"Yes, sir."

"We'll ask your dad."

Robert, Megan, and I are all quiet for a minute, trying to figure out what our father would say. He believes in the survival of the fittest, so I guess he'd agree, although I think he hates guns, so I wouldn't want to make a bet on it. I would bet, though, that Robert's got his fingers crossed so tight they hurt. You can see it in his eyes. All of a sudden he thinks Mr. Murphy is the greatest person in the world.

"Did you ever kill anyone in the war?" Robert asks, leaning forward on the couch, his comic falling to the floor. "Rusty told me you were in the war."

"No, I didn't kill anyone. But I tried, and I'll tell you, sometimes that bothers me. That I was trying to kill somebody I didn't know from Adam. We did the right thing, going over there, I know that, but me killing someone would have been a terrible burden. I got shot though."

"Where?" Megan and Robert ask.

Mr. Murphy puts his hands together like he's going to pray, then snaps his wrists so his fingers weave together, and all his knuckles pop. "I can't really show you. It's my left knee, got shattered to pieces. I'd have to take my pants off to show you. I think we've had enough people taking off their clothes for a while." He says this dead serious and we tense, ready for a stern lecture, but instead he bursts out in laughter. Megan and I share a look of total shock.

"Now, mind you, it was wrong what you did, and you should never do it again. I shouldn't be laughing." His eyes flicker to the picture of my mother. "Let's change the subject. What was your favorite place to live, Megan?"

"I liked Diamond best too," she says. "I liked the way people talked. And the trees had flowers."

"Sounds pretty. I'd like to see that someday. Mrs. Murphy and I are trying to save up for one of those trailers you can drive around in. Someday we'll drive all over the country, just like you." He relaxes against the back of the chair with a sigh, but he very carefully keeps his eyes lower than the picture. "And you, Tamara, what place did you like best?"

I'm thinking about Megan's and Robert's answer. I think they picked the last place we lived because it's the easiest to remember. But I never look back. "Here," I say.

"That's my girl." He grins at me, a warm and happy grin, like he's so proud of me, like he really likes me. I can't help smiling back.

The phone rings. I don't want to answer it, because I know it's my dad and I'm never going to talk to him again. He's mean and selfish and I hate him. He can stay in New York City forever. We'll live off venison, pickles, and canned tomatoes. It rings again. Robert doesn't seem to be able to move. His eyes are still glassy with the picture of him holding a gun. It rings again. Megan gets it.

"Hello. Oh hi, Daddy. Yeah, it's me. Yeah, I'm okay. I don't know, I just did. Yeah, I love you too. Uh-huh. We're talking to Mr. Murphy. Oh, okay. Just a minute." She holds out the phone to Mr. Murphy. "He wants to talk to you."

Mr. Murphy pushes himself up out of the chair and takes the phone, clearing his throat before he speaks. "Hello," he says. "Uh-huh. Uh-huh. No. No. You don't owe us nothing. It's been no problem at all. Oh, really? Well, that's nice. Sure, I'll get her."

"He wants to talk to you." He holds out the phone to me.

I shake my head no.

"Come on now. He has something to tell you."

I don't want to hear anything he has to say, but I take the phone anyway. "Yeah?"

"I'll be there at eleven-thirty tomorrow morning and I want you to have everyone ready. We're going to visit your mom."

I close my eyes against the sudden hot feeling inside them.

"Will you be ready, Tamara?" my father asks.

"Yes."

"See you then. Good-bye, honey."

"Good-bye." I want to say thank you, but I don't. I'm still too close to the moment when I hated him.

A few hours after Mr. Murphy leaves, Rusty and Brenda come over. They just open the door and walk in.

"We're okay," Brenda says. "We don't have TB. Mom made them do the test where they draw our blood and take pictures of our chest. That's what took so long. The lady that drew Helen's blood missed and had to stick the needle in twice and she's got this huge bruise now. Boy, is she pissed. But the X-ray tests were, were—shit, what's the word?"

"Negative," I say.

"Yeah, yeah, we don't got nothing wrong with us," Brenda says. "Did the vet come back? Is the cow sick?"

"Your dad's gonna let me use your rifle," Robert tells Rusty. "He's going to take me hunting."

"The vet didn't come back," I say. "So, is Helen still mad at us?"

"Oh, she's mad," Brenda says, picking up a comic book. "Wow! My mom won't let us read these! Cool!" She sits right on the floor to read it.

"Your dad really said that, Rusty, about the gun. He really did. Do you think he means it?" Robert says.

"Sure he does. My dad doesn't lie."

"When can we go?"

"In the fall. You have to wait for hunting season. But I bet he'll teach you to shoot at a target first." Rusty picks up a comic. "Boy! Look at all that blood!" I know for a fact he's looking at the girl's boobs, which are covered with just an inch of torn shirt.

"Hoo boy, I can't wait!" Robert says.

"Me neither," Rusty says, but he's not thinking about hunting.

Brenda and Rusty don't say anything else. They're too busy drooling over the comics. Robert and Megan join them. I'm suddenly disgusted with their fascination with blood and boobs. I go get an encyclopedia. M. I want to find some interesting facts to tell my mother tomorrow. There are no eggs to make cookies.

I open it up to the middle. Medicine. No. I skip forward. Michigan. No. I had to study Michigan last year. Molière. Okay. He wrote plays. He was the son of an upholsterer. *Tartuffe* was a satire on religious hypocrisy. She'll like this. He died of tuberculosis. I close the encyclopedia and pick up *Tomb of Terror*.

That night after dinner at the Murphys', Helen asks for a ride back to church. She wants to pray to God and ask Him how she can serve Him best after He saved her from tuberculosis. That's exactly how she says it. Saved her. As if she had it and He cured her. I know if my mother were here she would love to debate this with Helen. I guess *debate* isn't the right word.

It's not that Helen believes in God that bothers me, it's that she doesn't believe in herself, that she *was* healthy, that she can exist between prayers.

And there is the thought that if God did save Helen, then He could be making my mother sick. And then what about me? Would He let me get hit by a truck? What do I have to do to get His attention so He can save me too?

After Mrs. Murphy and Helen leave, Rusty motions me to follow him and we go out behind the tree with the swing and make out for so long I forget about everything. My father, my mother, the cow, Helen, even God. I am just lips and skin and tingles and warmth. This is my heaven, I think. It's not lust. It's probably not even love. But this touching, hugging, kissing, nuzzling, being-wanted stuff is great. When Rusty's father calls us to come in, it's like waking up. I look around at the dusky sky, the stars beginning to appear, the twinkle of fireflies, our farmhouse across the road, and I think, Oh, I'm *here*.

And it's like being hit, but at the moment it doesn't hurt. I want more than anything to *stay here*. It's an actual thought. I know what I'm thinking. I know what I want. Not to *not move*, but to *stay here*.

I want to graduate from high school here, sleep in Timothy's bedroom until it becomes mine, swim in the pond next summer and the next until the fish know me as well as I know the paths through the woods and the names of all the birds. I want to live across the road from the people in the tar-paper house, play around with Brenda, question Helen, and kiss Rusty every night. I want this and nothing more.

I wake in the morning just before light. The bright, anxious sounds of birds announcing the new day come through the open window and I think they are calling to me. I go downstairs. No one else is up. I go outside. The air is so crisp it's like washing my face with cold water; I am more completely awake right now than I can ever remember being. Last night I fell asleep quickly, into a place beyond sleep, deep and silent, the place I imagine caterpillars go to turn into butterflies. Now I feel as if I am a step beyond awake. Everything seems fragile and perfectly solid at the same time. I know this is a contradiction, but that's okay. I feel I have accepted something, and I look at my hands, half expecting to see a new thing, a spectacular thing, resting in the palms of my hands. They are empty. They are mine to fill.

Anything is possible. Maybe everything.

I laugh, because there is too much inside me. A crow caws out a series of sharp warning cries, and from the corner of the garden a chipmunk bolts out and crosses the lawn. The sky is crimson in the east, a pale blue-gray above, with hazy strokes of purples and pink clouds that blend into each other like water paints. I look at the sky until my neck hurts, thinking of my father, how frustrating it must be to paint things that are real. I understand how he must disdain abstract painters, how he must feel superior, how he will never be satisfied.

I am going to see my mother. I want to hug her and I want to yell at her. Just like I can't wait for my father to come home so I can kick him in the shins.

I walk across the road and go inside the house to get our good clothes off the basement line, then take them outside to dry in the morning sun.

A few minutes before ten, the Burns drive up and get out of their car. We are upstairs getting dressed. I look out the bedroom window at them as they stand around in their own front yard like visitors, too timid to knock on their own front door. They look awkward. Mrs. Burns adjusts something on Mr. Burns' shirt, and pulls at the strap of his overalls. He says something and she shakes her head, then pats him on the shoulder.

I go to my sister's bedroom and ask if she needs any help. She does. I fasten the fake pearl necklace she wants to wear. I don't say a thing about it being too dressy for a sanitarium, nor do I mention the ratty alligator suitcase she has packed that lies on the bed.

Megan and I go to Robert's room and ask him if he's ready. He has on his good clothes too: a white shirt and beige pants. I'm wearing a red skirt, white blouse, and my patent-leather shoes.

We come down the steps together, shiny and polished, Megan carrying her suitcase. When we come outside, Mr. Murphy is talking to the Burns. They stop talking and look at us as if we just sprouted wings.

"Well, I'll be, look at you all," Mr. Burns says. "You going to a wedding or is this all for the doc?"

It's only then I remember the veterinarian is coming this morning. He's going to think us crazy, dressing up like this. But I'm glad he'll see us at our best.

"My dad is coming," I say. "We're going to visit my mother."

"That's good," Mrs. Burns says. "And you look very nice. You tell her we said hello. Tell her the garden looks lovely, she'd be proud."

"I will."

Now another car rumbles up the drive. Dr. Ostrum. He gets out of the car holding a large black flashlight. "Hello," he says. He's just as handsome as I remembered. Mr. Burns says hello back, but his voice is soft, almost weak, and it's obvious he's worried. It's very quiet for a minute. Awkward. What breaks the silence is Rusty and Brenda running across the road.

"Is the cow sick?" Brenda yells. "Is he gonna kill her?"

"Did we miss anything?" Rusty asks.

"No, you're right on time," Dr. Ostrum says. "It's okay I go check her out now?" he asks Mr. Burns. Mr. Burns nods. Dr. Ostrum walks into the barn and we all follow, even Mr. Murphy.

I hear Mrs. Burns say, "Now, now," to something Mr. Burns must have said. I'm nervous myself.

I'm glad when we find Edith's still in the barn. We would have looked like fools walking through the pasture in our good shoes and clothes.

Mr. Burns helps the vet tie Edith to the post, then Dr. Ostrum stands to the side and behind the cow and lifts up her tail. He shines the spotlight at the cow's butt and stares for a while. Then he says, "Would you hold this, please," meaning the tail, to Mr.

Burns. He looks at us kids. "I'm now going to palpate both injection sites. Can you see?"

We nod. Once again, I think of my mother. She would love it that we are watching a veterinarian palpate an injection site. She'd be humming and rubbing her hands together with the excitement of it all. She'd be asking questions like there was no tomorrow.

The vet prods around under the tail, then shines the flashlight farther down. He has to bend to get a good look. Edith is moving from foot to foot and she gives her tail a good swish. It comes out of Mr. Burns' hand and swats the doctor on his shoulder.

"Just a minute more, my sweet," he says, then he straightens up.

Dr. Ostrum looks at each of us before he says a word, his mouth all tight and bunched up. We know exactly what he will say, but when he does, I think I hear him wrong all the same. He actually repeats it, as if he knows. "Positive. I'm so sorry."

"Damn it to hell," Mr. Burns says. "Are you sure?"

"Yes."

"Did my cow get her sick? Mrs. Anderson? Is that what you're saying? *My* cow?"

"Are you going to kill Edith?" Megan says, in a loud, frightened voice, a voice so scared we all stop. She repeats it, quiet this time. "Are you going to kill Edith?"

"All right, now. Let's just get her untied and let her out to the pasture, and then we'll go out into the sun and talk this over."

"Come on, kids," Mr. Murphy says. "Let's get out of the way."

We go stand by the cars and wait.

Dr. Ostrum and the Burns come out of the barn and walk over to us. A car drives by; the driver, a woman, glances at us. We must be an odd assortment of people: the vet in his good jeans and Hollywood looks, the Burns in ordinary farmer clothes, Mr. Murphy in a white shirt stained with grease, Rusty and Brenda looking like they slept in their clothes, which they probably did, and Megan, Robert, and me looking like we're going to church. I wonder what story that lady must have made up to explain us. I bet she would never have thought it all had to do with a cow that had tuberculosis.

"Now," Dr. Ostrum says, placing a foot up on the front bumper of the Burns' car, "your cow has a positive test result, that's certain. I don't know why. I don't know how long she's been sick, but my guess is, not long. Her breathing sounds fine and she looks healthy to me. But you never know. She has to be quarantined. Make sure she doesn't get near any other cattle."

"What's quarantined mean?" Megan asks.

"She has to stay here. She can't be transported anywhere except by special permit." He looks at Mr. Burns. He's trying to be kind, but Mr. Burns' face is all red. "A Bureau of Animal Industry employee will come and complete the necessary forms. It will take a couple weeks, then someone will come and take the cow. You'll be compensated."

Mr. Burns brightens. "You'll pay me for the cow?"

"Yes, sir, we will."

"I see," he says, nodding to himself. "Well, that helps."

"And everyone here will need to be tested for TB. Anyone who came in contact with the cow."

"We have," Brenda says, offering her arm for his inspection.

"What will you do to the cow when you take her away?" my brother asks.

Dr. Ostrum doesn't want to answer this. He looks at the ground for a minute, then at Mr. Burns, avoiding our eyes. "She'll have to be destroyed."

"We should have hid her," Megan says to me.

"There's still time," I whisper. But we both know we won't.

"I guess I'll be going," Dr. Ostrum says, running his fingers through his black hair. I wonder if he has to go read more cows' vulvas, or if one a day is enough.

Mr. Burns shakes the vet's hand, a big up-and-down hand-shake to show there are no hard feelings. "I am sorry," Dr. Ostrum says. "I hate to be the bearer of bad news. It's a rotten part of my job. But I was very glad to have met you all. I'll call you about making an appointment to test the cattle. I imagine they're fine, since they don't come in contact with the milk cow."

"Well, thanks, Doctor." Mr. Burns lets go of the vet's hand and folds his arms across his belly.

After Dr. Ostrum drives off we're left in two groups. The kids and the adults. The Burns and Mr. Murphy are talking about something, and Rusty and Brenda are asking us if we're going to tell our mother about the cow. I am trying to listen to the adults, because I think I hear Mr. Burns say something about the vet telling him maybe my mother gave the cow tuberculosis. I must have heard it backwards.

"So if you tell her," Brenda says, "it might make her sad. Maybe you shouldn't. Maybe you should all agree not to tell her. Like swear on a Bible or something, so it won't slip out. I don't think she should know, do you?" Brenda is tugging on my arm. She's pretty strong for being so skinny.

I yank my arm away from Brenda and go over to where the adults are still talking in low tones. "Did you say my *mother* gave Edith tuberculosis?"

They look at each other, then back at me. Mrs. Burns is the one who answers. "He said it was possible, Tamara. Cows can get tuberculosis from humans. But it doesn't matter, not really. No one's blaming anyone. We'll be paid for the cow."

But it does matter, to me. This way it makes my mother seem dirty. Unclean. Infectious. "She didn't get your cow sick," I say, but I don't repeat it, because I'm not so sure.

"It doesn't matter," Mrs. Burns tries to assure me. But it's not her mother we're talking about.

"I better be off," Mr. Murphy announces, then walks off, going back toward the car he was working on earlier. I can almost see his whole body relax when he gets across the road. He is a man comfortable only in his own boundaries. I'm glad Rusty isn't like him.

"We're going to go too," Mr. Burns says.

Mrs. Burns gives Robert, Megan, and me each a quick hug. "Give your mother our love," she says, and they drive off.

We are ready when my father comes. My sister has been ready for a month. She clutches the little alligator-skin suitcase that she brought to the hospital when we got our tests, when she believed she would be sick and could stay with our mother. This time I don't tell her there is no reason to bring it. I like it that she is so stubborn.

My father is so surprised to see us dressed nicely and waiting on the lawn that he gets out of the car and just stands there. We stay where we are for a moment, enjoying his surprise. He rubs at an eye with the heel of his palm and his lips tighten. He looks away. Not at anything, but just away from us. We are too hard to look at, standing here, dressed and waiting to be a family.

It's Megan who moves first. She walks toward my father, carrying her suitcase, her patent-leather shoes leaving flattened grass in her wake. "Hi, Daddy. Let's go."

"Can't I go to the bathroom first?"

"If you have to," Megan says. "But make it quick."

"Yes, ma'am." He touches her head and gives her a kiss, right on her hair, and I think that must feel nice.

"You're really ready," he says to all of us. He grabs Robert by the back of the neck and gives it a squeeze. He looks over Robert's head at me. "Hi, Tamara."

"Hi," I say.

He goes inside the house for a minute, then returns. "Let's go."

My father is in a jovial mood, which makes driving with him all the more dangerous. He turns to look at me as he talks, and, sometimes over his shoulder, at Megan and Robert. He drives in the middle of the road most of the time, unless a car comes at us, then we feel the loose gravel clang against the underside of the car as he weaves onto the berm. My teeth are clenched tight and I hold the handle on the inside of the door. My feet are pressed flat to the curved floor of the car. He is talking nonstop, so I don't have to unclench my teeth to answer him.

"It was so exciting," he says. "Unbelievable, really. Who would have imagined? A critic from *Newsweek* was there. He seemed to really like my work. He stood in front of *Through the Woods* for ten minutes, just stood there, without a word. Then he shook my hand." *Through the Woods* is a painting of the area where the pine trees meet the birch. In the branches of the birch are perched several little girls. One girl has flown into the pines, like an advance guard. There is something frightening about this picture, as if you want to call her back. My father's pictures have never been frightening. They have been pictures you want to walk into, peaceful, quiet, gentle. But now his pictures have turned darker, the colors toned down, grays filling in places that used to be blues. They feel more real than his landscapes ever did.

I know, from his letter, why he paints like this. Knowing it feels like a secret we share, even though he doesn't know I know. I feel like I belong in the front seat, next to my father, because I know this secret. It's a funny feeling, to like my father. To appreciate him. It's a bit scary. I feel like we might drive into a tree. I watch the road closely.

"I sold four pictures. I'm commissioned for two more and I got a promise for another show. I can quit painting couch pictures. God, what a relief."

We turn onto a highway, and now there are more cars. He grips the wheel tighter and drives on the right-hand side, as cars pass us on the left. It's fifty miles to the sanitarium, if we make it.

"I'm fifty-eight. I've existed in obscurity for so long now I never dared to hope. You don't know what this means to me."

This makes me wonder. What *does* it mean to him? That we might stay at this farm because it has inspired him? I'd ask, but he's stopped talking so he can concentrate on driving, which is a big relief. Still, I keep my eyes on the road.

It's a long car ride, but Megan never complains or asks how long it will take. She is so patient because she is somehow already there. I think if I spoke to her she wouldn't answer, wouldn't even hear me.

Even though I have read my mother's descriptions of the sanitarium, I can't help thinking that it is like a madhouse, with people tied to their beds, blathering, crying out for help, all skinny, with their bones showing, their eyes bulging, drool escaping from open mouths. I know this isn't true. Knowing doesn't help.

When we get there, the sanitarium looks pretty from the outside. It's a long, wide, wooden building painted bright yellow, and it has a porch that surrounds it on all sides, and acres of freshly mowed grass. It's big, like an enormous hotel, but I remember what my mother said, that just a few decades ago half the people sent here died. Right here. If any place has ghosts, this one does.

It's a day of blue, so blue the trees shimmer in applause. The warmth of the day comes right through our clothes. We stand outside the car looking around, and everything is so beautiful, so magnificent, that it feels false, like I have entered one of my father's pretty paintings and I will rip through the canvas if I make the slightest move.

Holding her suitcase, Megan marches through the parking lot and up the front walk. We follow.

Inside, there is a wide curved desk with a nurse sitting behind it, wearing a starched white uniform and a little white cap. My father explains who we are and she says we will need to speak to the doctor first. She tells us to wait, then walks off down a long hall. When the doctor comes back he shakes my father's hand and says he was expecting us, but he needs to explain some things to us before we see my mother.

"First off," he says, pausing to look at each one of us kids with one of those no-nonsense stares, "there is to be no physical contact with your mother. None. I am breaking some rules here, just allowing this visit. She has been moved to the lawn outside, to be in the open air. We have her seated facing the wind, which is slight. You are to sit in the seats provided, and that way, the wind will not blow any contaminants in your direction. Your mother has been very excited about this visit, almost too excited. Possibly I shouldn't have even informed her until you arrived, but I was worried what a sudden shock might do. Either way, you should be careful not to exhaust her with too many questions. Do you understand?"

We nod.

"Nurse Miller will lead you to her now. And, Mr. Anderson, after you visit your wife, may I have a word with you alone before you leave."

My father agrees and we are led by the nurse through silent hallways and out the back of the sanitarium to a parklike setting, where the grass is mowed like a golf course and shrubs are trimmed into perfect balls. There are thick wooden chairs scattered about, some in groups, some alone. There is one person painting on an easel. Two others are playing at lawn bowling. A lake of blue silver sparkles a quarter mile away.

The nurse points to a heavy wooden chair in the shade of a towering maple, a good football field away from the building. Someone is in the chair. There are also four empty chairs. "That's your mother, over there. She's doing better today. Your mother is a very charming woman. We all like her tremendously." She says this in a very sweet voice, as adults do when speaking to children. Before she leaves us she looks directly at my sister and her suitcase. "Can I take that for you?" she asks.

"No, thank you," Megan says, in that sweet voice children use to adults when they think them idiots. The nurse leaves.

As we get close, I see that my mother's eyes are closed and I worry that she is sleeping. But she must sense us coming, because before we say a thing, her eyes open and her whole face takes on an expression of delight, except her eyes, which are sunk into her skin as if the sockets are absorbing them. I take in a small gasp of air. I can't help it. She is so thin, and even though her face is flushed, her arms are white as paper.

"Hello," she says. Her chair is like a lounger. It has a place to rest her legs, which are stretched out in front of her and covered with a blanket. She doesn't get up. Megan runs to her, drops the suitcase beside the chair, and climbs into her lap. For a second my mother's face looks pinched in pain, but she buries her head into Megan's hair and when she comes out of the hug, the look is gone.

The rest of us stand by the designated chairs, then sit down awkwardly.

"I'm so glad you've come," she says. "I've missed you so much."

My father drags his chair closer to my mother. The legs of the heavy chair tear at the grass. No one must be watching us, because no nurses have come running out since Megan climbed in my mother's lap. But it makes me nervous.

"How's the farm?" she asks. "How's the garden? How's Edith? And the Murphys? Still taking you to church?"

I start to tell her the garden is fine but Robert interrupts.

"Edith has tuberculosis. A vet came and tested her. They're going to kill her." The way he says this I can tell he hates Edith, he blames her for the sunken face of my mother; that by saying they will kill Edith, he is exacting his revenge.

My mother's face turns suddenly white, like cold, dry snow. She puts a thin hand to her throat, as if to stop all the blood from leaving her head. "No," she says. Then she coughs. The cough is a full, watery-sounding thing that takes over her whole body. Her shoulders curve inwards. She bends over at the waist. Her legs shake. Megan hops off her lap as if my mother caught fire, tripping over her suitcase and falling backwards onto the grass. My father stands and puts a hand on my mother's shoulder, then he looks around, maybe for a nurse. No one comes. My mother's cough fades away in a minute, but she stays bent over, hands covering her mouth. When she pulls them away she wipes them on her white pants. She looks down. The plaid blanket that was on her lap is now on the ground. Megan pulled it off with her. There are red streaks on her pants. I think I will scream, but I don't. Robert is close to tears with embarrassment and shame.

"May I have my blanket, please," she asks Megan. Megan gives it to her, then sits in the last empty chair. She looks down at the grass, at her feet, at anything but my mother.

"I don't understand," my mother says. "You're saying Edith gave me tuberculosis? I can't believe it. No. I don't believe it. I was feeling bad before we got to the farm. Months before."

"You were?" my father asks.

"Yes."

"I didn't know."

"No, I guess you didn't." My mother smiles gently at my father. She forgives him even this.

"So, you've made friends here?" my father says.

"Yes. They baby me so. They're very kind. Most of them have privileges I don't, so they come to me, entertain me, tell me the most amazing stories. Mrs. Hyde was a publisher in New York. I love the stories she tells. I guess I miss it more than I thought."

My father tells her of his trip there, of his success, and she grins and nods and seems to get stronger just by hearing his news.

Her questions come out in a clear, unobstructed way that makes my whole body relax.

They talk like this for quite a while, as if they were sitting on the couch at the house, as if we were anywhere but here. She talks just to my father, finishing up what needs to be said before moving on.

"Good for you," she says. "But I never got to see some of those paintings you sold. Did you take photographs for me?"

"Renny did," my father says "The man's in second heaven right now. The way he talks you'd think it was his idea I paint these pictures. But let him have fun. Why not?"

"And you, Tamara? What have you been up to?"

I start to answer, but my father stands up. "The doctor wants to speak to me. Do you mind?"

My mother tells him to go on. He kisses her on the forehead and leaves us.

I tell my mother about the garden. She listens intently to the description of the tomatoes and beans. She asks what I've been cooking for dinners and I exaggerate, giving Robert a quick sharp look, daring him to contradict me. After my mother's reaction to his last announcement, I don't think he'll say a word.

"What about church?" she asks.

"I'm thinking of giving it up," I say just to please her. She smiles.

Next she asks my brother and sister what they have been doing, and Megan tells her about the night Kip chased a skunk and how the bomb shelter filled with water. Robert just says he's been doing a puzzle. Nothing else. His voice is jumpy again, as if it might start to squeak. She doesn't seem to notice Robert doesn't say anything else. With a nod, her eyes close. They stay that way.

We sit, and wait for my father.

.   .   .

By the time my father comes back, my sister is asleep, her body folded over like a wilted plant, her head practically on her knees. My mother sleeps with her head arched back, her mouth open. She snores.

"Let them sleep," my father says. "You two can go off wandering a bit. Not far." He sits in the chair he dragged over before, and stares at my mother. I look at Robert and he nods. We get up and walk off.

The lawn bowling is over and that group has gone. It's midday, a lazy heat slows us; we walk like older people. An orange monarch butterfly floats by, lazily rowing wide wings through updrafts of hot air. There is the smell of marigolds and daisies and fresh-cut grass. I imagine my mother must love this place. She has come so far from New York City, which she may still talk about missing, but I think she has forgotten how to live quickly. I think, if she could, she would stay here.

Robert and I whisper as we walk, even though there is no one near us. I imagine dead people listening to us. I imagine coming back to the chairs and finding my mother dead. I need to get out of here.

"I want to go home," I say to Robert, who has just asked me how I think our mother is, a question I don't need to answer.

"Me too," he says. "It's spooky here. Creepy. The village of the dead. Maybe the doctors are vampires. The people here are zombies. I wouldn't go to sleep here for a million, trillion dollars, not even a zillion."

"You read too many stupid comics," I say, although I have been thinking nearly the same thing.

"Yeah, well she's not getting any better here. She looks more like a zombie than the rest." Robert's eyes get watery. He looks away from me, at the lake.

We are walking on a cobblestone path that circles the building. Men and women dot the landscape in wooden chairs like pale fleshy plants set out to get some sun. I want to leave so bad I can feel my legs twitch.

"School's going to start soon," Robert says. "Who's going to take me shopping for clothes?"

"I will."

"Thanks. Dad could drop us off in town."

We both know shopping with my father would be a disaster. "Megan really needs new clothes," I say. "She's gotten taller."

"So have you," Robert says.

"Yeah." I'm surprised he noticed.

"So we'll go?" he says.

"Yeah, sure."

Robert nods to himself as if all his problems are now solved. "Good."

We walk around the building, stopping at a rose garden, and read a sundial. It takes us ten minutes to go in one big circle. After the third time we both agree it's been long enough.

My mother and Megan are still sleeping. "Are we going to stay much longer?" I ask my father.

"No, we'll go now. Megan, it's time to wake up." He reaches over and nudges her. She opens her eyes and wipes her chin.

"It's time we get going back," he says.

This is when Megan will throw her fit, I think, but she looks at my mother. "Okay," she says.

"Liz," my father says gently, but his voice catches on this simple word.

She jerks awake. "Oh my," she says. "Did I fall asleep?"

"Just for a minute," my father says. Her forehead is covered in droplets of sweat. He takes a handkerchief out of his pocket and wipes them off.

"Thank you," she says.

"We're going to go now, Liz. You keep getting better now, hear me? You keep eating. All right?"

"Yes, sir."

"That's my girl. Shall I get a nurse?"

"Oh, let me stay here a while longer. It's so lovely. They'll remember me eventually."

My father leans over to give her a kiss, but she raises her hand and stops him. "Please don't." He pauses, bent over, then stands up. We all say good-bye.

Robert cries.

"My poor baby," she says. "You're the sensitive one. Just like your father."

She must be crazy, I think. My father is as sensitive as a bag of rocks. But then I remember his letters, and I blush.

"You take care of them, Tamara," my mother says. "I count on you."

I tense. I don't want to take care of anyone, and she has no right to ask this, like she's on her deathbed and I have to honor her last wish. I nod tightly. I don't say yes or sure or anything like that, so it's really not a promise.

We leave. We walk away. I am aware for the first time how amazing my legs are. How they hold me up. How they move me where I want to go. I catch my breath, thankful for something too big to imagine, and, at the same time, scared of something I can now see all too clearly.

Fifteen

The car ride back to the farm is quiet. If my mother were with us, she would be pointing out the scenery and asking us millions of questions. *Look at that,* she'd say, as we drive by the steep side of a cliff, the layers of earth showing like muscles under skin. *What types of rocks might be found there?* Or she would have pointed out the dying trees in the swamp and asked us what animals lived there. What would they eat? Would they hibernate during the winter? Once, when I was ten, we smelled this terrible smell and it drove her crazy trying to figure out what it was. She saw a row of long, low buildings and drove us right up to them. It was somebody's property, with a house and a drive, but that didn't stop her. She got out of the car and went up to the house, just to find out what that smell was, so she could tell us. It was a pig farm. So now I know nothing smells worse than a pig farm.

But now, no one speaks until my father gets off the highway and onto the back roads. Then he clears his throat and says, "I have something to tell you. Please listen."

He pauses, for dramatic effect, or because a truck passes us on the left, going twice the speed my father is, our car shivering in the rush of air. Either way, my stomach turns.

"You listening?" he says, as the truck with long metal poles goes up the road in front of us, leaving us far behind. I'm sure the driver thinks my father a jerk for going thirty-five in a fifty-five-mile-an-hour zone.

"Yes," we all say.

"Okay now. Here's the scoop. The doctor says your mother doesn't have bovine tuberculosis, which is what you get from cows with tuberculosis. It infects the body differently, more in the stomach than the lungs. She's got regular TB, and the cow must have caught it from her. It's a miracle we didn't catch it, but these things happen. He says she probably got it from her father, but it's been dormant all this time, and now it's become active. There's no way to pinpoint why it didn't stay dormant. Sometimes it has to do with stress, or getting ill from something else first. But she hasn't been ill, not like he meant. So maybe it's stress. Not from you kids, not that I mean that. Probably from moving around. I have to admit it. It could be that."

We don't say anything. Our silence is more an accusation than anything we might say.

He clears his throat again. Another truck whizzes past, very closely. My father turns off the road, right into someone's drive, a house I have never seen before. The house is at the end of a long dirt drive that hooks to the right. There is a barn missing half its boards and looks like it will collapse if someone sneezes. A tractor is in the drive, but no car. My father pulls halfway up the drive, then shuts off the car.

He turns in his seat so he faces all of us. "Anyway," he says, as if this is a normal way to have a conversation, in some stranger's driveway, "she's pretty sick. The doctor says she has probably had active TB for over a year. It's not responding well to the drugs. It may have spread to her bones. They're doing their best, but they can't keep her there. The sanitarium is closing in a few months."

He stops, as if we might want to ask questions. He raises his eyebrows, and looks at each one of us. It's my sister who speaks.

"Is she going to come home?" There is not the great anticipation in her voice you might expect.

"No. Not yet. They're going to send her to another sanitarium, not really a sanitarium, actually, but a county clinic that specializes in infectious diseases."

"Where?" I ask.

"Outside Utica. It's a very good hospital. Very good. She can stay where she is another month or two, but then they will send her to this new place."

"Utica is pretty far away," I say.

"Yes. So we're going to move there."

"Utica?" my brother says.

"Yes. To be near your mother. The land is similar to the countryside here, so I can keep painting the . . ."

"We're moving?" I yell. "We're moving again! When?"

"Soon as I find a place."

"No! I'm not going. I'm not moving again! I'm not going. You can go, but I'm not. I'm staying here."

"Tamara," he says. "Please. We'll be able to go visit your mother more often."

I don't say anything, so he tries Megan. "You'd like that, wouldn't you, Megan? To see your mother more often?"

Megan only nods. She was scared by what she just saw; there is a limit to the fears we might enjoy.

I get out of the car. My father hollers my name, expecting me to walk away, cause a scene. But all I do is open the back door of the car and climb in next to my sister. I don't want to sit next to my father anymore. I have this feeling I might yank the wheel as he's driving. I can feel it in my arm. It's not that I want to.

Sometimes I do things I don't want to, but not this time. I am going to protect myself from me, until I calm down. And then I'm going to do something. I just don't know what.

My father starts the car and we drive home.

It's five-thirty when we get back to the farm. I'm hungry, but it's not food I want. Besides, the idea of sitting down at the table with my father makes me sick. I actually liked him for a few minutes. I'm so stupid. He'll never change. We'll never change. I'll never change. I want to reach up and tear at my hair. I can remember that bright, sharp, hot pain that took my breath away last time I pulled some hair out. It's a stunning feeling, so quick it's shocking that it goes away. It makes my heart beat hard. It makes me feel good. Tough. Alive. But then I remember last night, kissing Rusty, how my heart was beating then too, how it lasted and lasted until we stopped, and then it stayed with me. I get out of the car and walk across the road. I don't look back but I know my father is watching me, trying to decide to call me back or not. It's easier not to. He doesn't.

Brenda tells me Rusty's in his fort. She asks if she can come along and I tell her no. Her bottom lip is about to stick out when I tell her I'll pay her a buck to keep Robert away from the fort—play marbles with him, anything. A buck sounds good to her. She skips across the road calling his name in a nasal singsong voice. I figure I have about an hour before they both decide to sneak up on us.

When I pull aside the shower curtain Rusty is sitting on the sleeping bag with a big grin on his face. He must have heard me coming.

"Hi. How's your mom?"

"Not so good," I say. "They're going to move her to Utica."

"Utica?" He makes it sound as awful as it seems.

I nod. "Yeah."

"Why Utica?" he asks.

I tell him about the sanitarium closing, and about the place in Utica.

"Well, they might make her better there, huh?"

"Yeah." I don't want to talk about my mother anymore. It's too much to think about. "So what are you doing?" I ask.

"Nothing."

I sit next to him on the sleeping bag and it doesn't even take a minute before we're making out, my hands on the back of his head to keep him tight to me, his hands slipping under my shirt, around my back to unhook my bra, back to my chest, slipping up under my loose bra, and attaching like suction cups to my breasts. It's exactly what I want.

I'm wearing my skirt, which rides up my legs, leaving a space for a hand to find its way up. Rusty figures this out quickly.

He rubs at my crotch through my underwear, as if I were a lucky stone, but then he stops and I can feel a finger or two creeping between the elastic and my skin. He sticks one finger between the folds of my vagina and wiggles it. I turn slowly to the side, to make it easier for him. I can't believe what I feel. Like I might faint. Air comes in and out of me so quickly I don't think it's even getting to my lungs. I'm dizzy with a need for him to put his finger further in. I'm also scared out of my senses. Even in the midst of pressing myself closer I can see myself jumping up and running away. I shouldn't do this, I think, as my hand travels down his chest to the hard lump pressing against his zipper. As soon as I touch it, he moans, a guttural, sweet moan of pleasure that is like no other sound I've ever heard. I get wet, down there. I can feel it happen. His finger goes in further.

"Oh," I say.

It's not an ordinary *oh*, not an "Oh, by the way." But Rusty thinks I'm talking to him.

"Don't worry. I got a rubber. Stevie Miller gave it to me. It's not old or nothing," he says.

Our eyes are open now that we're talking, and everything seems different, less exciting. He takes his hand out from under my skirt. I glance at his hand. His finger is wet. I turn away.

"Do you want to?" he says.

"Yeah."

"So I should?"

I almost say no, don't use a rubber. If I get pregnant, Rusty will have to marry me, and I could stay with him. But he wants to fly. To see the world. I could trick Rusty into getting me pregnant, but it would just be a trick, like hitting a wall to take away the pain inside me. Tricks don't last long enough.

"Yeah, put it on," I say.

Before he does, he helps me take off my clothes, which is awkward, but we're both grinning, so it's not too awkward. Then he takes off his clothes and pulls the rubber out from under the sleeping bag. He puts it on with his back turned to me, then turns around. One look down and I close my eyes.

With my eyes still closed, I feel Rusty touching my shoulders, lowering me onto the sleeping bag so I'm lying down on my back. I feel the heat of his body right before I feel his weight. His chest is pressed on mine, and my breasts feel squashed, but then he raises up an inch and comes back down so now he's resting some of his weight on his arms. He uses his legs to spread mine open, so his legs are on the inside of my legs. My arms are just lying flat. I have no idea what to do with them. I'm afraid to put my hands on Rusty's back, or head, in case I stop him from moving some way he's supposed to move. I open my eyes quickly, and see that he's got his head bent, looking down at what we're about to do. I think he's trying to figure out where things go. I close my eyes again. A drop of Rusty's sweat lands on my chest.

Something soft and firm pokes me, but it's too high up. I open my legs a little bit more and feel his arm move. His hand is between us now, and I can feel it guiding his penis into my opening. It tickles, and feels strange, not at all like a finger, more gentle,

I think, but then something hurts. I'd pull back but he's pressing me against the ground and there's nothing to do but hold still. Then his body is tight to mine. I can feel his pelvic bones press against mine. He is making little sounds, like ahhhs, and starts moving up and down, not much, just short quick movements. I think he's afraid of coming all the way out of me. I can feel his penis, but not real well, and I'm not sure exactly what's happening. Then the ahhhs get quicker and he shudders and says, "Oh, oh God," and collapses right on top of me.

I feel warm and happy, but not like I did something as exciting as I thought it would be. Still, I feel very close to Rusty, almost motherly. I desperately want him to be very happy. I stroke the back of his shoulders and kiss his neck. I want to say something sweet, like *You're my baby* or *I love you,* but they sound stupid in my head and I don't say anything.

Finally he lifts himself up and says, "You okay?"

I say, "Sure."

He grins, showing all those small white teeth and pink gums, and I feel so much older than him.

"Thanks," he says.

"Sure," I say. We both look at each other, shyly and openly at the same time. His arms and chest are covered with freckles of all sizes, all different shades of brown. They are spattered across his skin like a Pollock painting, like the stars at night, like Morse code. I stare, wanting to memorize his skin. I want to believe that if years from now we were brought together on *This Is Your Life* and I was shown only his arms and his chest, I would know him.

We get dressed, more embarrassed by putting our clothes on than taking them off. We walk back to his house and right before we get to the gap in the woods where we will come out into view, he stops. "I really like you," he says.

"Thanks," I say. "I really like you too." But I don't feel like I think I should. I think I liked the touching part better than the sex part. I remember him kissing my neck that first time better than what it felt like to have him inside me. I hope he'll kiss my neck again, I think as he goes in his house and I go back across the road.

Kip greets me, sniffs my leg, and keeps sniffing as I walk, his tail wagging furiously. "Don't tell," I say.

I swear he nods his head. He's a sweet dog. I go into the house and open the refrigerator to get Kip something to eat. There is a bottle of ketchup, a jar of mustard, and a rotten apple. No one is here. The car is in the drive, but no one is in the house. I finally see the note; it has fallen on the floor under a chair. *We have gone for a walk up the hill. Please join us.*

I stand in the empty kitchen and stare at the note. *Us.* Us does not include my mother now. She will never come in this kitchen again. She will never walk up the hill. We will move to a new house and I will unpack the few kitchen items we possess. I will set up house. Cook. Do the laundry. Plan the meals. I can see this, like a movie, my moving through these motions, yet my body is empty like this kitchen.

All the good feelings from having sex with Rusty leave me, without even the memory of a kiss. I want my mom. I want her to want me enough to be healthy for me. But she has given up, and I have prayed and prayed.

I need God to save my mother. Maybe Helen is right. I have to do something for Him before He will do something for me. I have to show Him I trust Him completely.

I go upstairs. There is a trapdoor in the ceiling of the hallway that leads to the attic. I have to take the long, hooked pole from my parents' closet and reach up to pull the metal loop in the ceiling. The stairs topple down with a creak and a thud and a sifting of dust. The first step is more than a foot from the floor. When I put my weight on it, it shudders with a sigh of complaint. There is no light switch on the second floor for the attic. I assume it's up there someplace.

There are spiderwebs, but I've never been afraid of spiders; spiders are friends; living in the places we have, I can always expect them to be around. We even bring some with us, hidden in boxes; tiny stowaways. I wave an arm out, sweeping away the webs. A daddy longlegs clings to the wall.

The attic ceiling is low, with bare wood rafters slanting down to touch the floor. The light coming through the half-moon window illuminates the small, clean attic. Boxes are stacked neatly along one side of the room. On the other side are two old floor lamps missing their shades, a caned chair, a large black trunk, and a typewriter. There is no sign of a squirrel. No mice. Only Timothy, boxed and stacked. And probably pretty hot; it's close up here. The air is still. It's like being inside a lung, the rafters the ribs. I am inside a held breath, waiting for a shout.

I go over to the window. It's small, but I think I can squeeze through it. It doesn't lead out to a roof, since it's on the outside wall where there is no roof, but this isn't a dream. I don't need the roof. I try to open the window by pushing on the bottom. It's painted shut. Really painted shut. It's hard to tell where the wall ends and the window frame begins.

If I break out the glass, there won't be enough room for me to crawl out. I have to get the whole thing open, frame and all. I try to wiggle the window. Nothing. I bang on the frame with my fist. I find a nail on the floor and try to chip away at the paint, then push again. Nothing, but I'm building up quite a sweat. Finally, I sit on the floor and kick the frame with my feet, over and over and over. It doesn't budge. Suddenly, I am crying, doubled over, holding my stomach against the painful gulps of air my body takes in. The stuck window is God's message. He's saying, *I don't need you to believe in me. Don't bother.*

I'm not worth any miracles, big or small.

I tell God I don't care. He didn't punish me for the skinny-dipping, like Mrs. Murphy thought He should. He isn't saving my mother, even though I've begged Him. Helen is scared of getting

TB, even though she's saved. What good is He anyway? If there is a God, He's not the one I need. I can be just as miserable without Him.

I cry loudly, like a little kid, tears and snot running down my face. I cry so long it starts to feel good, like I deserve this. If anyone should cry it should be me. I can feel myself pushing it now, crying when I know I could stop. The self-pity doesn't feel good anymore, just feels stupid. I wipe my eyes and look around the attic at all the boxes. Everything left of Timothy is up here. If I had jumped and God hadn't saved me—which I bet He wouldn't have; I bet, if He exists at all, He's soaking up all of Helen's heady praises right now—there would hardly be enough of my stuff to pack into two boxes. There isn't enough of me to die yet. The thought almost makes me laugh. I can feel a grin at the corner of my lips.

If Timothy is up here in these boxes, he's trapped by that locked window and the trapdoor. It's hot and stuffy up here. He's all alone. Someone has to let him out.

I choose the first box I come to. It's taped shut with wide brown tape, so dry it tears off easily. Inside are clothes: blue jeans, flannel shirts, T-shirts, socks, underwear, a pair of flannel pajamas, a Boy Scout uniform. The clothes are about my size. He must have been small for his age.

I hold up a green flannel shirt to my nose. Dust and something else, something human. I stand and pull my blouse off over my head and take off my bra. Then I take off my pants. Before I put on his shirt I look down at my almost naked body. The skin of my torso is pale, while my arms and legs taper into tans of different shades mottled by healing scabs from my flight down the hill. Goose pimples form on my arms as I watch, even in the heat. My nipples get erect. I grin, thinking maybe God is looking now. Maybe God is a little bit like Rusty. Maybe He's a little bit like my dad too: blinded by His own light. Maybe God should be a woman and have to wash the dishes more often.

Still holding Timothy's shirt in one hand, I work off my underwear, dropping them on the dusty floor. I put on his shirt, then his
underwear. The underwear hangs around my hips but stays up.
Next, I put on his pants, which hang loose also. The pants have
been worn thin at the knees, which are at the top of my shins. The
bottom of the pants bunch up around my bare feet. The jean
material is soft and warm as skin. At the bottom of the box are
three rolled belts, like snakes. I put one on, hitching up the pants
as much as I can. Then I go through the rest of his boxes.

One has puzzles, at least a dozen, of animals and flowers and
cities. I carry it over to the open trapdoor to take downstairs.
Another box has just junk. Old notebooks, pencils, crayons,
combs, a wallet with scraps of paper with names and telephone
numbers, chewed-up rubber soldiers, some kind of army gog-
gles, a thick piece of wood with a battery wired to a flashlight
bulb, books about spaceships, used erasers, a small red rubber ball, a blue baseball hat with the insignia torn off, lots of
Cub Scout and Boy Scout badges, a blue wooden yo-yo, and,
wrapped in a kitchen towel, one glass, which must be the glass
that Timothy had his last drink from, the glass that made Mrs.
Burns move. A plain, clear, tall glass with a thick bottom. It
wouldn't tip over easy. But it would break if it fell.

The stuff in this box is just junk, really, the stuff we leave
behind or toss in Dumpsters the day before we go. But I think
this is the stuff that makes noises in the night; that needs him,
that defines him; the very stuff *we* leave behind.

I pick up the wallet and stick it in my back pocket.

The next box has comic books, hundreds of them, *Superman,
Batman, Donald Duck, Captain Marvel,* a gold mine for my
brother. I put this box by the one with the puzzles.

Then I open a box that has winter clothes in it. Hats, scarves,
gloves, a dark-blue snowsuit, green rubber boots. I don't need
this. I repack it neatly.

Another box has a set of miniature cars and trucks, houses and gas stations, a grocery store, a pharmacy, a bakery, and a little town hall complete with wide steps and sculptured pillars. There are tiny stop signs and yield signs. And scattered about, filling the spaces, are little people, their painted faces worn clear except for black eyes that are so deep the color can't be rubbed off. Everything is cast in metal. It is a town, for me. Without a drop of sarcasm, I tell God I'm sorry for all the mean things I said. I also tell Him I'm sorry, but I'm going to have to stop trying to believe in Him. If He's really there, I hope He's got enough people to believe in Him to keep Him happy. I'm going to give it a break. I don't even know if I'm going to be me for a while. I might give that a break too.

I carry this box over to the trapdoor. There are only two more boxes.

One box has clothes, but it feels heavier than clothes should feel, so I dig through it. Wrapped in shirts are three shiny silver trophies, each of a baseball player holding a thin bat. Each one has Timothy's name on it. Timothy Burns. I wrap them back up carefully, even though they should be on a shelf somewhere. I hope someday Mrs. Burns can look at them again.

The last box has about a dozen stuffed animals. I can't decide if I should take all the stuffed animals down, so I grab one middle-sized teddy bear and a soft, gray elephant with floppy ears. If my sister wants more, I'll tell her where they are.

They packed this stuff and kept it as if he might come back and ask where his things are. But no one ever comes back. It's hard enough just to stay.

I carry the boxes down the steps, moving very carefully on the wobbly stairs. The last step is too far away and I have to jump, landing on both feet. When I'm done taking everything down to the living room, I try to figure out how to close the attic steps. Every time I shove them up, they come back down. I'm making enough noise to wake the dead, which I don't want to do right now, especially since I'm wearing his clothes. Finally, I quit trying and leave the stairs down.

No one is back yet. It must be quite a sunset. I get a can of Spam from the basement for Kip and dump it in his bowl, but when I take it out to where he eats by the hydrangea bush, he ignores the food and circles me, sniffing the clothes I'm wearing. It's not the scent of sex he smells this time, but of love, his boy, good times. Kip looks up at me and tilts his head in question, his ears lifting up just as much as they can. Then his tail wags a thousand miles an hour. I can't get him to eat, so I sit down on the lawn and let him have a real good smell. Then I see Brenda running down the road toward me, my family walking slowly behind.

Brenda's going on a mile an hour about how my dad asked her to walk up the hill with them, but would I still pay her a buck since she did keep Robert away, when my father gets close. He looks at me, tilts his head, and raises his bushy white eyebrows. He's wondering where I got the clothes, but he's wary of me. He doesn't want to start something right now: he's had his quiet time on the hill and wants to hold on to it. I guess I do understand him a little, even though I don't want to.

Megan and Robert go inside and right away you can hear them. "What's all this stuff? Where'd this come from? Comics! A whole box of comics! Look at all these puzzles!" Brenda looks at me and I nod. She goes in. "Oh my God!" she shouts.

"What's going on?" my father asks.

"I've decided to live," I say. I don't mention it was old dried thick paint that saved my life. I don't want him to think paint saved me. What might he make of that? "The stuff in there is all part of the plan. It's the colors, you know. The reds and blues and greens. The indigo, emerald, and ultramarine."

I can see his recognition of the phrase by the way he freezes for a minute. "Tamara," he says. I guess he doesn't know what else to say, because he stops there.

"Maybe," I say.

From inside we can hear Robert, Megan, and Brenda exclaiming over all the stuff. "I . . . don't know about this," my father says. He must have figured out where the stuff came from. I'm pretty sure he doesn't believe in miracles. Not after visiting my mother.

"It's okay," I say.

"We'll have to put it all back tomorrow," he says.

"Over my dead body," I say, and laugh. It's tension, I know, but it's still a laugh.

My father shakes his head. "I better go look," he says, and goes in.

"Nice talking to you," I say, but he doesn't hear me. I'm a little giddy. It's been a long day. It sure seems like nothing happens here, or everything.

When Brenda comes back outside to ask me where all the stuff came from, I drag her into the barn. We sit on hay bales while I tell her about my father trying to make us move again. She gets properly disgusted, and we get carried away making up names for him. We start with jerk and build up to asshole, using up every swear word Brenda knows, then make up stupid names, like Jell-O Head and Lizard Tongue. My favorite is Cosmic Cretin. Then we go back to the swear words. When Brenda calls him a Toad Fucker, we know we have gone too far and go back into the house to work on a puzzle with my brother.

I tell myself if there are no missing pieces it means we will live here forever.

That evening, no one mentions moving. We eat Mrs. Burns' blueberry jelly with spoons, since there's no bread, and the last can of miniature hot dogs, which, frankly, I'm getting quite sick of. I bring in some tomatoes from the garden, but only my father eats those. Afterwards, Rusty and Brenda come over and we all read comics in the living room. No one mentions that they're not supposed to be in our house. I guess one hundred and forty-two comics—my brother counted them—is worth the risk. And I guess Brenda and Rusty's parents aren't all that different from mine; rules last only as long as the energy to enforce them.

My father sits and reads comics with us. Maybe this is his way of saying he's sorry we have to move.

The next morning my father doesn't go out to paint. Instead, he admits it's time to go to the grocery store. I tell him I'm staying here, but Robert and Megan want to go. "Please," he says to me, but I shake my head. "All right, fine," he says. I think he's saving his energy for the big fight he knows is still coming, when he tries to drag me farther than the local grocery store.

About ten minutes after they leave, the Burns drive up. It's Sunday. With all the commotion, we have forgotten that. And the Murphys didn't ask us to go to church with them. I don't know why. It also occurs to me the grocery store will be closed. My father doesn't realize this, since he hardly ever goes grocery shopping. He's going to be very confused when he gets there.

As the Burns get out of the car, I realize I'm wearing Timothy's clothes. It feels right to me, but I don't know how the Burns will take it.

"Well, hello there," Mr. Burns says, tugging on his ear. I wonder if his ears are so big because he always tugs on them. I tell myself never to do that. My ears are big enough.

"Hi," I say, standing back a bit, thinking maybe they won't see what I'm wearing if I don't get too close.

"No one here again?" he says, looking around.

"Nope."

"How was your mother, Tamara?" Mrs. Burns says. "Any better?"

"No, not really. She's not responding to the medication," I say. Mrs. Burns looks at Mr. Burns. Maybe it's more than they want to know. I know it's more than I wanted to know. I would have liked to think the way she looked was just a temporary setback, just a bad day, except they said yesterday was one of her better days. That I definitely don't want to think about.

"You know," Mr. Burns says, "I think I better look at that fence again." He nods to us. I bet if he were wearing a hat, he'd tip it.

"Might as well look at the garden while I'm here," Mrs. Burns says. "You want to come?" she asks me. Gardening must be another way of talking, like kicking Brenda under the table.

"Okay."

We stop by a row of tomatoes which have swelled in the last week, sucking up all the rain. Mrs. Burns bends down to get a better look. She turns toward me to say something, but instead takes in a breath of air and says, "Oh my." She is looking right at me. She straightens up. I look at the ground, unable to meet her stare. But she doesn't say anything, so I have to look back. She looks like she might cry.

"You are so very much like Timothy," she says slowly, as if she is letting out the words one at a time so nothing else can escape. For a minute I think we are both waiting to see if she will cry, but she doesn't. She just sighs, like my mother does, and goes on. "Sometimes he was so afraid, but he just wouldn't let us know. I think he was mad at himself for being sick. He blamed himself. He just wanted to be normal, so we wouldn't be so sad." She closes her eyes, as if she just can't look at me anymore, and I feel awful. I want to tell her I'm nothing like Timothy, that Timothy was a good kid. I want to say I'm sorry, but I'm afraid to speak. For just this moment, with her eyes closed, she looks so peaceful.

When she opens her eyes, she looks over at the house, and when she talks, it's as if she's talking to the house. "There're a lot of things you might get some use out of up there. It would make me feel much better if you children put them to some use. You'll know what not to get into, won't you?"

I nod.

"Good. There's so many puzzles. Please do the puzzles. There's one of zebras. That was so difficult. But what a picture it made. I left it on the table for days and we ate in the kitchen. We did that a lot. That dining room table's seen more puzzles than food. Mr. Burns pretended he didn't care for puzzles, but he'd sneak in a few pieces when we weren't around. You'll bring those down, won't you?"

"If you want me to," I say, not telling her they are piled on the dining room table right now.

"Yes, I do." The way she says this, slowly and firmly, I think she knows I already have. She reaches out a hand to me. She has bumpy knuckles and some of her fingers are bent. I take it gently, afraid of hurting her, but she squeezes my hand tight so I squeeze back.

"He's still here," I say. "I hear him sometimes. Sometimes I talk to him. I got his clothes out because I think he wanted me to. I think he saw I was unhappy and wanted to give me something. And I think he wanted to be remembered differently, not boxed up. I'm sorry I didn't ask. I guess, sometimes I just do these things . . ."

She stops me by raising a hand. "Those last weeks . . . I saw him everywhere, always just leaving a room."

"Do you think he'll stay here forever?" I ask.

"No. God will call him up soon. He's been very kind to let him stay around, but it's time, I think. It's time. I guess that's what the Lord is telling me, through you."

"But you'll never stop missing him?"

"No, never."

"I miss my mom," I say.

"I know."

Missing my mother floods me. It makes my knees weak and my head pound and my eyes burn. My arms ache. My stomach tightens. My ears ring. I must look funny because Mrs. Burns pulls me to her. Her stomach is soft. I put my head against her shoulder. I don't cry this time, but it's not because I don't let myself. I just like being hugged. It's good enough.

By the time Mr. Burns comes back we have picked a basket of tomatoes and Mrs. Burns is just explaining to me what we have to do to can them.

"My family is moving again," I say. "My dad won't want to pack glass jars of tomatoes."

"Leaving?" Mr. Burns says, very surprised. I guess I should have let my father tell him.

"They're moving my mother to Utica. He wants to be near her." And then I get an idea. How I can stay. I could be their child. They could adopt me. "Could I stay with you?" I say, knowing it sounds stupid, but the words come right out of my chest, passing right out the mouth that should have stopped them, waiting until I could think of the right way to say it.

They look at each other. They do that a lot, right at the same time. "Ahhh," says Mr. Burns. "Ummm . . ." Mr. Burns looks so uncomfortable I want to kick myself.

"That's a sweet thing to say," Mrs. Burns says. I hear the *but* in her voice before she even says it. "But you can't. Your father needs you, and Robert and Megan need you. And even though you're having trouble believing it, you need them." Then she turns to Mr. Burns. "Why don't you go get in the car? I'll be right there." He nods, like this is a very good idea.

"The fence was fine," he says as a way of saying good-bye.

When he's over by the car, Mrs. Burns starts talking again. "Remember I told you Mr. Burns and I argued sometimes? I said it was never meanly, but I glossed over that some. There were times we argued about, well, you don't need to know that, but Timothy heard. I guess you know this house is too small to hide such things. He was young, maybe ten, when we fought the most, and he didn't have any brothers or sisters to run to. He'd just stay in his room and, well, I don't want to think about what he'd do. But the thing is, I was so mad at Mr. Burns it didn't matter much to me what Timothy thought, I was too busy thinking what I thought. And, well, kids hear stuff like that, and they survive. I did. Then one day, Timothy ran away. He left a note and said he couldn't stand it anymore and not to look for him. He took off down the road, then decided to cut across the Jenners' place. He got lost in those woods for two days and a night and I thought he was gone. I thought somebody picked him up hitch-hiking and he was in Tennessee or Chicago, and my imagination went crazy. I cried so hard I thought I'd die, and I want you to know, if Timothy hadn't been found, I would have never stopped crying. I would have hated myself and Mr. Burns for the rest of my life. There is nothing worse than a child choosing to leave you. Nothing. And I know this for a fact. So I want you to never tell your dad you asked us this, because he hurts enough already. And I'm going to tell you one more thing. I'm so flattered by what you said that I'm going to go home and cry like I haven't for a while. Now you go play with Brenda or something, until your family gets home."

She stops talking, like she's going to walk off so I can think about it and not argue back, but then just as she turns away, she turns back to me. She doesn't say anything though. She reaches out and closes her hand over the flannel of the shirt I'm wearing, and rubs it between her fingers for a while. "You would have liked him," she says. Then she goes. The car backs down the drive, and they're gone.

.   .   .

The Murphys come home. Helen smiles and waves to me. It's such a warm, friendly smile, I smile back before I realize I'm still a little mad at her. Brenda starts to run across the road, but her mother calls her in.

"I'll come over after lunch," Brenda shouts. Rusty's the last one to go in. He looks at me and points in the direction of his fort. I shrug. He looks hopeful anyway. I decide to go work on the puzzle, but before I get inside, I hear my name called. It's Helen. I stand by the side porch and let her come to me. Her long hair is in a thick braid, but loose curls frame her face like a halo. She's smiling still, like her face was born smiling and will go on smiling forever. It's really catching. She motions for me to sit down on the step. She sits next to me and we both sit there for a whole minute, just smiling like idiots before we both start to talk at the same time.

"I'm sorry you tried so hard to save me, Helen," I say. "It was nice of you."

"I have something important to tell you, Tamara," Helen says. Then she laughs, both because we talked at the same time and because she's just so full of happiness. She makes me go first.

"I just want to . . . Well, you tried to . . . Well, thanks for teaching me about God, even though I'm more confused now than I was before. I guess what I like is you gave me the chance to be confused about what I think, not what my mom thinks. You were right. It was something I should know about. So I want you to know I'm not an atheist anymore."

Her eyes light up. "Really?"

I feel bad she's so excited, that she didn't catch my *but,* so I go on real quick. "No. I'm agnostic." I've heard this word before. My mother had mentioned it, I'm sure, but she must have breezed right by it. Now it feels like a word I discovered all on my own.

Helen thinks about this for a minute. "Well, I guess that's a step in the right direction. As long as you'll keep an open mind,

I'll feel like I've accomplished something. I'm very happy for you. Now for my news." She takes my hand. This is a lot of people taking my hand in one day, but I'm not complaining.

"First, I have to apologize. I'm sorry I overreacted. I was scared. But it was for the best, and I should have known all along God had His hands in even this, that it was a message, the message I was waiting for. Life is short and I can't waste a moment of it. I asked our minister today how I can become a missionary. I want to go to Africa, someplace they really need me. Anywhere they need me. He was so pleased. He said he knew all along I'd make this choice. God had told him so. He's contacting people right now. He said to put things in order here at home, and be prepared to go anytime in the next month. I have to go someplace for training in medical care, and all sorts of things. I'm so excited I feel like I'm floating. God's hand is lifting me up. Oh, Tamara, I wish you believed. I hope and pray you find God. I want to know I'll see you in heaven. I want you to know that no matter how far away you are, you and your family will be in my prayers."

Helen is flushed with more than the heat of the sun. She shines. I'm almost jealous of her at this moment. The other part of me is thinking about Rusty.

Rusty said he wanted to go to Africa too. People here want to go far away, and I just want to stay.

"Well, thanks, Helen," I say.

"Now, one more thing. I should have asked earlier. How is your mother?" I think I'm just going to say *not so good,* but instead I say, "My mother is going to die."

"Don't say that," Helen says. She pulls back and lets go of my hand.

"Why not? It's true," I say.

"It sounds cold. Heartless. There must be hope. They have medicine, don't they, that cures tuberculosis?" There is a slight sound of panic in her voice when she says this. Tests can be wrong.

"It's in her bones," I say. "She weighs like ninety pounds. There's not much left to cure."

Helen covers her mouth with her hand and stares at me. Then she leans over and kisses me on the forehead. "I will pray for her. God be with you, Tamara."

She won't give up. It's kind of a nice feeling.

My father comes home right after Helen leaves. He's carrying a box with carrots, lettuce, corn, green peppers, onions, and about a dozen zucchini. "The store was closed," he says. "But I found a roadside stand." Great, I think. Not only are we atheists, with one agnostic, now we're going to be vegetarians. What's next? Nudists? I sure am going to be popular next year.

Sixteen

The next day my father, Robert, and Megan go back into town. I stay here. I have my curse again and I just want to lie around and listen to music. I sing along, but not too loudly. I know it's stupid, but I think Timothy's listening.

Along with some real food, my father brings me home a present. It's really for all of us, he explains, but he's putting it in my charge; we are always assigned the things we own, that way someone is responsible for packing them up. It's a camera, a Brownie camera. He even bought three rolls of film. This is something I have wanted for a long time. I say thank you so many times he finally says, "Why don't you go take some pictures?" and shows me how to load the film. I tell Robert and Megan to come outside with me and we go across the road. I make everyone pose for me. Brenda on the swing. Rusty by the maple. Helen holding her Bible to her breast—her idea. Robert and Megan on the side porch with Kip, who won't face the camera, no matter what we try. Helen takes a picture of me and Brenda, then me and Rusty, then me and Megan and Robert, and we all make faces even though Helen says to smile nicely. I take a picture of Helen, Brenda, and Rusty out in front of their house, then I make Mr. Murphy come out and I pose him by the rusted cars. He smiles because Brenda's jumping around behind me yelling, "Smile, Dad!" It's a goofy smile, all teeth; I can't help thinking it's a great picture. I'm finished with the first roll in a half hour, but my dad says to save the rest of the film for another day. I'm already thinking of the next pictures I want to take. I better get a picture of Edith before they kill her. And the bull. If Mrs. Murphy comes home when it's light out, I might ask her too.

In the evenings we still walk up the hill to watch the sunset, like we used to when my mother was here. Tonight, while Robert and Megan play in the open field by the road, my father calls me over to where he stands—on the berm. There are words, like *berm,* that have my mother's voice no matter who says it. Sometimes I say *berm* over and over as we walk up the hill, and it's like she's right here, invisible, talking in my ear. *Dinner* is a word like that too, but I'm afraid that might not last, since I have to say it so often now. No one ever comes to dinner the first time I call, except Kip. Even Robert doesn't run to meals anymore. They are the times when my mother's absence is most present.

"See the way the road goes down, then back up that next hill," my father says. "Then there's a dip you can't see, and then it rises again. Each hill looks higher, but we're really higher where we're standing right now. It's an optical illusion. There are all these optical illusions in nature, and when I first started painting landscapes, I couldn't make them look right. I tried and tried. For years, a road like that would look like just a black line when I painted it, nothing at all like a road going someplace. It drove me crazy. I was painting when I was in my twenties. After teaching all day, I'd pack up my stuff and drive out of the city just in time to paint an hour before the sun set. I'd get the hills all right, I guess—I wasn't great then . . . I'm not great now either, but that's beside the point. Anyway, I'd get out my black charcoal, or my tube of black oil paint, and I'd study that road. The angles. The length, the curve. I knew what that road did in my head, mathematically. Realistically. But I couldn't draw it. I don't know what changed me, I wish I could tell you that, but one day I drew it with a gray charcoal, lightly, freely, not exactly as it was, but where it wanted to go, as if the road wasn't made of asphalt, but of light and movement. And it looked, well, better. I was pretty happy. I've drawn roads a hundred times since then. Sometimes they are wide and practical, sometimes potholed and well used, sometimes mysterious. Sometimes they're Prussian blue, sometimes burnt sienna, sometimes a mixture of copper and Payne's gray, and they change color as they rise and fall; they're never all one thing. Never just black. You know, there are some oil painters who feel you should never use black, it's deadening to a painting. I don't think that way. There is no doubt some things need black. It's just there are so many other choices. So many ways to see something." He pauses here, seeing something; hoping I'm seeing the same thing, I guess. I don't say anything. I'm getting good at this listening thing. Well, better.

He continues. "I know you read my letters. I wish you hadn't, but what I want to say to you is, who I am to you, the bad guy, is not all of who I am, and even if you can't see that now, I know you will, and I want you to know that no matter what happens, I know you love me. And I love you." Then he kind of trembles. I can see his hands shake, because all this time I've been looking down at his hands and his feet and sometimes his shoulders, and the road. Then those arms, which are still shaking, rise up and move around me like wings, and he hugs me. After a little bit, I hug him back. Then we stop and step back.

"God, that's been building for a long time." He laughs.

"Guess so," I say.

Robert and Megan come over and we run down the hill.

.   .   .

One more letter comes from our mother. It's addressed to my father and I don't open it. After he reads it, he says there's a note inside for each of us. They are very short notes.

Dear Tamara,

It was so good to see you. You looked beautiful. You have such a pretty face, but I could tell you are mad at me. I don't blame you. I have only recently realized I have been mad at my father for dying, and I have never forgiven my mother. If she drove into that tree on purpose, which I will never know, it was the act of a coward. If it was an accident, I wonder what distracted her. Not thoughts of me. I suppose I need your forgiveness now for my not being there, and your understanding. I know I ask too much of you. I always have. But I ask you to be brave. Be always brave.

Love,
Your Mom

It's not fair I can't tell her she's asking too much, that being brave hurts. If she just asked me not to cause too much trouble, I could probably do that for her. She thinks she's being comforting, but all she's comforting is herself. Still, I'm glad she wrote. That she had the energy to write.

I don't ask Robert or Megan to show me their letters. Maybe someday I will.

After we are done reading our notes, my father calls us into the living room. I hope it's not another analogy about art and life. I appreciated his effort, but once was enough.

We sit down, expecting the worst. What could be worse than our mother dying of TB and our moving to Utica is beyond me, but I bet my father can think of something.

He pulls the floral chair around, so he's facing all of us, then begins. "I have promised your mother something she has asked of me. Here it is. I am to find a house *in* Utica, not far out in the country. She wants you to be able to walk to school and the stores. And she says we have to live there until Megan finishes high school. If I have to travel to paint, then I'll have to travel. I imagine there are some interesting places nearby I can paint. She says when she comes back she won't have the energy to move, and I agree. So that's that."

No one says a word. This is too good to be true. And it's too horrible, because there is no doubt my father would never have agreed to this unless he thought her request was the kind you can't refuse.

The very next day my father starts his farewell painting of the farm. He sets up his easel on the lawn, close to the road. The ditch is right behind him. I wish he would step back to look at his picture from a distance, and fall in that ditch. He will. It's just a matter of time.

The manila envelopes come. Pictures of houses, cut-out ads, scribbled notes from the man who is helping my father find us a new place. It feels so familiar, these manila envelopes. They mark the endings and beginnings of my years—except they have come much too soon this time, less than six months since our last move. It throws me off. I can't remember what month it is. I wake in the morning thinking I should be getting dressed for school. I expect it to snow. I laugh when I'm sad. I eat when I'm not hungry.

Looking forward to leaving here makes me angry at myself. I am a traitor to my own desires. I am frightened by how easy I am swayed, how what I believe in my heart can change at the turn of a few words, the trading of dreams. It feels too easy and I fight every moment I look ahead. I find the only way not to think about it is to stay busy. I do puzzles and play records. Talk with Brenda. Play marbles and hide-and-seek. Weed the garden and take pictures. My father has to buy six more rolls. He complains, but absently, as if he's complaining because he thinks he should.

I tell Rusty I don't want to have sex again, and even though I can see he looks pretty disappointed, he just nods and asks if he can still kiss me and do other stuff. I say sure, and we do, mostly behind the big maple. Sometimes we wrestle in the grass, groping at each other, nipping at ears, bending back fingers until someone says uncle, and sometimes we walk up Valley View Hill and run down it, hand in hand, until our fingers separate and we spin off at our own speeds.

One day, Megan convinces all of us to have a tea party in the bomb shelter. Even Helen agrees to come. Megan puts an old blue woolen blanket down on the cement floor, which is dry now and covered with fine brown dust. We make Kool-Aid because we don't have tea, and carry out a package of gingersnaps, mugs, and real plates. Helen makes us say grace before we start to eat. Drinking Kool-Aid with our pinkies held up, we talk in high silly voices about the weather and pretend movie stars are our best friends. Robert imitates Mae West, and does a great job of it, until we are laughing so hard the cookies spill from our mouths. Brenda shows us how she can blow Kool-Aid out her nose, and Rusty throws a cookie at her and it bounces off her chin and falls down her blouse. The cookie slips right down, since there's nothing much to stop it, and it comes right out the bottom of her blouse and lands in her lap. We all try throwing cookies at Brenda, to see if we can do that again, like playing basketball. Kip eats the cookies off the ground, wagging his tail madly. It's a perfect day.

My father wouldn't know if we went to the moon during these days. He paints his farewell picture, reads ads, makes phone calls, gets phone calls from New York, opens manila envelopes. He eats whatever I cook with a nod of thanks.

· · ·

Over a dinner of deviled ham sandwiches and pickles my father tells us he's found us a house.

"I haven't seen a photo, but it sounds perfect," he says. "It has a bedroom and a bathroom on the first floor. It will be easier on your mother when she comes home. She'll have to take it easy. And there's a room with all windows that can be a studio. There are two large bedrooms and another bath on the second floor, and a large attic, Tamara, your bedroom, if you want, with an outside staircase, so you can have some privacy. Doesn't that sound like a good idea?"

I nod dumbly.

"We can move in September 2nd," he says, then drinks his Kool-Aid.

It's Saturday, August 28th. He's talking about less than a week away. No one but he is still eating. He takes a big bite of deviled ham and chews, looking at us expectantly. There is no sadness in his face. No sense of loss.

"When are we going to leave?" Robert asks.

"Wednesday. We should pack Tuesday. I was thinking of asking Rusty to help. I'd pay him. Do you think he'd like that, Tamara? A little extra spending money?"

I shrug, refusing to let any of this be easy for him, even though I'm already picturing that attic, the outside stairs.

"Can we take the comics?" Robert asks.

"I don't think so," my father says. "They don't belong to us."

"The Burns won't mind," I say. "They don't need comics anymore."

My father nods. He can see the logic in that. "Well, you'll have to ask them, Robert."

My brother's face clouds over. He won't dare ask the Burns.

"I'll ask them for you," I say.

"Thanks," he says.

"Who will live here?" Megan asks my father. "Who will take care of Kip and the cows?"

"They'll find someone." He finishes his food and gets up.

"Want to go up the hill?" I ask Megan and Robert.

They say yes. We do the dishes first. We leave the kitchen spotless. It isn't ours to leave a mess. It never was.

At the top of the hill we walk into the tall grass. Together we stomp down a circle of the rough, spiky grass. When we sit, we are invisible from the road; the grass surrounds us, bounds us, makes everything simple. There is nothing but us.

Before, being alone with my brother and sister made me crazy; long car rides and faraway lonesome places with only them and always them. But right now it feels good, comfortable, just right. They are the only ones who know exactly how I feel. We are all three of us torn between anger and hope. Fear and hope. Hope is on the other end of everything I feel right now.

"Do you think we're really going to stay at this place? For years?" My brother says this with all the disbelief of someone asking if it might rain elephants.

"He says he promised her," I say.

"What if she dies?" Megan says. "He'll move us if she dies."

"She's not going to die," Robert says. "Don't say that."

"He can't break a deathbed promise," I say. "We'll have to stay there anyway." We sure are being practical about all this. I guess that's our mother in us. I bet we'll keep finding bits of her in us for a long time.

The night is coming quickly now that the summer is almost over. The light fades, as if in a hurry to go somewhere. A bat swoops low, just above our heads. I wonder if we stayed here in the tall grass how long it would take for my father to come looking for us.

As a gentle breeze makes the grass whisper a constant *shhh*, one star appears in the sky. I try to memorize the way we are sitting, the sky-blue color of my sister's eyes in this light, the way she waves the mosquitoes away with her small little kid's hands, the defiant tone to her voice when she repeats after me, "We'll have to stay." I try to hold inside me the exact length of my brother's hair, the way he sits with his knees bent, the lines of pebbly scabs on his shins from a fall down this hill. I close my eyes and we are here, inside me.

The day before we leave, two men with papers to be signed and a slat-boarded truck come to take Edith away. Rusty and Brenda run across the road as Mr. Burns leads Edith out of the barn, a rope tied around her neck. She refuses to move and Mr. Burns tugs and jerks on the rope as Edith twists her head and snorts so loud it sounds like she's struggling for each breath. The two men help drag Edith up the ramp and into the truck, then they swing up the ramp and latch it shut. The truck is made of slats with open spaces, so the air can get in. Edith moos steadily and stumbles about inside, bumping into the sides of the truck. I want to pat her, tell her we love her, but there is no time. The men are professional cow movers. She is gone in minutes.

Mrs. Burns keeps her head bent, eyes on the ground. Her cheeks are red. Dr. Ostrum and some people from the Animal Bureau are coming next week to test the rest of the cattle and the bull. They will have to tranquilize the bull first. I'd like to see that.

My father drives our car around to the other side of the barn and hooks on the trailer. With several stops and starts, he manages to back it up by the side porch. I hate this trailer. I hate it worse than liver and snakes.

"We better get going," Mr. Burns says. "We don't want to get in the way. Unless you want some help?"

My father says no. "We have everything under control," he says, nodding at all us kids. "But thanks anyway."

Before they go, I ask about the comics, the puzzles, and the little metal town. Mrs. Burns says to take them, take anything we might want, including the bike. My father waves his hand and says, "No, no, please, we shouldn't," but he hasn't got a chance.

Robert, Megan, and I are working together, thanking the Burns, saying how much we appreciate it, we'll take such good care of everything, we'll always remember them. Mrs. Burns' eyes get all wet and my father ends up shaking his head, then shaking their hands.

Mrs. Burns gives me a hug. "Bye, honey," she says. "Take some jam too." I grin as my father rolls his eyes.

She gives Robert and Megan hugs also. Mr. Burns shakes everyone's hand with a strong, tight squeeze. "Drive carefully," they both say, more than once. They leave, with Kip in the car, his head out the window, his ears flopping in the breeze. They have decided to chance his living with them, even by the busy road.

We pack. Rusty and Brenda help. Helen is at church, talking to the minister. We have to move everything around in the trailer several times to make sure the bike isn't near any of my father's paintings. He is frantic that the bike might shift and the handlebars poke a hole in something.

When we're done, we have packed everything but a few clothes, some comics, and three packs of gum.

We all eat dinner together at the Murphys' picnic table. Mrs. Murphy acts like I brought her a pot of gold when I hand her a jar of Mrs. Burns' pickles, so I go back over and get her two more. She refuses to accept them, so when she's not looking, I put them in her cupboard. I counted twenty-six more pickle jars in the Burns' basement pantry.

When Mr. Murphy says grace, my father lowers his head, but doesn't close his eyes or fold his hands together. Silently, I thank him for bowing his head. My mother wouldn't have, but I believe the Murphys deserve this bit of pretense for all the nice things they have done.

Just as dinner is over, I get a gigantic splinter stuck in the palm of my hand. It's the size of a spike. Brenda says she'll get it out and tugs at it with her fingernails. It breaks off, leaving a slash of wood deep under my skin. Brenda wants to dig that out with a needle but I don't let her. She pouts the rest of the night until I give her my going-away gift, my peach-colored dress with the white-trim collar I wore to church with her family. I've almost outgrown it. Helen says she can take it in, where needed. Brenda gets all sappy and says she'll be my best friend forever. If we were staying here, she probably wouldn't be speaking to me next week for some reason, but I tell her she'll be my best friend forever too.

School starts tomorrow, so we have to say good-bye to Rusty and Brenda tonight. Rusty gives Robert a wood gun with a shiny tin handle. Helen gives us a Bible. Brenda gives me a half-used bottle of perfume. Rusty tells me to write. It's ten o'clock at night when my father calls us in, saying we have to get some sleep for the big day tomorrow. I hug Helen and Brenda good-bye. Rusty takes my hand and walks me across the road, almost to the porch, even though everyone's watching. I tell Robert and Megan to get inside the house now before I beat the beans out of them, and they go in. I can see the curtain I put back up yesterday sway as I kiss Rusty good-bye.

When I wake in the morning, my hand hurts from the splinter that is still stuck under my skin. It's not just my hand that hurts, though. My chest is tight, my jaw aches, and my stomach's sour. Pretty much like I always feel the day we leave. The splinter's just an extra. I'll have to soak it out when we get to Utica. There's no time now. My father hustles us about as if a flood were approaching, as if our very lives are at stake if we don't leave by ten o'clock on the nose.

I pull the sheets off my bed, noticing for the first time a brown stain on the mattress the shape of an ear. Blood, maybe mine, from my curse, or maybe it's Timothy's. I guess it doesn't matter. We have both bled here. This is what I leave behind then, not a ring or a brush or anything as simple as that. I like the idea. I tell myself it is both Timothy's and my blood, mixed together. I put on his black T-shirt and my blue jeans. Last night I put his wallet back in the box upstairs. That's when I took the glass. I wrapped it in layers of newspaper and packed it very carefully. I did it for Mrs. Burns. I think she'll understand.

I imagine I am taking Timothy for a ride to a new place, like the spiders that stow away in our boxes. I know Timothy isn't here anymore, if he ever was, just like I figure God isn't real, but still, it's a nice idea. Like flying.

My father yells at Robert to get out of bed and start moving, so I go in his room and pull the bottom sheet off the bed while he's still in it. Robert tumbles to the floor and looks like he might cry. Probably not *just* because he fell off his bed. I put the sheet over my head and moan like a ghost. Robert laughs. My father actually thanks me and I pretend to have a heart attack from the surprise, falling on the bed and clutching my heart.

"Okay, that's enough," he says. "Let's move." He means let's get going. He doesn't even realize what else it means. Robert and I get quiet and carry the sheets down.

I make a breakfast of scrambled eggs, toast, and Kool-Aid. My father won't stop for anything once we get on the road. He may not stop at all. He is so anxious to leave, he carries around the car keys in his hand, sure we will be ready any minute. He's not usually involved in all these last-minute maneuvers and can't quite understand what's taking so long. I tell him to sit and eat. "Then, when you're done," I say firmly, "take a paper bag and go pick the rest of the ripe tomatoes, while we finish cleaning up." He looks at me like I'm crazy.

"There's room for a bag of tomatoes," I say, sounding so much like my mother he nods and says fine.

"Just hurry," he says.

After we eat, Robert and Megan do the dishes while I wring out the sheets and take them outside to hang on the line. This is what we agreed to; Mrs. Burns will come and take the sheets down. Which means she will have to go back in the house. Maybe it will be easier than she thinks.

As I lift up the damp sheets and carefully fold them over the clothesline I realize I need to name this house. I try to think back, to remember one thing that sticks out, and suddenly my arms go limp and my lungs take in too much air. Four months, and I remember them all. Kip eating the puzzle piece, all of us running down the hill, teaching Brenda math, watching the bonfire, Rusty's mouth and Rusty's freckled arms, the tea party and—

Tears come out of my eyes and I tilt my head up to feel them run down my cheeks, not wiping them off until they hit my chin. I feel sad, but it's a strange sad, like my mother's letters describe, a clear sadness I can examine, understand. But at the same time, I see a large attic room. I'll tape posters to the wall. I'll make curtains. I'll buy a blue vase.

I look around. My father's in the garden picking tomatoes and I can tell he's taking this job seriously, holding a tomato in his hand and staring at it before pulling it from the vine as if he's waiting for the tomato to say, "I'm ripe." He needs my mother.

The wind tugs at the sheets and they make a snapping sound, as if they are mad at me. "I'm sorry," I say, to the sheets, to my absent mother, to the house and hill beyond. "I have to go." My father comes over, carrying his bag of tomatoes, and says, "It's time now." But I knew that.

As we pull out of the driveway I turn and look back at the pretty little farmhouse with the hydrangea bush and the lace curtains. Always before, when we left, I would say good-bye with a shrug, with my jaw tight, believing the places I left to be as transitory as I, and as fickle. This time, I know that this land will stay here, that it holds a bit of me in all that it is, and that's okay, because it's an even trade, a good trade; I take it with me, the shape and slope of the hill, the house, and the people who live here. I imagine myself coming back sometime to say hello. For the first time, I understand that just because we leave people behind doesn't mean we love them any less, or they us.

My mother's voice says, "Say good-bye," so I do.

I decide to name this house The Last House. The next one I'll call home.

Acknowledgments

My sincerest thanks to:

Dr. Jay E. Graber, for his invaluable expertise in bovine tuberculosis

Charles Oberndorf, Paul Ita, Pat Brubaker, Maureen McHugh, Meg Guncik, Roc and Barb Bonchek, Harriet Slive, and Moira Roth, for all of their thoughtful suggestions

Karen Joy Fowler, for her inspiration, encouragement, and belief

Cindy Roche, for her enthusiasm, hard work, and for finding a wonderful home for my story

John Glusman, for liking this "quiet" story, then helping me make it even better

The Cleveland Heights Public Library, for patiently helping me find the answers to all my strange questions

The East Side Writers Group, for always being there

Matt, for turning down his music

And finally, for everything possible and impossible, my parents